An inde

Abigail Shaw is a proper young lady, hardly the sort to boldly offer a deal to London's most distinguished and perfect duke. But Abigail, desperate to save her father's newspaper business, is after a good scandal. She'd have the sensational headlines that would keep the *ton* talking—and the family business thriving—if only she could uncover the secrets of Christopher Cabot, the Duke of Madingley. What better way than a pretend romance? Yet, with all his seductive glances and stolen caresses, she somehow has to keep from succumbing to temptation.

Christopher finds Abigail—and her proposal—intriguing. A fake romance with the stunning commoner would allow him time to choose a suitable wife from among the would-be duchesses nipping at his heels. It seems like the perfect plan . . . as long as he can keep her from uncovering his one deep, dark secret. But as he falls for the cunning beauty, he will be tempted to reveal all—his secret, his heart, and his soul.

GAYLE CALLEN

Never Dare A DUKE

An Avon Romantic Treasure

A V O N

An Imprint of HarperCollinsPublishers

AVON BOOKS
An Imprint of HarperCollins*Publishers*
10 East 53rd Street
New York, New York 10022-5299

Copyright © 2008 by Gayle Kloecker Callen
ISBN 978-0-06-123506-1
www.avonromance.com

First Avon Books paperback printing: December 2008

Avon Trademark Reg. U.S. Pat. Off. and in Other Countries, Marca Registrada, Hecho en U.S.A.
HarperCollins® is a registered trademark of HarperCollins Publishers.

Printed in the U.S.A.

10 9 8 7 6 5 4 3 2 1

To my aunt and godmother, Marilyn Cox: You and my mother showed me how close sisters can be, and I learned a wonderful lesson from that. Thank you so much for all the great visits, the laughter, and your support, which made me feel like a daughter rather than just a niece. I love you.

Chapter 1

London, England
1845

"There he is!"

Miss Abigail Shaw craned her neck in the most unladylike fashion. "Where?" she hissed. "Are you certain it's the duke?"

The driver of Lady Gwendolin Warfield's open carriage continued to maneuver down the crowded lane in the middle of Hyde Park. Much to Abigail's frustration, Gwen waved and smiled at the passing carriages, her black hair shining in the sun beneath her neat little hat.

"Gwen!"

Still holding a smile and speaking between her teeth, Gwen said, "He is riding his horse with no one else in attendance. Do you see him now, coming toward us? The dark-haired man who just tipped his hat to the Fogges."

Abigail saw him now. Christopher Cabot, the

duke of Madingley, had the black hair, black eyes, and olive complexion of his mother's Spanish heritage. He rode his horse with the grace of a king, and she knew that all of the *ton* in attendance this afternoon admired him greatly for all his good and noble works.

But Gwen had said there was more in his background, something covered up with money and the threat of nobility—something scandalous.

Normally, Abigail would not let herself be caught up in gossip, but everything had changed, and she was floundering.

Being the daughter of a newspaper publisher who prided himself on championing justice, Abigail had grown up wanting to make a difference, to be a journalist herself. All people deserved to be treated fairly and to have access to the truth. The world was changing, and the peers were not the only people who mattered anymore.

But as a woman, she faced an even more difficult hill to climb. Even her father didn't know she was a writer for his paper—yet. But he would. Writing anonymously, she had started with small pieces, literary reviews at first, and had next graduated to become the drama critic. But when the managing editor recently told her that he could no longer pay her, she had learned of the *Morning Journal*'s financial problems. Although the implications for her family were grave, she did not let herself panic. She thought she could help.

Abigail had researched all of her father's competition and realized that what lured the readers was gossip. Middle-class people loved to read about the foibles and scandals of the *ton*. The *Journal* had to do a better job of giving readers the important news of the day—mixed with a little gossip.

Gwen had told her that the most scandalous family of all were the Cabots. For at least three generations, they'd been a journalist's dream. The most recent cousin, Daniel Throckmorten, had just been married, after having won his wife in a wager. The *Morning Journal* had only reported the marriage announcement rather than the details of the scandal itself, an opportunity lost, in Abigail's opinion. But, then, everyone had written about the Cabots, and yet the public was still ravenous for more.

The duke was the only member of the Cabot family who portrayed himself as above the many scandals that seemed to follow the rest of his relatives. He had no reputation except that of a sought-after, titled bachelor. But according to Gwen, there were rumors that he was hiding a dreadful secret and that exorbitant money had been given to pay for that secrecy.

Abigail was offended that he could pretend to be so perfect, that people could look up to him when his reputation was founded on lies. She owed it to honest readers everywhere to uncover his secrets. With this new story, she would increase the circu-

lation of her father's paper tenfold, lure wealthy
advertisers—and save the *Morning Journal* from
ruin. Her father's reputation would be restored,
and he could continue to help people. And she had
Gwen to thank for the idea although Abigail had
not yet confided in her friend the real reason why
she had to write this article.

"What did I tell you?" Gwen said in a low
voice, still smiling at her many friends. "Is he not
handsome?"

"Yes, he is."

And it was very true. She had been prepared to
find the duke sinister and arrogant but had been
unprepared for his handsome looks, dark as sin.
She noted his tall, correct posture, the cutaway
riding coat that emphasized his broad shoulders
and lean hips, the trousers that hugged his muscled
thighs and disappeared into his perfectly polished
riding boots.

"He is almost too perfect," Abigail mused.

Gwen glanced at her with amusement. "For your
article, you mean?"

"I guess that's the point," Abigail said. "No one
is perfect, and no one should be allowed to deceive
others."

But as the duke continued to approach, she felt a
little light-headed. It was surely the warmth of the
summer sun, not the way his dark, impassive gaze
swept over them.

And returned. Something in her tightened when

he looked at her. Though it was a brief glance, it was penetrating, and she knew what he saw: a short, plump woman, with plain brown hair and brown eyes. Nothing that would interest a duke. And it was a good thing, too, she reminded herself. If she was to investigate him, he must not notice her.

And then the moment of his intense regard was gone, and he was tipping his hat to them both.

"Good afternoon, Your Grace," Gwen called, waving to him.

"It's a fine day, Lady Gwendolin," the duke said. His gaze touched on Abigail again as he nodded. "Miss."

His deep voice held no trace of an accent, although she had already learned that he spoke fluent Spanish.

To Abigail's shock, he slowed his horse, and the alert coachman did the same. She was fairly new to journalism and felt almost embarrassed facing the man she would soon investigate.

She returned his nod, keeping her smile simple. *Let him move on, please.*

Gwen leaned forward. "Your Grace, allow me to present my dearest friend, Miss Abigail Shaw. Miss Shaw, the duke of Madingley."

Once again she was forced to sit still beneath the duke's perusal, praying that he wouldn't associate her very common name with the newspaper. She could not curtsy, so she nodded again, feeling like a bobbing puppet. And then she met his eyes, determined not to start her new assignment with cowardice. He did not seem to show any recognition.

"It is a pleasure to meet you, Miss Shaw," he said.

She hated how much she enjoyed the sound of her name on his lips. How could she so easily fall into the trap of admiring a man simply because he was a duke? She was no better than her naive readers.

"And I you, Your Grace." To her relief, her voice sounded normal, cool rather than fawning.

But that made him look at her with even more intent, as if he wasn't used to levelheaded women. She bit her lip to keep herself from doing anything to make the situation worse.

"Miss Shaw is new to London, Your Grace," Gwen said. "She was raised in Durham."

Abigail stiffened. Now Gwen was *lying*? What was going on?

The duke gave Gwen a brilliant smile. "Then I am certain she is with the proper companion, Lady Gwendolin. Surely you have been sightseeing. What have you seen?"

Gwen seemed momentarily stunned at the unexpected question.

Abigail quickly said, "The new British Museum, Your Grace. I enjoyed the reading room."

"Books, Miss Shaw? Not the paintings or sculptures?"

Oh heavens, could she have made herself seem any more plain and boring? But the duke's smile never faded, and she imagined that he had plenty of practice at hiding his pity.

Gwen opened her mouth as if to cover the awkwardness, but Abigail spoke without thinking. "If I had said I admired the paintings, Your Grace, surely you would have teased me by asking if I preferred the nudes or the landscapes."

He only blinked, Gwen stiffened, and Abigail thought surely time had frozen into a long moment of hot embarrassment.

At last, he chuckled. "A clever response, Miss Shaw. Do enjoy yourselves as you tour the city, ladies."

He swept on past them, and the tight knot in her stomach slowly uncoiled. The carriage lurched back into motion.

Gwen broke into a peal of laughter.

"That was all your fault!" Abigail said, glaring. "You didn't even warn me that you planned an introduction!"

Gwen only took her hands and squeezed. "You certainly captured his attention. But never mind that. Remember that everyone will want to read about him," she said in an excited voice. "He is a handsome mystery. Surely your father will see that you deserve to write for the paper!"

"But you lied to him about me! Why was it important that he think I'm new to London?"

"Trust me, Abby. I will explain everything. I only have your best interests in mind."

"But—"

"Don't you want to interview me for your story? I could be your anonymous source."

Though Abigail wanted to cling to her suspicions and questions, she helplessly shared a laugh with Gwen. Abigail thought the world of her friend, whose progressive father had sent his daughter to be educated in a school with daughters of the middle class. Gwen had never thought herself better than the others, and she'd proved herself a trusted friend through all sorts of mischief. Once, Abigail had convinced herself that a hated teacher was really a highwayman in disguise. It was Gwen who'd commandeered a carriage from the school stables at midnight, so that they could ride up and down the roads for hours, all to prove Abigail's theory. She only shuddered to imagine what could have happened to them if the man had been a highwayman in truth instead of a distracted suitor secretly courting the local vicar's daughter.

Abigail knew that she herself was far too inquisitive, prompting Gwen to throw herself into any adventure. Did Gwen now have a new one in mind?

Forcing herself to be patient, Abigail took out her pencil and notebook. "How long has the duke held the title?"

Gwen sobered. "His Grace was only eighteen when his father died, or so my mother told me.

That was nine years ago, and I was still in the schoolroom, so I do not remember much. He was supposed to go to university like his ancestors, but of course he could not, what with his new responsibilities."

"You would think a young man would feel overwhelmed," Abigail said thoughtfully, wishing she dared to look over her shoulder and study the duke.

"If he did, I never heard that he revealed it. He took over the reins of the family. He spends most of his time at Madingley House, the family home in London, while his mother oversees their country seat outside Cambridge. She is not one for London."

"The old duke fell in love with her in Spain, did he not?"

"And what a scandal it was, since she was a poor commoner as well. The *ton* can be brutal, and she never did fit in. But she and the duke were very much in love, so I imagine she did not care."

"And now you're saying that this newest duke, someone supposedly so perfect, has a scandal of his own."

Gwen shrugged. "It is up to you to find out. I only know about the rumors that someone had to pay someone else on the young duke's behalf. Could it be blackmail, do you think? Or an illegitimate child? Or even bribery of a government official?"

"We cannot continue to guess wildly," Abigail said sternly. "We must gather the facts before we form a conclusion."

"And I have the perfect way for you to do that." Gwen took Abigail's hand. "Now, Abby, I know you've never done anything like this before, but I want you to give it considerable thought."

"Done what?" Abigail asked in confusion. "Give what considerable thought?"

"I received an invitation to Madingley Court, the duke's country seat, to attend the first house party that the dowager duchess has ever given. I believe it is to benefit her only daughter, who recently made her coming out to the queen, and now needs to be introduced to eligible gentlemen. My aunt will be attending to chaperone me, and I am sure I can convince her that my dear friend, a gentleman's daughter who happens to be visiting me, should come as well."

Abigail gaped at her. "You cannot possibly mean *me*. Was that why you told him I was new to London?"

Gwen laughed, twirling her parasol. "And how else did you plan to investigate a private man such as the duke?"

"With my talented investigative skills, of course."

"Did you think he would agree to an interview? That his relatives would gladly tell you everything that—"

"Oh Gwen, hush! You planned this! You deliberately suggested the Cabots as my target because of this party invitation." Abigail crossed her arms in a huff. "Approach him in his own home and lie to him?"

"That you are a gentleman's daughter? Is not your father a good man?"

"He is the owner of a newspaper! Regardless of his genteel manners and his wealth, the *ton* would never call him a gentleman. He works for a living."

"My father says that only calling large landowners gentlemen is nonsense."

"As an earl, your father can afford to be different."

"You know that my father considers all men equal, that he—"

"Gwen," Abigail interrupted, "you know I adore your father. If not for his progressive ideas—he might almost be called an American—you and I would not have met. I will be forever in his debt for the gracious way he has treated me and my family."

"Then let me do this for you. It is only a little lie. And it will be such fun to have my dearest friend with me. These affairs can be so dreary, especially if the weather is bad. How many letters can one write to while away the day? And remember, the duke seldom visits the country this time of year. Parliament is in session, and he is far too busy to attend a house party."

"You're sure he won't be there," Abigail said, shuddering as she remembered how she'd just humiliated herself.

"I am certain." Gwen grinned. "You will simply be another guest, rattling around in their home as you talk to his family and servants and learn all about him and how he grew up. Isn't that what you do when you interview people?"

"Of course, but I haven't had the chance to interview many people. Remember, all I usually do is see the play and write my review." Abigail heard her own tired bitterness. Only a year ago, she'd been thrilled to write anonymously for her father's paper. It had been her own secret, her chance to prove her skill. But if the paper closed, she wouldn't even have that—and her father might be ruined, the most important consideration of all.

Gwen grinned. "But now you'll have the chance to show the world what a talented woman is capable of."

Abigail sank back on the padded bench in the carriage, closing her eyes against the sun's brilliance. "Oh, Gwen you are making this far too tempting."

"It is as if fate, in the form of a rare invitation, gave you this perfect chance. And before you protest that you were not invited, if you are visiting me for a month, they would expect you to come as well. And you are my dearest friend. I am not lying to them about that either. Say yes." Gwen blinked her persuasive eyes, smiling with hopefulness.

Abigail hesitated, and in the end, good sense won out. "I . . . will think on it."

Gwen pouted. "Can you not think quickly? I need to send my response within the next day or two."

"I will tell you my decision tomorrow."

With an exaggerated sigh, Gwen flounced back on the bench, tilting her parasol to block her face from Abigail.

"And will you forgive me if I do not go along with this insane plan?" Abigail asked, trying not to laugh.

Gwen dipped the parasol to peek at her with narrowed eyes. "Probably not."

"Then that is even more reason to give this great thought."

"You think too much. Now stop thinking, and begin to nod regally. You never know if we'll meet someone who might be in attendance at the duchess's country house party."

Abigail's smile died as she stared at the crowded lane, full of beautiful carriages and beautiful people. Gwen could not possibly imagine that Abigail could fit in, that she'd even know what was expected of a gentleman's daughter.

That night, Abigail settled into her well-loved role by her father's side at a paper-strewn table in the drawing room. He was a beefy man, given to living a good life with the money he'd worked hard to earn, with sparse gray hair on top of his head and a mouth that seemed incomplete without a cigar. Several times a week, he brought home articles that his writers were working on and sought her opinion on how they appealed to women. She couldn't help but be flattered since he was a man whose newspaper sparked discussions in Parliament, bettering society.

"What about this one, Abigail?" he asked, putting another paper before her though she hadn't finished the last one.

She skimmed the article, trying not to wince at the plight of solitary women immigrants and what they did to survive. She would never have such problems, she knew—she had plans for her life, talents that would aid her. Surely she'd inherited her skill from her father. For just a moment, she thought about confiding everything to him.

Suddenly, he snatched back the article. "Wait, I did not mean you to read this one. I haven't edited it yet, and it is far too graphic for feminine eyes."

"But Papa, I'm an adult now. I have been reading your paper for many years. You don't need to protect me from life."

He gave her an absent smile, still engrossed in his work. "That is what a father is for. And then it will be your husband's duty."

She sighed. Until she proved herself to him, she would always be his little girl rather than a talented woman. Her investigation into the duke could accomplish that. She thought again of Gwen's offer to take her to Madingley Court and the risks involved. If she had it in her power to help the *Morning Journal*—and her father's reputation—shouldn't she do all she could?

The bell at the front door rang, and neither father nor daughter paid attention to it.

A few minutes later, a feminine voice said, "Excuse me, Lawrence."

Abigail looked up with a smile. Her mother, Henrietta, stood in the doorway, thin and delicate, her hair a light brown that had begun to fade. She was the daughter of a tailor and had never quite accustomed herself to the luxurious life her husband had lavished on her.

And then Abigail saw that her mother was not alone. A young man wearing an earnest, hopeful expression gave her a tentative smile. He was of middling height, pleasant of features, trim enough to indicate an active life.

Her father rose to his feet, fairly beaming between Abigail and the young man. Abigail hid her resigned sigh. Though she'd grown up worshipping her father, she was dismayed that his newest project was her respectable marriage to a man above their station. What else did a businessman's plain daughter have to offer a nobleman—but money?

But never did her father mention his problems at the newspaper as being one of his motivations to marry her off. How could she not love him, regardless of the controlling nature he softened with his love?

When she rose, her father urged her forward by the hand, displaying her. "Abigail, may I present Mr. Wadsworth? He is in town for the season and owns ancestral property in the Lake District."

Her father looked a bit too proud of himself, and she understood at once: Mr. Wadsworth was a "gentleman" in the truest sense of the word. She curtsied in resignation.

"Mr. Wadsworth, my daughter, Miss Shaw."

Mr. Wadsworth bowed to her.

"And how are you and my father acquainted, sir?"

Mr. Wadsworth's florid face blushed even more. "I am a new member of Parliament, Miss Shaw, and the *Morning Journal* has been a staunch supporter of several bills I am sponsoring."

Abigail smiled at her father. "He is always so interested in helping people."

She glanced at her mother, who hid her amusement behind her sudden concentration on the embroidery she'd picked up.

"I invited him to dinner," her father said, "and he could not wait to agree, especially when he heard he could meet the whole family."

Including my marriageable daughter, were the unspoken words.

Was this going to be her future? Married off to her father's ideal prospect while he still had the dowry money to make it happen? Was she going to succumb to his desperation and just give in, hoping that with a good marriage, she could support her parents when they no longer could? How would her father survive the humiliation of bankruptcy?

No, she could not let this happen.

While her mind still worked, while she could still write, she would work on the gossip story that would bring readers back to the *Journal*. She would give her father back his respect and save her family. The Cabots had land and wealth and power but still thought they could use illegal means to hide their crimes. It wasn't fair to good people everywhere. The truth—and justice—had to come out. She would take Gwen up on her offer and visit the country house of a duke.

And suddenly, the thought of disguising herself as someone else, *being* someone else, was a very powerful lure.

Chapter 2

∾‿‿∾

"**W**hat is it?" Gwen asked with concern in her voice.

With a sigh, Abigail looked away from the hedgerowed countryside that seemed to roll past their carriage. She was trying not to show her emotions, but with Gwen, even a twitch of her eyebrow could be a signal.

They both glanced once more at Miss Imogene Bury, Gwen's elderly spinster aunt, who'd spent almost the entire morning dozing.

Suddenly serious with determination, Gwen said in a quiet voice, "You have been . . . strange all week, when you should be excited. After all, your father thinks you're on a visit with me—and that's the truth!"

Abigail looked at her lap, fingering her reticule, which matched the green of her gown. "Something has been on my mind and I . . . I did not know how to tell you."

Gwen took both her hands and leaned close. "Tell me what, my dear?"

"The *Journal*'s circulation has been decreasing the last year. My father would never be the one to tell me. His managing editor, my 'employer'"—she gave a bitter smile—"did so. I know I should have told you the truth, but I did not want you to know how much rested on this assignment I've given myself."

"Oh, Abby," Gwen murmured, rubbing her hands. "Your poor parents."

"I don't even know if my mother is aware of the situation. But this is why I am so desperate to succeed. If it were just about me and my need to prove myself to my father, I would never have gone through with it. My stomach is already full of angry butterflies at the thought of looking into the duchess's face and—" She glanced at Miss Bury and couldn't continue.

Gwen nodded. "It is just an article, you know. You are not committing a crime. And they're hiding something illegal—"

"Are they?" Abigail interrupted bitterly. "We don't even know for certain. Would you want your private problems to be told to all of London—to all of England?"

"But I am not a duke," she said, as if that explained everything.

Abigail groaned, sank back on the bench, and closed her eyes.

"We are almost there," Gwen said, patting her leg again. "Do you not want to see where we'll spend the next week?"

Abigail opened one eye. "I am certain I will see it when we arrive."

But then she was caught by something out the window, and she found herself lowering the glass, regardless of the dust, so that she could have a better view.

"Are those Greek columns?" Abigail asked, leaning out the window to see the impressive columns fall away behind them.

"They are," Gwen said solemnly, though her eyes betrayed her by twinkling. "It will be a while yet before we see the house."

Abigail tried to pretend she wasn't nervous. She looked at the pastureland spread out even to the hills, filled with roaming white clusters of sheep. A stream cut through the earth, and gradually the trees growing near it thickened until they blocked much of the view.

Abigail frowned. "But how will we see—"

As the carriage followed a bend in the road, leaving the trees behind, at last she saw Madingley Court. She was used to elegant homes, but she could not stop the gasp that emerged from her throat.

"Sumptuous, isn't it?" Gwen said, looking out the other window. "I've always wanted to use that word."

"It's the perfect word," Abigail whispered in awe.

It was not just a mansion, but a castle and palace

NEVER DARE A DUKE   21

all rolled into one. There were pointed turrets and battlements like those of a medieval castle, but spread up five floors and across a swath of countryside. Hundreds of windows reflected the glittering sun. The lane led past the house as if it took forever, until at last they turned into a courtyard and pulled beneath the columned portico. Another carriage, empty now, left the courtyard.

"Other guests have arrived," Gwen said.

Abigail realized again the enormity of her task, for she would not only be fooling the duke's mother and sister. "How many guests will there be?" Her voice was almost a squeak.

Miss Bury awoke with a start as the horses came to a stop. She smiled between the two young ladies. "Oh, Miss Shaw, do not fret. This is the duchess's first house party. I am certain it will be a small affair, surely not more than twenty-five or thirty guests."

Abigail tried not to gulp too audibly.

There was a footman to open the carriage door and assist them down, a footman to take Miss Bury's arm and escort their small party up the stairs, and another waiting to open the door for them. All wore the knee breeches, short brass-buttoned coats, and white wigs of the duke's ancient livery.

If there were this many servants in the courtyard, imagine how many were in the entire castle, Abigail thought in awe.

But that's how the Cabots expected visitors to feel, she reminded herself: awed by their title and money and power. If one were full of awe, one might ignore the scandalous underbelly. But not Abigail. She would notice everything, talk to everyone, be they duchess or scullery maid, and discover the *real* duke.

Inside the great entrance hall, two stories high, statues stared blindly at them from alcoves in the wall, and beneath their feet was the most intricate marble inlaid floor. It took everything in Abigail not to gape about her. She did peer into the next massive room, a great hall, with scattered groups of furniture, overlooked by ancient swords and shields on the walls between medieval tapestries.

They were met by a housekeeper, an older woman dressed in a black gown, white apron, and lace cap, who pleasantly told them that luncheon would be served in one hour. A maid was dispatched to show them to their chambers to refresh themselves.

And then Abigail had to tax her brain to try to remember the many stairs and corridors they used.

The young maid bobbed her head as she said over her shoulder to Gwen, "This wing will house the young ladies—milady."

Abigail and Gwen exchanged a grin, then Abigail casually asked, "So there is another wing for the gentlemen? Does the family itself split into these two wings as well?"

"Oh no, miss. There is also a family wing."

Abigail nodded thoughtfully. There was much to learn about Madingley Court, and if she wanted to explore it unobtrusively, she would need to study the layout well.

At last they reached their chambers on the third floor. Gwen and Abigail had rooms next door to each other, and Miss Bury was situated directly across the hall. The maid promised to send someone up immediately to press their gowns.

Miss Bury patted Gwen's hand. "Come fetch me when the maid arrives to take us to luncheon. You know how tired a journey makes me."

When the two of them were alone in Abigail's room, Abigail said, "I also have to feel guilty about lying to sweet Miss Bury. Will it ever end?"

Gwen went to the tall windows, which spanned almost floor to ceiling. "If it helps you to know, I have heard old family stories that 'sweet Miss Bury' was wild in her day, but did not want to settle on just one man, so she never married."

Abigail's mouth sagged open. "Really?"

Gwen grinned wickedly. "Now you know why I asked her to chaperone."

"And are you planning to follow in her wild footsteps?" Abigail asked, arching an eyebrow.

"Why, no, my dear, but you are. At least this week. Now let us pick out the perfect gown in which to greet our fellow guests."

"And our hostess," Abigail murmured, wondering about a woman so in love with a man that she left her homeland to live among intolerant strangers.

"It is a good thing we have each other," Gwen was saying. "I did not want to bring a maid—who knows how many poor dears are crammed into the servants' quarters for an event like this."

"And the other reason you didn't bring a maid?" Abigail prodded.

"Oh very well, because she would have known your true identity."

Abigail only grinned and shook her head.

At last, their gowns were pressed, and the first maid arrived to show them to the drawing room. Miss Bury joined them in the corridor, looking refreshed and excited.

"Ah, to see the reclusive duchess is such a treat!" she whispered to her charges.

The drawing room was a bit more intimate than the intimidating great hall. There were still several clusters of furniture, but the guests had gathered before the intricately carved hearth, where naughty-faced angels held up the massive mantel. The ceiling was dominated by painted frescoes clustered above each chandelier.

A dozen or so guests openly or surreptitiously glanced at Abigail and Gwen as they arrived, and Gwen's expression brightened with pleasure at the people she must already know. The guests were an interesting mix, from a fresh-faced girl wide-eyed with wonder at being newly come out, to an older gentleman wearing a frown that looked like it was etched into his face. Some were standing, some were sitting, but Abigail thought it was quite easy to pick out the duchess, seated on a sofa. The duchess had the deepest black hair, now threaded with silver, and the darker complexion that she'd passed on to her son. Seated beside her must be her daughter, Lady Elizabeth. The young woman had her mother's black hair but the paler, peach skin of her father's family. They each had dark eyes, with a strong nose in a handsome face. Where the duchess's gown was conservative in color and cut, her daughter wore bright summer yellow. These were two women with whom Abigail would have to become well acquainted, in order to hear as much as she could about the duke.

Lady Elizabeth gestured subtly to Gwen, who took Abigail's arm and led her straight to the duchess. Miss Bury trailed behind. Abigail didn't need any prodding to curtsy at Gwen's side.

"Mama," Lady Elizabeth said, "may I present Lady Gwendolin Warfield."

She stressed Gwen's name oddly, and Abigail and Gwen exchanged a curious glance.

The duchess nodded regally. Abigail began to wonder how she would ever be able to talk to such a woman.

"Your Grace," Gwen said demurely, "thank you so much for this invitation."

The duchess smiled, which softened her noble features into kindness. "It is my pleasure." Her voice held the faint melody of a Spanish accent. "My son speaks highly of you."

Abigail barely kept herself from frowning in surprise at Gwen. No wonder Lady Elizabeth had emphasized her name.

"And my thanks as well for extending your invitation to my guest," Gwen continued. "Your Grace, may I present my dearest friend, Miss Shaw?"

Abigail sank into another curtsy. "My thanks for your gracious invitation, Your Grace."

The duchess waved a hand. "You've seen Madingley Court, Miss Shaw, so you know we always have room for another guest. Miss Shaw, allow me to present my daughter, Lady Elizabeth."

The young woman stood up, and they curtsied to each other. There was no pretension in Lady Elizabeth's eyes, just open curiosity and happy anticipation, as if the start of the party was already more than she'd dared hope for.

"It is so nice to have more ladies close to my own age," Lady Elizabeth said.

Her mother rolled her eyes. "And exhausting for the chaperones. Is that not right, Miss Bury?"

Miss Bury came forward and made a spry curtsy. "Good day, Your Grace. And I do not mind being a chaperone. It reminds me of how wonderful it was to be young."

"Ah yes," said the duchess, arching an eyebrow,

"I seem to remember hearing a story or two about your youth."

Miss Bury only smiled, her eyes twinkling with secret memories. At last the three of them left the duchess and her daughter, and Gwen brought Abigail along as she reacquainted herself with the other guests. Abigail paid attention to everything she heard, not knowing what—or who—would prove useful in her investigation.

Abigail learned that the rest of the family was absent, which might hinder her. The duke's two aunts, Lady Flora and Lady Rosa, were in London, along with Lady Rosa's two unmarried daughters and her widowed daughter-in-law. How sad that the duke had a cousin who'd died so young.

Also in attendance were two other unattached young ladies, Lady May and Lady Theodosia, closer to Lady Elizabeth's age of eighteen than Abigail's twenty-three. There were five bachelors, most likely for Lady Elizabeth's perusal: Mr. Tilden, a redhead who blushed at making Abigail's acquaintance; Lord Keane, who seemed to think himself above most of them; Lord Paul Delane and Lord Gerald Delane, the younger sons of a duke; and Mr. Wesley, who was introduced as the local vicar. Abigail couldn't help but see how he stared at Gwen before he caught himself with a faint blush.

There were also two other married couples: the

marquess of Swarthbeck and his wife—the parents
of Lady May—and the earl and countess of Greenwich. An elderly gentleman, Mr. Fitzwilliam, was
nodding off in his chair—until Miss Bury tapped
his shoulder, and the two smiled at each other as
old acquaintances.

The butler appeared in the doorway, paused
until it was quiet, then intoned, "His Grace, the
Duke of Madingley."

Abigail gaped. He wasn't supposed to be here!

The duke himself still wore his traveling clothes,
spattered with rain, and he had not yet looked into
the drawing room. Abigail thought how much
larger and powerful he seemed within the confines
of his home rather than the outdoors.

She would *not* be intimidated.

As he handed a leather satchel to the butler, he
said, "Hamilton, would you please take this to my
room yourself?" Then he added with amused exasperation, "And I certainly do not need an introduction to my own mother and sis—"

He broke off as he caught sight of the eager
guests.

"Chris!" his sister cried, walking swiftly to him.
"I mean—Madingley! What a pleasant surprise
you've given me. I did not know you were coming
to my house party."

He gave her a tight smile. "Elizabeth, how could
I miss your first Society event?"

He bent to kiss her cheek, but Abigail saw him

aim an impassive look at his mother. The duchess only inclined her head, wearing a look of faint amusement.

Abigail would lay money on a wager that the party was an *un*pleasant surprise. There were several eligible ladies here, after all. Even the mother of a duke could play the matchmaker for her son.

Chapter 3

Christopher had no difficulty hiding his dismay and anger. He'd always done his duty as the sixth duke of Madingley, even if it meant riding down Rotten Row in London, displaying himself like a stuffed peacock for the well-dressed masses. His sister Elizabeth had just come out, and he knew how important it was that she marry happily and well, and his own behavior affected that. After all, he should be used to hiding everything he felt behind a mask of civility.

But he did not like surprises, and his mother knew it. A crowded house party, for God's sake, just when he'd come home hoping for a peaceful week to untangle his thoughts.

He could not miss that Lady Gwendolin, Lady May, and Lady Theodosia were in attendance, the three women he'd mentioned to his mother. He had thought he was safe discussing his future wife with the woman who'd borne him, but apparently not. There were also bachelors scattered in the crowd, and he knew they must be meant to interest Elizabeth.

But although his sister was glad for such help—he wasn't.

He strode forward into the drawing room, watching as people hastily drew back to allow him easy access to his mother. It always made him tired to watch them scurry away from him. He nodded politely to the guests lining each side of him, and a wave of curtsies and bows followed in his wake. Lady May looked as if she hadn't dared hope for his attendance. Lady Gwendolin, on the other hand, wore only her usual lovely smile, which seemed to hide so much. He'd had several intriguing conversations with her, leading him to think she had an unusual mind, full of contradictions that a young woman normally didn't have.

At her side was the same brunette woman he'd seen with her in Hyde Park the week before. She was short and well curved to Lady Gwendolin's lithe height, and seemed to eye him with purpose, as if she would discover the kind of man he was by considering him long enough. Was she simply another woman interested in snaring a duke? As he remembered her amusing comment about nude portraits, he found that he watched her a moment too long, for he almost stepped on his mother's hem when he reached her sofa.

The duchess was trying not to chuckle as he bowed his head to her. He lifted her hand to kiss it.

"Mother," he said simply.

She cocked her head, as if trying to read his emotions with that one word. "Madingley," she answered, "I am so glad that you were able to put aside your busy schedule to attend."

"And how perfect that you were able to plan this around the week I told you I would be home."

There was a faint dimple in one cheek as she tried not to smile. "Yes, indeed."

She bent her head, and he knew she was hiding the triumph in her eyes. It was an old game between them. She had wanted him settled for several years now, though he was but twenty-seven. He'd put it off, needing to improve the tattered reputation from his youth. Only now was he coming into the height of his power in Parliament and at the queen's side.

Then he'd made the mistake of confiding in his mother the names of women he was considering as a future duchess. And now here they were, the three noblewomen—and Lady Gwendolin's friend. Was she perhaps a companion? He ruled that out because her clothing, although not extravagant, still spoke of wealth, and she was mingling with Lady Gwendolin and the other guests.

It had been a long time since he'd felt as intrigued by a woman. They were always so transparent in their eagerness to court his favor—or his bed. Surely once they'd had more than one conversation, the mystery of her would no longer sway him.

The guests were seated male and female, so Abigail had a gentleman on each side to converse with. On her right, Lord Greenwich spoke rather loudly across the table to his wife, as if she were hard of hearing. On her left was Lord Keane, the bachelor with the sardonic expression and a knowing look in his eyes as he studied each woman. Gwen was on his other side, talking to the duke at the head of the table. Lord Keane watched them for a moment, then shook his head.

"Is there something wrong, my lord?" Abigail asked, as she looked with approval at the lamb cutlets and asparagus set before her.

"Of course not," he said with a grin. "It is simply that we bachelors will have little attention now that the duke has arrived."

"And you do not receive enough attention?"

He blinked down at her in surprise, then said lightly, "Why, no, we don't, Miss . . ."

Though he'd forgotten her name, she let him off with easy grace. "Miss Shaw. And certainly Lady Elizabeth cannot be distracted by her brother."

Lord Keane nodded and looked down the table at the duke's sister, who laughed aloud at something the blushing Mr. Tilden was saying.

"Very true," Lord Keane said. "And there is you, of course."

"Me?" she asked with a bit of apprehension.

"The other ladies, obviously summoned for the duke, are the daughters of noblemen, but you are not."

Thinking of Gwen as a possible duchess had never entered Abigail's mind, and she would have to think of the ramifications to her story—and to her dear friend—later. "I cannot be grouped with them as a duke's future intended," she said ruefully.

Lord Keane laughed, causing the duke to glance at them from the head of the table. Abigail found that, for a moment, she couldn't look away from that penetrating stare. Why did he keep looking at her? The foolish words she'd spouted in London kept echoing in her mind. He was making her feel confused and uneasy, two things she seldom felt. And she didn't like it.

"Then why are you here, Miss Shaw?" Lord Keane asked her.

She was glad for the distraction, even though his question was rather blunt. "To be honest, I was visiting Lady Gwendolin when the invitation arrived. I offered to return home early, but she would have none of it."

"Ah, brave of you to admit it."

If the duke heard what she was saying, he would know she was an accidental guest. Of course, he was one himself, she thought with amusement.

"There is an interesting light in your eyes, Miss Shaw," Lord Keane said.

She blinked at him. "Pardon me, my lord?"

"I think you are not one to take all of this too seriously. Perhaps you can even enjoy yourself over the next few days, while the rest of us are jostling for notice between the respective ducal siblings."

"And you are that desperate for notice, my lord?" she asked wryly. "Why does that ring false with me?"

He laughed again. "You are a sly one, Miss Shaw. I will keep an eye on you."

At last he turned to speak with Gwen, and in that moment of changing conversation, the gazes of both Abigail and the duke collided once again. He arched a brow at her. What did he want? And could one look away from a duke? After all, she could not converse with him by shouting across two other people. She offered a polite nod and turned to her other luncheon companion.

Excitement warred with her nerves. Although she had the rare opportunity to interview the subject of her article himself, she would bide her time. She would be able to form her own conclusions rather than just relying on the opinions of others. But how easy was it going to be for a woman of her lowly status to pursue conversations with the duke without making anyone—especially him—suspicious?

When the luncheon was over, Lady Elizabeth rose to her feet. "Ladies and gentlemen, we were going to retire to the garden for dessert and relaxation, but I fear the rain has spoiled our plans. Instead, we will adjourn to the conservatory. And then later tonight, I will announce a special surprise. Our house party is to have an unusual theme."

Several people voiced approval and excitement, and casually they all arose and began to follow the duchess and her daughter back through the drawing room and eventually out a door at the far end of the library. Immediately, a warm earthen smell touched by the intangible scents of dozens of exotic flowers wafted toward Abigail. On the glass roof, rain beat softly, running in streams down the windows, blurring the view of the park.

"Beautiful, isn't it?" Gwen said softly as she took Abigail's arm.

"I have never seen a conservatory so large." Abigail tried not to gape as she saw the stone paths disappearing deep into ferns and shrubs. The occasional small tree rose above the rest of the greenery, and vines wound their way up the walls.

Gwen led her toward several tables overflowing with a selection of fruit and cheese and tarts. As they stood with plates in hand, trying to choose between one delicious item after another, Abigail casually glanced around.

"The duke did not join us," she said in a quiet voice.

Gwen frowned and looked over each shoulder. "I thought I saw him come through, but perhaps I was wrong. Since he did not know of the party, he might have had other plans."

"Or perhaps he wanted to show his mother that he could not be controlled all the time."

Gwen gave a soft gasp.

"I'm sorry," Abigail quickly said. "Just knowing that he might have been protected from suffering the consequences of his actions, all because he's a duke, makes me assume the worst of him. That is unprofessional of me."

As others approached the refreshment tables, Abigail inclined her head, and Gwen followed her until they were standing alone beneath an orange tree.

"Lady Gwendolin!" Lady Elizabeth waved as she came toward them. She lowered her voice. "So what did my brother say to you during luncheon? I am so excited for you!"

Gwen glanced at Abigail with wide eyes and answered cautiously. "We simply spoke of people we knew in London. Why are you excited for me?"

"Because Mother invited you to spend time with the duke." And then she frowned in dismay. "Oh, dear, perhaps I was not supposed to say that. I am forever speaking before I think."

To save her friend from having to answer, Abigail said, "So the duke is at last planning to marry."

Lady Elizabeth blushed. "Well, he has begun to hint such a thing to Mother. And it is time, you know. I keep telling him that once he marries, I might actually have women friends who like me for me!"

When Abigail and Gwen winced in sympathy, the young woman only shook her head and chuckled. "Do not worry for me. I have good friends I can rely on."

"Then forgive my curiosity," Abigail said, "but beyond the obvious, why has he suddenly changed his mind about marriage? Is there some mystery we ladies should know about?"

Abigail was hoping for her first clue into the mind of the duke. Even Gwen seemed frozen, waiting for the answer.

Lady Elizabeth only chuckled. "He is seven and twenty, Miss Shaw. I think he has finally realized that a woman can help him, perhaps even be a comfort in his busy life." She patted Abigail's arm. "You are so amusing!"

And then she sailed away, and Abigail felt like deflating.

"Good try," Gwen said, taking a sip of her lemonade.

Abigail sighed. "I'm sure the answer would have helped you, too."

"What do you mean?" she asked, her brow wrinkled in confusion.

Abigail looked around, but the duke was still nowhere to be seen. She lowered her voice. "My purpose here will not make things easy for you."

"What are you talking about?" Gwen asked, wide-eyed.

"Well . . . he is looking for a wife, is he not? And his mother said he 'speaks highly' of you. There are only three eligible women here. Don't you see—he favors you!"

Gwen stared at her for almost a minute, then burst out laughing. Lady Swarthbeck and Lady Greenwich both turned to stare, but Gwen's merriment took a moment to die down.

"Oh, Abby, dear, you know me by now," she said, wiping tears from her eyes. "Why ever would I be interested in becoming a duchess?"

"Because you could marry *him*. I mean—look at him!"

"Well, he is not here to look at, is he? And I know that he is a handsome devil, but I feel nothing for him except pity."

Abigail gaped. "Pity!"

"Well, of course. Wealth and privilege and power are fine, but the responsibilities of his position are not to be taken lightly. If I were a duchess, I would have to support everything he did, wouldn't I? Do you know how much time it takes to entertain? My charity work would suffer! And the thought of people treating me as almost a princess, 'Her Grace' this and 'Her Grace' that—ugh. And I thought being the daughter of an earl was tedious." She sighed. "I imagine if I loved him, I might feel different, but . . . he is so aloof, so mysterious. Too much work for me."

She patted Abigail's arm, and Abigail almost didn't feel it, so full of disbelief was she. How could Gwen not be lured by the thought of being the woman in the duke's life, the focus of his intensity, the one who shared his bed at night?

Good Lord, what was Abigail thinking? Her cheeks felt scalded. What happened to journalistic objectivity?

"Now you see that pleasant vicar standing alone over there?" Gwen said.

Abigail turned to see Mr. Wesley at the refreshment table, looking at the food as if he didn't know where to start. He was a nice-looking young man but seemed a bit too shy and out of his element.

"That is a man whose purpose I admire," Gwen said. "His sole focus is to save men's souls." She giggled. "I can be so amusing. Now enjoy yourself, Abby!"

She left Abigail standing alone, feeling foolish and confused.

And . . . relieved. She would not have to worry that whatever her investigation turned up would harm Gwen or her future.

After setting her plate down on a little table beside a bench, she decided to explore the conservatory. As she followed the winding path, the sounds of people seemed to fade, muffled by the immense ferns and flowering camellias. The stone path took a sharp turn when she reached the glass wall and a door to the outside. She could see a stunning garden, glistening with rain, and she followed the wall to see it better, before coming to a stop at a large shrubbery that had grown up against the glass.

Suddenly, she could hear voices nearby. She froze, feeling guilty. Just because she was at Madingley Court under false pretenses, she shouldn't jump at every little—

But it was the duke's deep baritone she heard. He *had* come into the conservatory but had not bothered mingling with his guests. Her first instinct was to politely walk away, like a well-raised young lady.

But as a journalist, she was being given the perfect opportunity. She had to take it.

Staring into the wall of shrubbery, she realized if she ducked her head a bit, she could just catch a glimpse of the duke—and his mother. Guilt seared her again, and she almost ran. But clasping her trembling hands together, she forced herself to stay.

The duchess was seated on a bench that faced out toward the beautiful view of the park. Abigail could only see half of the duke, but it was enough so that his exasperated expression was plain.

"Mother, you should have let Elizabeth be the center of this party. She—and I—would have enjoyed it better."

"Nonsense, Christopher," the duchess said with an elegant wave of her hand. "Your sister was thrilled to share this first event with you. I know she is a brave girl, but she is still overwhelmed at being the sudden center of focus in Society."

Why was he so upset? Abigail wondered. Gwen had told her this was the first house party the duchess had ever given. Perhaps her son had taken for granted that this house—this palace—was his sanctuary.

"Mother, you are deliberately misstating Elizabeth's excitement. She is not fragile."

"And neither are you, Christopher. It is time for you to do your duty to the family and your ancestors. These are the young ladies who specifically interest you. It will not cause you untold agonies to spend time with each of them."

"Mother, I have plenty of time to find a bride. You always said I would know her when I met her, that you and Father shared a single stare and knew that it was destiny."

Though there was sarcasm in his tone, his mother did not take offense. Abigail rather thought she should. But then again, how could Abigail be upset with his attitude when she herself wanted nothing to do with her father's matchmaking?

"And it is not just your future marriage that concerns me," the duchess said with admirable patience. "I worry about you. You seldom come home, and when you do, you are distracted and distant."

The duke crossed his arms over his chest and glanced out the window. He was avoiding meeting her eyes—he was hiding something.

"You know how many things I have to attend to," he said patiently. "I am surprised that I manage enough hours to sleep."

"You have always been busy," the duchess said in a gentler voice, "even when you were a boy."

A smile quirked his lips. "But then I was busy doing inappropriate things."

He had not always been the model of a gentleman, this perfectly controlled duke. At least he admitted it.

"You need to relax and enjoy your good fortune more," the duchess said. "You have more than made up for the past."

The faint smile slid away from the duke's face. For just a moment, Abigail glimpsed a stark bleakness in his eyes, but it was gone so quickly that she knew he was well practiced in hiding his emotions.

In a brisk tone, he said, "Mother, the past is long put to rest. Shall I tell you what I have been doing lately to distract myself?"

Abigail didn't think she'd breathed, let alone moved, but suddenly the duke's head lifted, and their gazes clashed. He had seen her. If she ran, he would know of her guilt. If she stayed, could she bluff her way out of it?

Heart pounding with excitement and dread, she knew she was about to find out.

Chapter 4

C hristopher caught a glimpse of bright blue in the middle of greenery. Someone was listening.

"Christopher?" his mother said, when he didn't continue. "What have you been doing to distract yourself?"

He gave her a brief smile. "I'm not sure that you deserve to know after what you've done here."

She rose to her feet, scowling. "You cannot tease me, then withdraw. It is . . ." She looked like she was struggling to find the right word.

"Maddening? Now you know how I felt when I arrived today."

She reached up and pinched his cheek as if he were five years old. "You never could keep a secret from me for long." And then she whirled and walked away.

Christopher remained still, staring into a woman's wide eyes, waiting for his mother to be gone. The woman didn't run away, and reluctantly, he had to admire that. And then he reached for her and pulled her right through the bushes. He heard her gasp, saw the way a strand of her hair caught on a branch before pulling out of her chignon to trail across her shoulder.

It was Lady Gwendolin's friend, Miss Shaw. She stared up at him. And he realized that along with her brown hair, he'd thought her brown eyes would match—but he'd been wrong. They were flecked with a warm gold, like hidden treasure. He thought a guilty woman would tremble, but she didn't. She was breathing fast; if he put his hand on her heart, he would feel its frantic pace.

He suddenly realized the strangeness of his thoughts. Hand on her heart? By God, her family would be demanding marriage before the day was through.

He gave her a little shake before he let her go. "What do you have to say for yourself?"

"Forgive me, Your Grace," she said, and bit her plump lower lip as if with chagrin.

What would those lips taste like?

By the devil, the girl had been spying on him, and all he could think about was kissing her?

"I did not mean to catch you unawares," she continued. "I was exploring, and when I heard you with your mother, I did not want to disturb you and have you think that I . . ."

She trailed off, fluttering her hands as if with

helplessness. Why did he get the feeling that she was anything but helpless?

"I mean . . . we have only recently been introduced," she finished lamely.

Christopher didn't understand his anger. This was nothing a half dozen women hadn't tried before. He almost felt . . . disappointed in her, and he wasn't certain why. He didn't know her—he didn't *need* to know her.

But he kept noticing random things, like how her voice was pleasantly modulated, a bit deeper than normal, but without a northern accent, though Lady Gwendolin had said she'd come from Durham.

"Surely you visit Lady Gwendolin often," he said.

She looked baffled at the direction of their conversation. "Uh . . . yes, I do."

"But with this recent visit to London, you have won the prize of a stay at Madingley Court," he said sarcastically.

She cocked her head. "I am not quite sure that feeling uninvited and bothersome to my dear friend and her hosts counts as having 'won the prize.'"

He arched a brow as he stared down at her. From their first meeting, he had appreciated that she was a woman who could still speak coherently when talking to him.

"My mother would not have included you if she

hadn't wanted to," Christopher said shortly. "You are not bothersome to her, or I'm sure to Lady Gwendolin—only to me."

"It will not happen again, Your Grace," she said softly.

But she did not lower her head in meekness, only continued to stare at him. And in that moment, he had an insane urge to push her back against a tree and kiss her, to discover if her body was as soft and welcoming as it looked. There was a crackling moment of tension between them, and what brought him out of it was that she seemed just as surprised as he was.

They both took a step back.

"Might I leave, Your Grace," she said, "before my face is so red that I shan't be fit company?"

"You may."

She turned and left, not hurrying, and he was able to watch the sway of her hips, the way her skirts almost seemed to shimmer. Between the lush curves of her hips and breasts, she had a narrow waist that made her almost look delicate.

But he guessed that Miss Shaw was not the delicate sort.

Had she gotten away with a deliberate offense against him? He would have to keep an eye on her—and subdue his impractical thoughts. He had not had a woman in several months; surely that was the reason he was noticing everything feminine about her.

* * *

That evening before dinner, Abigail was trying to decide which gown to wear to give the impression that she was slightly repentant but not crushed. Was that even possible?

It had been far too thrilling to face down the duke of Madingley though she'd been in the wrong. He'd been furious with her, she knew, but somehow they had not been able to stop looking at each other. She didn't know what to make of the strange sensations that had buffeted her contrary body.

Just before they'd parted, had he actually been staring at her mouth?

She had to stop thinking such ridiculous things. The duke had three beautiful women waiting for his attentions. She had to concentrate on what was important—that he'd long felt he had to make up for the past, according to his mother.

What had happened in his past?

She was relieved to know that she was on the right track. The duke had a secret. What could have happened that no one but family knew about? Abigail couldn't imagine quizzing his sister. At least not in a bold manner, she amended. But if his family wouldn't talk, there were always the servants, many of whom must have begun their employment when the duke was a child.

But she regretted how much harder she'd made things for herself by being discovered eavesdropping. The duke was bound to remain suspicious of her. She would have to tread very carefully.

There was a knock on the door, and Gwen peeked in.

"Might I come in?"

"Of course. You can help me choose a gown."

Gwen looked radiant in gold for her first dinner at Madingley Court.

"If you don't want the duke's attention," Abigail said dryly, "you might want to wear a less stunning gown."

"Stunning?" Gwen echoed happily. "What high praise! But there are other men here to impress."

"All of whom are interested in Lady Elizabeth."

"I do not believe that is true," Gwen said, primly lifting her nose in the air. "While you were mysteriously absent, I discovered that the vicar, Mr. Wesley, had only been invited to even our numbers at the dinner table."

Abigail gasped. "And he knew that? How sad!"

"No, no, he always volunteers his services. He says he owes the family a great deal and regards them highly." Gwen rolled her eyes. "He did like to go on about them."

"Or perhaps he didn't know what to say to you."

Gwen actually blushed before clearing her throat. "So where did you disappear to this afternoon?"

"I already told you," Abigail said, turning away to look at her gowns again.

"To explore the conservatory, I know. Then why did I see the duke reappear just after you did?"

Abigail turned back to face her friend and could not stop the grin that overtook her face. "I encountered the duke—in a rather unusual way. He caught me eavesdropping on him."

Gwen gave a shocked gasp, followed by an admiring grin of her own. "You deliberately followed him!"

"No, I stumbled on his mother and him by accident. And I didn't hear much, only that the duchess says he has to stop making up for the past."

"Ooh!" Gwen said, coming even closer. "And then they caught you!"

"His mother didn't. He let her leave before he pulled me out of hiding."

"He laid his hands on you!"

"By your excitement, I can't help wondering if you wish you were I," Abigail said hesitantly.

"No, no, I told you, I have no interest. But the duke is so very careful with women. You can imagine what one might do to marry him."

"I'm not surprised. But he seemed to believe my apology." Abigail found herself far too embarrassed to confess she'd had foolish, romantic thoughts about the duke. "I think I've made things much harder on myself."

"He will be suspicious," Gwen said in agreement, but she spoke almost absently.

"But I will manage it."

Gwen said nothing as a frown narrowed her eyes.

"Is something wrong?" Abigail asked.

"Talking about the women who'd do anything to marry a duke has me thinking. Lady Theodosia and Lady May are the perfect candidates for a duchess."

"Not yourself?" Abigail said with a grin.

Gwen only waved her words away, still without a smile. "But there is one other woman whom I am surprised is not here—at least if her own subtle boasts can be believed."

"Who is that?" Abigail asked with interest.

"Madeleine Preston. She is a gentleman's daughter, with a family fortune and lands that are quite impressive. Her brother went to school with the duke, although we don't often see him in Society since he prefers the family home in Scotland. But Miss Preston is frequently seen dancing with His Grace. She has made it clear to several of her friends—who told *me*—that the duke is interested in her."

"But she's not here, so his mother must not know. She is a lead I will follow when I return to London."

"You are so confident, Abby," Gwen said fondly, "even though that has not always stood you in good stead."

Abigail gave her friend a little push, and Gwen pretended to stagger.

"Don't say that. There is too much at stake. Now help me choose a gown!"

After a lovely dinner, where Abigail sat between brooding Lord Swarthbeck and shy Mr. Tilden, the ladies retired to the drawing room, leaving the men to their drink and stories. How she wished she could eavesdrop on that! But she sensed that His Grace was just as reserved with men as he was with women. Something had made him that way, but she couldn't imagine what.

Though Abigail said little to the women, she did not feel excluded, and even enjoyed their gossip about who was engaged to whom. At last the men rejoined them. She felt an expectancy in the air. The single ladies and gentlemen confronted each other as if occupying a battlefield rather than a sedate drawing room.

She was standing with Gwen when, to her surprise, the duke approached them. Abigail wasn't certain how she was supposed to feel as he bore down on them, all dark shadows and unreadable eyes. Had he told his family about her audacity? Would he even now scold Gwen for bringing her?

She and Gwen curtsied as he gave them a short bow. Abigail was strangely unnerved and told herself it was because she was keeping a secret from him. Before their encounter this afternoon, she'd thought him a reserved man who would be appalled and angered if he knew what was going on. To counter that, she'd been telling herself that he was a public person and that the public had the right to know, especially if a crime had been committed.

But when he looked into her eyes again from his great height, she felt a little catch in her breathing that didn't have anything to do with her nervousness over her investigation. It was the same feeling as this afternoon all over again, and she'd thought she would be better able to control it a second time. But no. She had to be honest with herself: He was a stunning man, so exotic in his features, so composed—too composed?

"Lady Gwendolin, it is pleasant to see you again," he said.

Even his voice set off delicious little shivers inside Abigail. There was nothing to indicate that he was not British through and through, but his very differentness intrigued her.

"It was so kind of your mother to invite me," Gwen said, smiling up at him.

He nodded to Abigail. "Miss Shaw."

Abigail curtsied again. "How do you do this evening, Your Grace?"

"Fine, thank you," he said in a clipped manner.

"Really?" she found herself saying. "I would not have thought so this afternoon, when you first entered the drawing room and saw all of us."

Instead of repairing the damage from the afternoon, she waded in deeper. Gwen was almost gaping at her. Behind her, she heard a lady's gasp and the sound of a cup rattling in its saucer. But Abigail didn't turn away from the duke to see whom she'd offended. At least *he* wasn't offended, if his interested expression was any proof. And maybe that was something she could like about him.

The duke arched a brow as his eyes, so dark and hidden, delved into hers. "Miss Shaw, you have no problem saying whatever comes to mind, do you? I also prefer honesty."

"But you are not willing to say if you knew about this party given by your mother."

At last he gave a faint smile, and the devastating effect of those white teeth in his dark face could not be underestimated. Her heart didn't seem to know its correct beat anymore.

"You're setting me up against my mother, Miss Shaw," he said. "Stark honesty does not always work best in such a relationship."

Abigail tilted her head, smiling in return. "Does she agree with you?"

At last, the duke freed her from the capture of his gaze and glanced at Gwen.

"Lady Gwendolin, I do believe that your friend is accusing the duchess of manipulation."

Gwen only laughed and patted the duke's forearm. "Your Grace, every mother is entitled to do what she must to see to her children's happiness.

And I think your mother believes you would be happiest spending time with all of us."

The duke glanced back at Abigail, as if including her. "I can hardly deny that her methods work, not without appearing the cad."

"Or appearing as if you are too set against her plan," Abigail added.

He bowed. "This has been an enlightening conversation, ladies."

He meant to leave them, Abigail knew. But before he could, his sister rose to her feet.

"Excuse me!" Lady Elizabeth called.

Her face was even more flushed with excitement, and Abigail saw Mr. Tilden regarding her with unabashed awe.

"Ladies and gentlemen, I am ready to tell you about the special theme I've chosen for our house party. It will give us all a chance for merriment together, but it is nothing too strenuous. In fact, you may participate as much or as little as you wish—"

"Can you not tell us?" Lady May interrupted plaintively. "I cannot bear the suspense!"

Everyone chuckled.

"Very well," Lady Elizabeth said. "I am glad you are as excited as I am! Madingley Court is an ancient house, and like so many others, it has a reputation for being haunted." She clasped her hands together. "So we are going to hunt for the ghost!"

People leaned together to laugh or talk, but Abigail thought there was a general air of curiosity, regardless of the silliness of the task.

When she glanced at the duke, she saw a frown flicker in his eyes, then quickly masked. He was obviously accustomed to hiding whatever he was thinking.

"There have been sightings of a ghost for at least two hundred years," Lady Elizabeth continued, "although I myself have never been so fortunate as to witness it." She shared a smile with her mother. "But Madingley Court is over two hundred and fifty years old, and the castle ruins on the grounds are even older. Both might be full of fascinating ancestors who could have decided to linger in the afterlife. Whoever discovers the most stories about the ghost will win a prize."

Regardless of the duke's displeasure, Abigail thought it a wonderful idea. It would give her even more reason to be wandering the house, looking into old secrets best left undisturbed.

"You may form teams," Lady Elizabeth added, "or work on your own."

Abigail noticed that both Lady May and Lady Theodosia were eyeing the duke with interest. Abigail knew there would be resistance if he tried to withdraw from the competition. The two ladies glared at each other, as if they were about to make their move. Abigail debated maneuvering him into choosing her, but after the awkwardness in the conservatory this afternoon, she doubted he would trust anything she did. She needed to win his trust. No, she could not be his partner.

But whom would he choose?

Chapter 5

After Elizabeth's announcement, Christopher saw many female eyes turn toward him, while his sister blinked at him with studied innocence. She didn't know that he'd wanted peace and quiet for the week to finish his project. She wanted something different, success in her first house party, and he could not begrudge her that. Yet now strangers on a ghost hunt would be running through his home, prying into things that didn't need to be disturbed.

To avoid the expectant look in the three eligible ladies' eyes, Christopher found himself glancing at Miss Shaw. She looked intrigued and excited, and he didn't know why he should feel disappointed. Women loved a mystery.

He waited for the others to begin choosing partners, but there was an unnatural silence, and more than one glance his way. Even the men hesitated, as if waiting for Christopher to make the first choice.

He resisted a sigh. "Elizabeth, I am not sure how much I will be able to participate, so it is best I work alone."

Of his three possible brides, Lady May pouted, Lady Theodosia sighed, but Lady Gwendolin looked away as if unconcerned. He couldn't decide if perhaps she had a very different strategy for winning him. It was always refreshing when women didn't openly pursue him.

"After all, ladies," he said, raising both hands, "how can I play favorites among you?"

Did Miss Shaw's lips quiver in a smirk before she, too, turned away? She and Lady Gwendolin moved off together, arm in arm, speaking softly. He felt that regardless of what he said, Miss Shaw sensed the real truth beneath his words, almost as if she read his mind.

Lady May and Lady Theodosia now took their turn, advancing in a line like battalions taking formation for battle.

Lady May said, "Your Grace, what an amusing idea your sister has proposed! But surely you cannot enjoy it all alone."

"Yes, it will be terribly difficult," he said gravely, "but it only seems fair."

"Your Grace," chimed in Lady Theodosia's calm voice, "perhaps you do not have to choose. Your sister said we could work in teams, so the three of us could—"

"Ladies." He cut them off with practiced charm.

"I will make a poor teammate. I have far too much work to do while I am here. Perhaps the two of you could work together."

He extricated himself as they gaped at each other in disbelief. These were the women he'd thought interested him the most?

But it was not fair to judge them so harshly. When he'd first met them, they'd seemed so sweet and biddable, lovely and desirable, ideal young women with the right backgrounds. He wanted an innocent, demure noblewoman whom he could easily take care of, as he'd been trying to take care of his family, a woman who would reflect well on everything important to him.

Lady May and Lady Theodosia had had few chances at conversation with him, with their chaperones usually keeping close watch. But now they were showing him a different aspect of themselves. He imagined the pressure they were under from their families to attract good husbands. If it was anything like the pressure his mother was putting on him . . .

He didn't want to be here making small talk, not when his mind was elsewhere, and there was work to be done. As the teams were formed, he managed to slip out of the room and reach his own chambers. Rather than enjoying the peace of his home over the next week, he would be dodging ghost-hunting and duke-chasing women.

As he loosened his cravat, he reminded himself

that the women he was interested in were still so very young. When he was young, he had never cared how his actions affected his family. He had been wild and hot-blooded, acting before he thought, a Cabot through and through. It had taken a terrible mistake and dire consequences for him to see that he had to make his father proud, to be the one Cabot in control of the family.

Christopher had spent his youth waiting in line for his destiny as a duke, to be respected and held in awe by everyone. But he hadn't imagined how solitary he would feel, as if he weren't just a man but an object desired for social betterment, for political assistance—or for marriage.

So he held himself under the strictest command, doing his duty to the king, his country, and his family, holding back every impulse churning to be set free. He knew where such undisciplined emotions led. Only with the occasional willing female did he allow himself to experience true passion. He had never had a mistress—too many chances for difficulties that would reflect badly on him. But to certain willing women, of a lower class than his own, he could be quite generous, with both his money and his body. But only for a night or two, never more. Those rare moments of passion, when he indulged his senses, forgot who and what he was, were a release in more ways than one.

But the rest of the time he only let most people

see what they expected, the proper duke of Madingley, in control of his family and their independent ways. He'd grown up close to his cousins, Matthew Leland and Daniel Throckmorten, who'd been at his side from his wild youth to his proper adulthood. But Matthew had died last year serving the queen's army in India, leaving a grieving bride, and Daniel had just married last month. Christopher was on his own. Even Daniel did not know the secret that Christopher had been keeping, the newest way he'd found to release the part of himself that yearned for expression. And Christopher planned to keep it that way.

Someone knocked on the door, and he gave a start. Since it could not possibly be one of his bridal targets, he called for the person to enter.

His mother closed the door and leaned against it, watching him with concern. "You retired rather early."

"I have so much ghost research to do," he said lightly.

She finally smiled. "Do not tease your poor sister. She was looking for a way to make her house party stand out, and she has certainly done so. You should allow yourself to relax."

He shrugged. "I'll try."

And they both knew it would be a feeble attempt. He had spent his adult life working too hard.

The duchess looked away, almost as if with hesitation.

Christopher casually rested an elbow on the desk. "Out with it, Mother."

"Sadly, we are not so far removed from London here that we can avoid the dark mutterings of rumors."

He arched a brow. "Surely we are used to those. It cannot be my cousin, Daniel, causing problems. His marriage has surely settled him."

"I am not so sure of that," she said, a smile twinkling in her eyes before she sobered. "But no, it is not Daniel. It is Madeleine Preston."

Christopher leaned his head back against his wingback chair and sighed. "What has she done now?"

"She is rather open in her pursuit of you, is she not?"

"She is. So I am grateful that you did not invite her."

"Yet you feel guilty," she answered shrewdly.

"How could I not? Her brother is my good friend."

"And he wouldn't want you to consider his sister just because of that friendship."

"But *she* wants me to," Christopher said darkly.

"I knew she was using your past against you," his mother said.

"Mother, please do not worry. I have made it clear, as gently as possible, that I am not interested in marrying her, regardless of how she believes we're connected." He held up a hand when she would have interrupted. "But if it makes you feel better, I will write to Michael and enlist his help with his sister."

She studied him a moment too long but only nodded instead of saying more. His mother had always been good at letting him run his own life—until his need for a bride had become too much for her. He went to her and kissed her cheek, still regretting the sorrow he'd put her through when he was young.

"I will make a good choice, *Madre*," he said softly.

"Soon?"

"Soon. But probably not this week."

She smiled and patted his chest. "Then can you not enjoy yourself with our guests?"

"I will, I promise. But not every moment of every day. And you cannot make me hunt for imaginary ghosts," he added, pretending sternness. "Whatever gave Elizabeth such a crazy—"

"She is young, Christopher."

And if that was the most foolish thing his sister did in her youth, then she had him bested.

Though Abigail had stayed awake far too late, writing down every conversation and conclusion she'd drawn from the evening, she made sure that she was, but for the servants, the first person up in the morning. She wore a front-buttoning gown, so she wouldn't need the assistance of a maid at dawn. She wanted to be alone in the dining room for breakfast, the better to begin her casual interviewing of the servants. Luckily, Miss Bury was an easy chaperone, who seemed to assume that her presence somewhere in the household was enough to make her charges behave.

But while guests came and went through the morning, planning their ghost-hunting strategies, haunting the library to look for old family histories, or already writing home about the intriguing house-party theme, Abigail grew more and more discouraged. No matter how cleverly she worded her questions, how brainless she made herself appear to ease suspicions, she could not persuade a single servant to speak about the Cabot family. From the footmen at breakfast to the maid sweeping out the coal grates to the laundress to whom Abigail took a stained gown, no one had anything to say. Of course their livelihoods depended on the Cabots, but Abigail was good at seeing beneath a veneer to the truth behind words. To her, it seemed they had absolutely nothing to complain about and loved working for this "perfect" family.

How could they be so perfect? Abigail had done her research. The current duke's grandfather had neglected his children so much in pursuit of expanding his fortune that all of their marriages had created scandals. One daughter had married a poor composer and been accused of killing him for a symphony; another had married a professor caught up in an anatomy scandal with corpses; and the duke's father had fallen in love with a common Spanish girl, thumbing his nose at Society's expectations for a duke's marriage.

Yet although she had received hints of squabbling among the family, it seemed they all treated their servants so well that they inspired great loyalty. And normally Abigail would admire that. But it did not help her investigation.

The duke was obviously not going to take the ghost hunting seriously because Abigail never saw him throughout the morning. She'd overheard that he had meetings with his steward and several bailiffs of neighboring properties. Yet he put in an appearance at luncheon—probably for his mother's sake.

From across the room, Abigail watched the way the Ladies May and Theodosia latched on to the duke from both sides. They were opposite in temperament, the first demanding and emotional, the second more reserved and mature, but they were after the same thing and did not seem to care who knew it.

Why should Abigail feel sorry for him? He had a perfect, comfortable future all laid out before him. He could choose whomever he wanted as a wife, while Abigail might be forced to marry a man she didn't love. She would have a boring life she didn't want, and only this story could save her from that.

Today's luncheon was to be a picnic in the park, Lady Elizabeth announced, then a tour of the grounds, including the ruins of an ancient castle, the original stronghold of the Cabots when they were mere earls. There was certainly enough history to sponsor an occasional ghost. Abigail saw the duke's lack of reaction to the announcement, and she imagined he was planning ways to escape.

And then she lost sight of him as Gwen took her arm and hurried her down the corridor at the end of the crowd of guests.

"Where have you been?" Gwen asked with quiet urgency.

Abigail frowned at her, and whispered, "You know what I am doing. I've been trying to interview the servants, and not a single one would speak to me about the family."

"You cannot be surprised."

"No," Abigail agreed heavily. "But I had to try. I will have to think of another method to encourage people to talk."

"Well, right now, you have to listen to what I've been doing about the ghost."

Abigail rolled her eyes. "Gwen, you cannot believe that I—"

"Just listen! Mr. Wesley says—"

"The vicar? Is that who you spent your morning with?"

To Abigail's amazement, Gwen blushed again. Side by side, they followed the others through the main door outside and down the stairs into the courtyard. Though the sun was shining through dappled, fluffy clouds, Gwen continued to hold Abigail's arm as if to ward off a chill.

"We were both in the library together," Gwen continued, "and Mr. Wesley had managed to find the one remaining book on the Cabots, a very ancient one about the old castle ruins and the start of the family."

"The one remaining book?"

"Those silly girls beat us there," Gwen said, tossing her head toward the ladies vying for the duke's attention. "They've decided to work together, the better to keep an eye on each other where the duke is concerned. They'll probably hide all the books, so the rest of us can't use them."

"Devious *and* intelligent," Abigail said. "I'm impressed."

Gwen sighed and looked ahead toward the duke, who was escorting his sister across the wide green expanse of lawn. "That poor man."

"Well, I imagine you'll have him trailing you soon if you keep avoiding him. It will be a refreshing change from the other two. But there is the vicar," Abigail amended, seeing Gwen's narrow-eyed look.

"We are just helping each other research the ghost," Gwen insisted, "since I couldn't find you."

"I will be a poor teammate," Abigail said regretfully.

"And I understand why. I've told Mr. Wesley that you are not in the best of health, that you suffer headaches and require rest. He's quite concerned about you."

"Do I look ill?" Abigail demanded with exasperation. "What will he think when I keep reappearing in the best of health?"

"That your headache is gone. Try to look fatigued occasionally. Meanwhile, I'll do our research. It is rather fun, you know."

Abigail grinned. "Especially with the handsome Mr. Wesley."

"It is not like that," Gwen said hotly. "We will simply be helping each other."

To Abigail's surprise, the walk went on far longer, down a wide path in the center of the sculpted gardens. At the edge of the park, a pavilion had been set up, facing a large pond, the woodland beyond, and the castle ruins on the water's far edge. Blankets had been spread out for the guests, along with several chairs for those who did not wish to sit on the ground. Lord Swarthbeck, Lord Greenwich, and their wives sat with the other older guests around a table.

In the rush to be near the duke—or for the men, near Lady Elizabeth—Abigail found herself sharing a blanket with Gwen and Lord Keane, who did not stoop to open pursuit even if Lady

Elizabeth was the sister of a duke. At the refreshment table, they filled their plates with pigeon pie, salad, and jam puffs, then returned to their blanket, where Lord Keane sprawled on his side to eat, while Gwen and Abigail folded their legs beneath them to sit. Ginger beer in flasks slaked their thirst.

Though arrogant, Lord Keane could be an amusing man, and they laughed their way through the meal. Abigail stole occasional glances at the duke, who naturally shared a blanket with the two young ladies. Unlike Lord Keane, His Grace did not seem to be at all relaxed, although his expression was pleasant as he spoke to his admirers.

"It is a shame he cannot enjoy it," Lord Keane said.

Abigail turned her head in surprise. "You mean the duke?"

"Yes. Wasn't that who you were looking at?" he said, his lips turned up in the faintest smirk.

Abigail controlled even the impulse to blush. "Yes, it is difficult to ignore the tableau of a man being hunted."

"And neither of you ladies is on the hunt?" Lord Keane asked, his hand propping up his head.

Gwen and Abigail exchanged a look, then a laugh.

"We are not on a hunt," Gwen said. "We are here to enjoy ourselves."

"What about you, Lord Keane?" Abigail asked. "Besides the chance to socialize with Lady Elizabeth—your own hunt, shall we say—do you know the duke well?"

Smiling, Lord Keane folded his hands under his head and looked up at the willow leaning low over them. "Though we were not in the same year at school, I have known Madingley since our youth."

It took everything in Abigail not to demand answers to all her questions, but she had to show restraint. A good journalist must be a master of the interview. "He is a very dignified man, and I hear quite successful in the House of Lords."

"Dignified," Lord Keane said with obvious amusement. "Yes, he is that—now."

"But not always?"

"Even we peers had our foolish youth to overcome. For someone not on the hunt, you are very curious, Miss Shaw."

Before Abigail could respond, Gwen cleared her throat and looked abashed. "She is only inquiring for me, my lord. I had no idea that the duke had any interest in me. How can I help but be curious about him?"

"Though he is rather staid now," Lord Keane said, "he was once considered reckless. They used to call it his 'wild Spanish blood,' but since it seems to be a trait of the Cabots, we should not slur his mother's unusual lineage, at least among us." He grinned, as if they shared a joke.

Gwen glanced at Abigail, and said in a hushed voice, "What did he do that was wild? I have heard nothing of this."

"You are too young," his lordship said. "And he did little more than what any young buck does, fresh from the control of his parents and tutors. It is not fit for feminine ears, of course."

Abigail barely resisted a groan. She wanted to shake the man and demand answers. But not now, not yet. She could be patient.

When the luncheon was over, the duke strolled toward the ruins, a lady on each arm, and Abigail couldn't resist following. The remnants of the ancient castle were composed of parts of walls, some still high enough overhead that she avoided walking near them lest they fall. Moss and ivy overran much of the stone, yet there were still areas that were passable, because she saw the duke and his escorts disappear within. She followed.

As she remained near enough to hear their casual conversation about the chance of a ghost in the ruins, Abigail didn't have to pretend interest in exploring the old castle. She had always had a vivid imagination, and as she entered the round turret, part of the defensive wall, she imagined knights in armor guarding the home of their lord—the home of ancient Cabots. What must it be like to trace one's family back so far? As far as she knew, her paternal grandfather had been a poor boy hawking newspapers on London streets.

Light grew dim within the castle, only peeping through the occasional hole in the wall. The voices of the two women ahead of her echoed with giggles, and Abigail hesitated, not wanting to alert them of her presence. To her surprise, the duke suddenly appeared in front of her, and as she gaped at him, he put a finger to his lips and pulled her aside, deeper within the gloom. He was far too close, capturing her between him and a wall, so that she was trapped. If she moved, their chests would touch. The air settled around them, with dust glimmering in a beam of light beyond them. And inside her, warmth spread like wildflowers.

"Where did he go?" came Lady May's plaintive voice.

"He said he saw something in the shadows and went to investigate," Lady Theodosia said with caution. "He didn't want us harmed by following him. Surely there are loose stones."

Abigail could see them now, looking about in desperation. But she said nothing, conscious of the duke's large hand still holding her upper arm as if she would flee.

"You do not suppose it was the ghost." Lady May's voice came out like a squeak. "His Grace wouldn't want us to remain where we might be in danger."

Abigail's nose began to tickle. She stopped breathing, trying desperately not to sneeze. Pressing her free hand beneath her nose, she saw by the duke's frown that he was aware of her situation. The tickling was becoming unbearable, and her eyes went wide and watered. If she revealed the duke's location, she would lose a chance at his trust.

"Let us leave," Lady Theodosia said. "The duke knows his way out."

"If the ghost lets him go," Lady May countered.

The absurdity of that, coupled with her need to sneeze, had Abigail shaking. Her shoulders brushed the wall, dislodging even more dust. At last she gasped for air, and the duke stepped back.

"They are gone," he said with relief.

She started to sneeze and couldn't stop. She felt a handkerchief pressed into her hands, and she made use of it with only a little embarrassment.

"Thank you," she finally said, wiping the tears from her eyes.

"No, thank you for not revealing us," he answered, looking down on her with faint amusement.

She chuckled. "You seemed quite desperate for my silence. I do not know why you don't simply ask them to give you a measure of peace."

"It is not necessary to hurt their feelings."

"Or your mother's feelings."

His teeth were a white flash in the gloom. "You think me a mama's boy."

"No, I think you're a man who is considerate of his mother."

When he didn't answer, their silence became awkward. Now that the ladies were gone, Abigail realized they were alone in a dark place and that he could think she was—

"Spying on me again?" he asked almost conversationally.

She sighed, meeting his dark eyes. "We came here to eat and tour the ruins. I'm touring the ruins, just as you are. Or as you were forced to, anyway."

"I was not forced to. It is only right for me to converse with everyone."

"Especially the eligible young ladies," she said, not bothering to hide a smile.

"I am conversing with you, am I not?"

"But I am not the same."

He leaned his shoulder against a column as he studied her. "And what do you mean by that?"

"We both know that I am not the sort of woman who could be your potential wife. In a sense, you're safe with me."

One side of his mouth curved up. "Safe, am I?"

There was a deep timbre to his voice that almost made her shiver. He was teasing her, she knew, but she ignored it. A plan had come into her mind, and she didn't have time to give it more than the briefest consideration.

"Safe," she answered firmly. "I am not interested in marrying you—the thought of becoming a duchess frightens me to no end."

"You, frightened?"

He was almost grinning now, and she was startled by how much more appealing it made him. He suddenly seemed like a different, very dangerous, man rather than a responsible duke. And he was far too intriguing like that, for it made her remember his wild side. Where had it gone?

"I have only been raised on the fringes of your world, Your Grace." And that was the truth. "I like the anonymity. But I have a proposition that might appeal to you."

His smile vanished, and his eyes moved languidly down her face. "A proposition?"

A blush of mortification heated her cheeks. "Do not read more into that word than is proper. I only meant that I had an offer for you."

He arched a brow, and then she really started stuttering.

"I—I mean that I'm making a proposal you should consider." She closed her eyes so she didn't have to look into his handsome, amused face. "Let me just say it then. I have no wish to marry a duke, and I know that you are going to marry a woman from your world, someone far above me in consequence and dowry."

"So now I'm a snob looking only for money."

"I know you don't need money," she said with exasperation, waving her hands about as if two castles were not enough proof. "But there are certainly expectations for a man in your situation. Lady May and Lady Theodosia both realize this.

And though it has obviously not occurred to them, their open pursuit of you is ruining their chances of either becoming your wife."

He cocked his head. "Is it now? Do tell me what I'm feeling."

She ignored his sarcasm. "I only have to study your expression to know that. You are not quite as enigmatic as you think."

He suddenly put a hand on the wall beside her head and leaned too close. "Then do tell me what I'm *thinking*, Miss Shaw."

She was glad that there was still a playfulness about him, but she knew that this situation could easily get out of hand if he wished it to.

"You are looking for a wife," she said, inwardly wincing at how her voice had become a bit breathless. She had to force herself not to look at his arm, so close to her, his hand, which was so large, splayed against the rough stone wall. He was making her feel trapped again, but now it was a far-too-intriguing sensation. "You want to look at your leisure, and make a logical, well-thought-out decision. But with the two ladies pursuing you, you can't even think, let alone relax. How can you possibly make a choice when their behavior is annoying you? I can help you with that."

"Do tell."

She didn't understand what was happening between them, why he was looking down at her from his great height, standing too close. He had women trailing after him, for heaven's sake. Why was he teasing her like this?

"You could pretend that you wish to spend time with *me*," she finished in a rush. "The other ladies will be disappointed, but they will leave you alone to make your decision in your own way, in good time. And they would hardly choose another man as husband, not until you've made your decision. And since we both agree that there is no future between us, you will be safe."

But would *she*?

Chapter 6

Christopher stared down at the surprising Miss Shaw. Was she actually offering to allow herself to be used, to be gossiped about, and someday to be pitied when he didn't choose her? It made no sense.

And though he didn't know her well, he already guessed that she was too smart a woman not to realize the consequences.

So why was she doing it? He didn't trust her motives, but he would discover them.

Though he had her backed against a wall, she didn't seem afraid. There was a forthrightness and courage about her that he wanted to admire, yet his suspicions kept getting in the way.

She thought she understood him, did she? After only twenty-four hours in the same house? She obviously trusted him in naïveté, for he could do anything he wanted to her, and only his version of the truth would count. He could be a lecher out to deflower her, by God.

Yet she stood there so brazenly offering her services.

And he found himself thinking about what a real offer from her would be like. For just a moment, he said nothing and let himself look his fill. She was not a classical beauty, but that gave her an air of openness and honesty, as if she were used to men seeing her as she was rather than fantasizing about her.

And there were those eyes, the deepest brown, lit by gold from within. A man could lose himself in there, forget everything. Her eyes looked wider and wider, and he suddenly realized he was bending too close.

He straightened and stepped away from her, disappointed by his own behavior. Again, he'd wanted to kiss her though he knew nothing about her. All he had was her word that she had no wish to marry him. That was so rare a proclamation that he didn't trust it.

Oh, he was beyond thinking about himself as quite the handsome catch, although he'd been that stupid briefly in his youth. When one married a duke, the groom was only a part of the package, which included wealth and comfort, luxurious homes scattered across several countries, and, of course, the title of *duchess*. He had long since gotten over the notion that a woman would ever love him for him. And as long as he and his wife got along well enough, and they desired each other, that would suit.

Miss Shaw cleared her throat. "So my suggestion has shocked you into speechlessness."

It was too easy to smile around her, so he resisted the urge. "I was only considering the merits of the idea."

She wrinkled her nose. "While you're considering, can we move into a different chamber? My sneezing is threatening a violent return."

"And how foolish of me, but I only have one handkerchief."

He lifted a hand toward the far wall, where a perfectly preserved arch led into the next chamber. He'd been there with the two ladies, but he had not taken them beyond. He found himself ushering Miss Shaw through, up several stone stairs into another room, where part of the wall had fallen away. The roof was long gone, and sunlight warmed them. The hedgerowed countryside spread out before them, uneven squares of farm and pastureland.

"It is lovely," she murmured. "Do you own it all?"

"Almost all. Not quite as far as the eye can see—in this direction."

She smiled, even though she didn't look his way. And he wanted her to look up, so he could look into those darkly fringed eyes again.

He had to get this foolish lusting under control. He'd never taken a woman of his own class to bed, and he wasn't about to start now, especially an innocent virgin under the protection of his own roof.

As they stood side by side, Christopher asked, "Why are you making this offer of your services, Miss Shaw? You must know that when I choose someone else, Society will pity you."

"And perhaps even ridicule me," she added in an unconcerned voice.

"And you do not care how it might look to your family?"

"My family is in Durham, Your Grace. My parents are unconcerned with the *ton* and seldom visit London. Even if they somehow hear a rumor, they would be grateful and amazed that I was even being considered by a duke."

"How will it feel to *you*?" he asked in a softer voice.

She glanced up at him. "You need have no worries about my tender feelings. I will see it as an adventure in my otherwise-boring life. And then I'll return home and find a sweet country squire to marry, someone as settled and simple and dull as I am."

"Dull?" He resisted the urge to tip her chin up to face him. He didn't want to feel how soft her skin might be, how warm. "I would not call you dull."

She suddenly seemed a bit skittish, as if she was surprised by his attention. "Then settled and simple."

He laughed, and it felt strange to do so with a woman who wasn't related to him. He had become so guarded, so careful, all out of need.

He could not allow himself to feel so relaxed, not even with a woman who professed no interest in him—and whose motives he still didn't understand.

"I will give your suggestion some consideration, Miss Shaw," he said at last.

She nodded gravely, but her eyes were alight with amusement. "Please do so, Your Grace."

He turned to face her. "You, too, should understand what you are getting yourself into."

"I already said I did." Her expression was full of confusion.

"I will be taking your hand often." He did so now, her small, gloved hand nestled within his. "I will lean near and speak to you in an intimate fashion."

She licked her lips, her only betrayal of uncertainty, yet her nod was firm.

"I have already considered that. I will use it as practice for when I return home and look for my own husband."

He considered her with amusement. "I have never before been used as a 'practice' suitor."

"That you know of," she countered.

And then she winked.

And something inside Christopher flamed higher with a need that had to be fought.

* * *

As the duke returned her to Gwen's side, Abigail couldn't help but notice the stares they received—the stares she'd been receiving ever since they were seen walking from the rear of the castle ruins. She took it all in stride, congratulating herself on coming up with the perfect way to remain conspicuously in sight and yet at the duke's side to listen to—and decipher—everything he said. She had not been lying when she'd told him she didn't care what people thought about her. Other than Gwen, she would never see these people again, for her world in London might as well be on the other side of the country from theirs.

Abigail allowed Gwen to pull her a little away from the party because it fitted so perfectly with the scene she'd staged.

Gwen spoke through smiling teeth. "How did you end up with the duke? I saw him leave with the ladies."

"And he abandoned them for me." Quietly, Abigail told her friend everything that had transpired. Well, not quite everything. She couldn't explain how it had felt when the duke had backed her up against the wall and leaned over her. There weren't words to describe such tumultuous and breathless feelings—and she usually knew how to come up with words!

"You've found the perfect way to remain close to him," Gwen said, admiration shining in her eyes.

"Do not congratulate me yet," Abigail said, watching as Lady May and Lady Theodosia bore down on the duke from opposite sides. "He has not agreed."

But His Grace turned and gave Abigail an impassive look, and she had the triumphant feeling that he was gladly going to accept her suggestion. She would have him to herself, she thought gleefully, and she could discover everything about him. After all, they would have nothing to do *but* talk.

Which only made her think of the other thing men and women did together. She firmly suppressed a shiver. They *wouldn't* be doing that. She would only go so far for her story. Deceiving the man was bad enough.

"Cold?" Gwen asked. "Would you like my shawl?"

"Thank you, no," Abigail answered, looking away to avoid her friend's eyes. "I don't think we'll remain outside for long. Lady Elizabeth looks like she's going to speak."

When the young woman stood alone in the center of their gathering, blankets and tables filled with people surrounding her, she clasped her hands together and smiled. "I have brought you all here because this is where the recorded history of the Cabots began."

She gestured gracefully to the ruins behind her, which reflected into the pond, a dual image of a savage and distant past, when even then, the Cabots were nobility.

"Over four hundred years ago, my distant ancestor became the earl of Chesterton, a title my brother still holds—until he has a grandson, that is."

Everyone laughed, and Abigail tried to imagine an infant with such a title.

"Chesterton had been a knight in the service of his king, Henry V, and won renown at the Battle of Agincourt against the French in 1415. For that he was given the title and this land, where he built a magnificent castle." She glanced with amusement to the ruins behind her. And then her face grew almost serious, as she said, "I am showing you this because there are those who believe that the ghost could date from the period of the first earl."

"Does the ghost appear here?" Lady May asked in a high voice.

Lady Elizabeth smiled. "I do not know. I have only heard about servants' sighting the ghost inside Madingley Court itself. I myself have never been lucky enough to see it." She glanced at her brother mischievously. "Madingley, did you ever see the ghost?"

The women on either side gaped up at him, and although there were chuckles, everyone seemed to wait expectantly on the duke's answer, as did Abigail. Was he the sort of man who would see ghosts—or even admit such a thing?

"No, my dear sister, I never saw a ghost."

There were sounds of dismay from around them, and Lady Elizabeth's happy expression faded a bit.

The duke sighed. "But my father's valet said he once woke up in the night with it above him, face-to-face—or so he claimed."

As Lady Elizabeth brightened, Gwen leaned close to Abigail. "What a nice man to help out his sister."

Abigail felt uncomfortable, as if she didn't want him to be such a nice man. But *she* was the villain here, much as she wished to lay blame on the duke.

Lady Elizabeth continued, "I wish you all to start on equal footing, so I will say that the ghost is a male figure, dressed in old-fashioned clothes. No one was able to date when the garments might have been in fashion."

"How very convenient," Lord Keane said dryly.

Abigail exchanged a glance with Gwen and had to resist a chuckle. It was almost as if they were in school again, exchanging stories to frighten each other.

"The ghost appeared concerned, even agitated, but not in a threatening way. And the strange thing was"—Lady Elizabeth added dramatically—"he was always carrying a quill pen."

The guests murmured to each other with animation.

"Could he have stabbed someone with it, and the victim had his revenge?" Gwen called out, and her question inspired good-natured laughter.

"No dripping blood, I'm afraid," Lady Elizabeth replied, smiling. "Just one agitated male ghost who might have been making a shopping list when he died."

Abigail watched the Ladies May and Theodosia begin to pester the duke. The next time he looked up at Abigail, she gave him a smile and a raised eyebrow. Like magic, he excused himself and made his way toward her. Suddenly she understood his concern about her feelings, because for just a moment, the heady sensation of being able to attract this enigmatic man overwhelmed her. And then she remembered who—and what she was. Their relationship was all business.

Eyes bright as if she were trying not to laugh, Gwen quickly excused herself, leaving Abigail standing alone. Watching the duke approach, his dark eyes intent on her, she imagined for a breathless moment what it would be like if he really wanted to be with her. If those eyes smoldered with sensual, rather than practical, need.

But she was a practical woman and did not let such wistful dreams tease her for long. She curtsied to the duke and did not look beyond him to the jealous expressions of the other women.

"Your Grace," she murmured, biting her lip to keep from smiling her triumph.

"I accept your terms on what we discussed."

She almost said, "You mean my proposition?" But if someone overheard and misunderstood, she would not be helping her cause. Instead, she nodded. "I am happy to be of assistance. You'll have to tell me how to proceed, because I'm not certain what people expect."

He cocked his head as he looked down at her. "Surely a lovely woman such as yourself is often courted by men."

She didn't have to fake her blush at his flirtatious words. "Society in Durham is rather limited. And after all, shouldn't being courted by a duke be far more exciting?"

He briefly frowned at her, and this time she could not help chuckling.

"You are so easy to tease, Your Grace, because you take everything I say at face value. If I cannot tease you, what fun will this be?"

She thought he would smile then, but instead his eyes seemed to roam her face.

"If you can tease me, then you must expect that I will do the same," he said in a low voice.

Her smile faltered. She wanted to tell him to stop doing that with his voice, but she could not so easily reveal her vulnerability. "How does a duke tease?"

"You shall find out. After all, we have to make this fascination with each other look real."

"*That* is definitely teasing," she admonished him.

He laughed, and she saw the Delane brothers watching with astonishment. It was a good beginning.

He turned and began to walk back toward the gardens, inclining his head to her. She realized she was supposed to go with him. They walked sedately for a bit, she very conscious of his presence, he remaining quiet, as if her presence was all he wanted from her. She was thinking too much about him as a man rather than the subject of her investigation, admiring the smooth, determined way he moved, as if he knew every inch of the vast property. But if they didn't talk, she would learn nothing about him.

"Were you raised here, Your Grace?" she finally asked.

He glanced at her with curiosity, and she waited with disappointment for him to say that conversation wasn't part of their arrangement.

"I spent much of my childhood here, yes."

To his own surprise, Christopher felt inclined to answer her questions. He usually deflected such discussions, preferring to know a person better before revealing anything of himself.

And after all, what did he know about Miss Shaw and her motives toward him? But he wasn't going to discover them if he offered nothing of himself. "And my cousins lived here as well," he added.

"How many cousins do you have?"

"My aunt Flora had one son, Daniel Throckmorten."

"Ah, the one who just married."

"They heard about that all the way in Durham?" he asked dryly.

"It is not every day that a man wins a wager against a woman's mother. I hope for their sakes that they are very happy."

"They are," he said, his tone softening. "And I never would have believed it of my rakish cousin."

"He is not as reserved as you?" she asked, her gaze taking in the expanse of roses and the two gardeners working among them.

"He would laugh at your suggestion that I am reserved." And why had he said that? It was the image he strove so hard to project.

"Ah, then you are one way with the public and another with your family," she said. "That is not so unusual."

He couldn't seem to stop watching her, where she seemed to see nothing but the scenery, as if she were just passing time. Her arms moved briskly at her sides as she walked, no mincing steps for her.

"So you like to keep yourself apart from Society," she said, when he had not spoken. "Is that the mark of a secretive man?"

"A cautious one."

"Then you have had reason to be so. How sad."

The path they trod now wound its way through a series of trellises spanning overhead, draped with ivy and twining vines. The sun dimmed, the air grew cooler.

"You do not strike me as a very cautious woman, Miss Shaw," he said.

She glanced up at him in surprise. "When caution is necessary, I exercise it. But here, amidst the cream of the *ton*? Why should I be?"

"And that is what is perplexing. I am still curious about your offer to help me."

Now she looked away. "You must be used to dealing with people who want something from you. I do not want anything besides your companionship, and the gratifying feeling of being useful. So tell me about your other cousins."

Suspicion always lingered too much in him, and he pushed it away. Miss Shaw was surely an eccentric, and that was all. "My aunt Rosa has two daughters younger than I, and a son, Matthew, who has since died."

The dappled sunlight revealed the sadness on her face. "You have my sympathy, Your Grace. How did your cousin die?"

"He was an army officer, serving the queen in India. He died a hero, although that does not ease his parents' pain. They have only just emerged from mourning, along with Matthew's widow. And besides my sister and myself, that is the last of my cousins."

"Not all that many, for such a large house. You could easily not see each other for days."

"We made sure that didn't happen."

"Three young men about the same age," she mused. "You must have been a handful, if your cousin Mr. Throckmorten had any say in the matter."

"I held my own," Christopher said, remembering with bittersweet fondness the many governesses they'd driven away.

"When we need a topic to discuss, you'll have to tell me of your adventures."

They were almost to the end of the trellis, and he wanted to take her hand, to stop her from emerging back into the world, back before prying eyes. But he'd always been so careful with virginal misses, and he would not stop now.

The sun almost blinded them, and he saw that several more of the guests were wandering back toward Madingley Court.

Miss Shaw gave him a rueful smile. "I would politely ask you what your plans are for the afternoon, Your Grace, but I sense you do not like people who pry into your privacy. So I give you leave to return to your duties before the other ladies waylay you."

"Then I wish you a good afternoon, Miss Shaw," he said, nodding to her.

As he watched her walk away, he found himself wanting to pry into *her* privacy, to know things about this strange young woman. No one could be so altruistic—not without a purpose.

Chapter 7

I t was too easy to follow the duke, Abigail thought, as she walked quietly through the garden, keeping shrubbery and trees between her and the guests, and peering between them to follow the duke's path.

She'd passed the first step, where he'd accepted her offer of help. So while she slowly earned the next level of his trust, she could not waste the opportunity to learn more about him.

So she followed him up to the house, watched him enter through the double doors off the stone terrace. When she stepped into the coolness of the house, she saw him at the far end of the corridor, where he left the public rooms and headed toward the family wing. She turned a corner just in time to see the duke disappear behind double doors at the far end of the wing. The master's bedroom, by chance?

And then she waited behind draperies for what seemed like hours. What was he doing in there during the day? Sleeping, or trying to escape the guests? If he was working, why was he not in his study? It was a mystery she had to unravel.

At last she made herself leave, knowing she would soon have to dress for dinner. She returned to her own room, silently congratulating herself on finding it. She hadn't been inside for more than a few minutes when someone knocked at the door.

Miss Bury peered inside. "Might I come in, Miss Shaw?"

Abigail blinked at her in curiosity. "Of course. What can I help you with, Miss Bury?"

"Oh, my dear, it is I who'd like to help you," the old woman said, closing the door behind her and leaning against it to consider Abigail. "I saw you in the castle ruins with His Grace."

A feeling of unease tightened her stomach, but Abigail reminded herself that she had no reason to be afraid. "Yes. We were exploring together."

"Good for you!" Miss Bury said with cheerful enthusiasm, walking spryly across the carpet.

Abigail smiled. "I am not certain what you mean."

"I know my practical Gwendolin does not wish to be a duchess, so I would love to see you try for the position!"

"I—I am merely spending time with him, Miss Bury. I know it will not lead to anything other than friendship." Abigail's face felt overly hot.

"You do not strike me as the pessimistic kind,

young lady. I will help you catch the duke's notice in any way I can. Those other two girls are far too silly for a man such as he."

Abigail could not help laughing quietly. "And what sort of man is that?"

"Why, a man who bears great burdens every day but does not show the strain. He has spent his adult life working hard to improve his family legacy, to care for his cousins as if they were his brothers and sisters."

"You make him sound like a mother hen," Abigail said lightly.

"Then I do him a great disservice."

"Perhaps he is a man who is far too involved in other people's concerns." She almost shuddered, knowing how much she resented her father's attempts to decide her future.

"It was not easy to be raised a Cabot, to bear up beneath the weight of intense scrutiny and expectations. And so far he has succeeded wonderfully. But he holds himself so correctly, and I sense great loneliness in him."

The stab of guilt took Abigail by surprise, but she was getting used to ignoring it. "He is a duke, Miss Bury. He is surrounded by many people every day."

"Too many people, if you ask me."

"Then he should relinquish the title."

Abigail spoke playfully, but Miss Bury looked puzzled.

"You know such a thing is impossible, Miss Shaw."

"Miss Bury, please, I was only jesting."

"Oh . . . well, I can see you do not believe that I am serious about the possibility of your catching the duke's eye."

Instead of being disappointed in her, the old woman just looked determined.

"Miss Shaw, I know something of waiting too long."

She spoke without bitterness, and Abigail couldn't help but be intrigued. "Then you . . . wish you would have married?"

"At times. But I never felt the moment was right, and I let my chances slip away. But do not mistake me—I have no regrets. I lived my life as I wished. I just do not want to see you throw away a chance at happiness because you do not think it is possible."

Miss Bury claimed to have lived life as she wanted—Abigail was doing the same. But she didn't see the purpose in contradicting the old woman aloud. After all, how could she explain what was *really* going on? She had to remind herself that if Miss Bury thought she had a chance to be a duchess, then her ruse with the duke as her pretend suitor was already working.

Christopher leaned back in his chair, rubbing his tired eyes. He had been hunched over the desk in his bedroom all afternoon. It was time to distract himself with letters that he'd long neglected to write. Only when he was looking up the address of a London friend, who prided herself on knowing information about every notable family in England, did he think of Miss Shaw. Would his friend know *her* family?

He was curious about Miss Shaw—and suspicious. And since he was considering Lady Gwendolin as a bride, should he not know all about her friends and their motives?

Before he could change his mind, he wrote a brief postscript, saying he'd met Miss Shaw and asking his friend if she knew of the Shaw family. He sealed the envelope and affixed a stamp. He would have it sent to the post office immediately, and it should reach London the next day by the railways. He wouldn't have long to wait.

And what did he intend to do if he found out the Shaws were hiding a secret? Tell Miss Shaw he didn't want her assistance? Or simply watch her, which wasn't terribly difficult to do. At least it gave an air of excitement to the usual house party.

He sighed and looked back at his desk. Procrastination. He was good at it. And Miss Shaw made thinking about her far too easy.

When Abigail and Gwen entered the drawing room, Abigail saw the duke speaking with Mr. Tilden and Lord Keane. She knew the moment that he saw her over their shoulders. She thought with some irritation that he was quite the actor, so pointedly did he take in her gown with a dark sweep of his eyes. She thought she might have to force a maidenly blush, but it came quite naturally.

More than one person noticed the duke's attention on her, and to heighten their curiosity, she gave the duke a brief nod, as if she took note of his interest and approved.

Mr. Wesley approached them, wearing a pleasant smile. There was no mystery to this young man, no tension that made a woman restless with longing. She imagined that everyone in the room thought he was the man she should focus her attention on, the younger son of gentry, as high as a gentleman's daughter should reach.

But Abigail saw the way Gwen straightened when the vicar looked at her. Did Abigail imagine that the vicar quickly looked away because he shouldn't be caught staring at an earl's daughter? It was all so very interesting.

"Ladies," Mr. Wesley said, "what did you think of Lady Elizabeth's ghost stories?"

"They were a good beginning," Gwen said, "but did not give us a historical period to concentrate on."

"Perhaps someone in the family can give us dates when the ghost was spotted?" he asked.

Abigail nodded almost absently, feeling only a little guilty for letting Gwen bear the brunt of the ghost research. Seeing her bright eyes upon the vicar, Abigail didn't think she would complain. They continued to talk about research strategies, and the vicar's revelation about old diaries he'd discovered. Abigail's gaze wandered away.

The duke was watching her again, and she lifted her chin as if in challenge. Flirting was not so difficult after all.

Vaguely, she heard Mr. Wesley say, "Perhaps they even invited me to exorcise the ghost!"

The two of them laughed rather breathlessly, and Abigail for a moment thought them silly. But not for long, for suddenly the duke excused himself from the two men and came striding across the room toward her. She found herself not breathing, watching with wider and wider eyes as he moved past the ladies, nodded absently at Lord Greenwich, who spoke to him, and even walked right by without seeing his approaching mother. He was breathtaking in his dark coat and trousers, all shadows and intensity.

And then he was standing beside her, his face above her, and she felt far too dainty. And silly, as she realized what she was doing. She sneaked a glance at Gwen, who looked as if she was trying not to laugh. Only a moment ago, she had found Gwen silly!

And then the duke reached forward, and she realized she was supposed to offer her hand. Awkwardly she did so, and to her surprise, he bent over and pressed his lips to the back of her gloved hand.

And inside her, a blaze caught fire and smoldered, though she tried to put it out.

People were openly staring, including his mother and sister. Lady May and Lady Theodosia fumed and sulked, whispering to each other. Their enmity toward her had suddenly made them allies.

He paused, his face just above her hand, his eyes full of a dark heat. She wished she had forgotten her gloves, so that his lips would have touched her bare skin. And then as if on cue, since only she could see him, those eyes seemed to light with secret amusement. They were fooling all the guests, and he was enjoying it. How often was it that he did such things since becoming the proper duke of Madingley?

"Good evening, Miss Shaw," he said in his deep voice, straightening at last to his full, impressive height.

"Good evening, Your Grace," she answered breathlessly.

He glanced at Gwen and Mr. Wesley, and Abigail was impressed that he let them think he was startled by their presence. He nodded to them both, then turned back to her, his smile fading. It was almost rude . . . or as if he couldn't be distracted.

Gwen put her hand on Mr. Wesley's arm, and he gave a little start. "Come, Mr. Wesley, we can continue our discussion," she said. They smiled at each other and disappeared into the crowd.

Leaving Abigail alone with the duke. Or almost alone, since they were in a drawing room with over a dozen people. Abigail looked up at him again, and any words she was thinking seemed to fade away. They shared a strained, tense silence. She licked her lips, and she could have sworn the duke's eyes followed her tongue.

"Your Grace, I am quite impressed," she murmured, wishing she had a glass of lemonade to hold up so as to disguise her words from others.

He arched a dark brow. "And all I did was walk over here and greet you."

"But you did it so superbly. Perhaps you could not see the reaction to your single-minded attention to me, but everyone else did. And the way you so easily chased away Gwen and Mr. Wesley—"

A frown flickered in his eyes. "Chased away?"

She smiled. "Very well, I think Gwen wished to be away from you, but you made it look like she was chased away."

But that had been the wrong thing to say, for the duke's eyes, a moment ago so full of smoldering warmth, seemed to turn into a winter night.

"Why would Lady Gwendolin wish to be away from me?"

"Oh, it is nothing personal, my lord," she hastened to say. "I think even *she* believes that you are interested in me." Another lie to add to her tally.

"But that is not all of it," he countered.

She might as well tell him some of the truth, and save him from feeling like he was coming between her and Gwen—if he even cared. "To be honest, she is not . . . interested in becoming a duchess."

He cocked his head. "I do not mean to sound arrogant, but this is the second time today you've told me such a thing. In my own experience, that is usually not true."

"Oh, I am sure that *most* women think that being your wife would be the most fulfilling life imaginable." Abigail blinked guilelessly at him.

One side of his mouth slowly turned up in a smile. "You are an amusing woman."

She put a hand to her chest. "Why, Your Grace, such flattery will turn my head."

A moment later, she regretted bringing his notice to her bosom, for it rather strained against the bodice of her gown in far too common a fashion. But he didn't seem to mind, for it took him a moment to look back at her face. She did not take his interest personally, for her abundant figure was something she could not control. Men always looked when offered the chance. It didn't mean anything.

He linked his hands behind his back. "So explain to me why two friends do not wish to be a duchess."

"I already explained my own reasons to you,"

she said matter-of-factly. "As for Gwen—Lady Gwendolin—"

"I like the way you shorten her name. I might call her Lady Gwen from now on."

She smiled. "Gwen is a different woman than you're used to. Her father brought her up to believe that people are of equal merit, regardless of their station in life." She waited, wondering his opinion on the topic.

He only nodded. "Many believe money or position differentiates among people, making some more worthy than others."

"And what do you believe, Your Grace?"

"Worthiness itself is meaningless. A person's actions are all that matter."

She wondered to what actions he was referring. Surely he had some actions he wished he had not committed. She hadn't realized she was staring thoughtfully at him for so long until he said, "Miss Shaw?"

She gave a startled laugh. "Gwen's father believed she should see all of life, from the factories to immigrant housing. As a child, she often played with the children of her father's secretary. She says she pities you for the responsibilities of being a duke."

He smiled. "It has been a long time since I've been pitied."

"She believes her charity work would suffer were she to become a duchess." Abigail did not bring up the fact that for some strange reason, Gwen did not share her attraction to the handsome duke.

He took a deep breath and nodded. "You have certainly made my future decision easier."

She felt a pang of remorse and anxiety. "Have I . . . disillusioned you? I would hate to think you felt drawn to Gwen and that you are saddened that she doesn't return your feelings."

He gave her a perfunctory smile. "On the contrary. I have always known I would marry for duty and suitability. But a duchess needs to understand and desire the position, not just the man."

"But . . . is it not also about love?" she asked softly, then regretted her foolish display of emotion.

"Love, Miss Shaw? How could love play a part in uniting one great house with another? I will be content if my future wife and I tolerate each other well enough, and if she understands the need for decorum."

"Tolerate?" she echoed, fascinated. "But . . . do you not *believe* in love?"

Why ever was she goading him? What did this matter to her article? Then she reminded herself that to write authentically about him, she should know everything she could.

And she found herself far too fascinated—and sad—to stop.

"Love?" Now he was the one echoing her, and he wore a smile that said he was the one pitying her. "There is too much at stake to hope for something so remote, so ephemeral. Your friend Lady Gwen seems to understand what is at stake. But not you? Or do you believe you will be lucky enough to marry for love?"

"I hope to, Your Grace," she said in a quiet voice. "I was told that your parents fell in love and did not care that your mother would not suit Society's expectations."

"My parents were a rarity, Miss Shaw," he said.

She saw him glance fondly at his mother, who was speaking with Lady Swarthbeck.

"And you do not think you can repeat their success?" she asked.

His gaze returned to her face. "Success?"

She was startled to realize that perhaps he did not think their marriage a success. His parents had love and children and security—was that not enough? For a moment, she and the duke simply looked at each other, and there suddenly seemed to be a chasm between them, but not of stations so much as expectations. Love wasn't important, but "understanding decorum" was. She didn't know what to think.

Suddenly the butler intoned that dinner was served.

Abigail smiled awkwardly. "Well, though we might not believe in stations separating us, I do believe you must lead the highest-ranking lady into dinner."

"And that would be my mother," he said. "Unless the queen is here."

"Does she visit you often?"

He shrugged. "Once or twice a year."

With awe, Abigail watched him take his leave of her. She took a quick, startled breath when he glanced back at her over his shoulder. He smiled in far too intimate a manner.

As if they were coming to an understanding.

Abigail remained alone, knowing she was being looked at, spoken about, with curiosity, surprise, or envy. At last Mr. Wesley came to join her, the lowest man of rank, to match her as the lowest female.

He looked about. "So, you seem to be of interest this evening. You have succeeded in capturing the attention of the duke."

She wanted to say that it didn't mean anything, that it wasn't true. But her ruse did not allow her. She could only smile and blush—and feel a bittersweet triumph.

Now if only she could handle the results of the charade she'd begun.

Chapter 8

A fter dinner, the men decided to retire to the
billiards room for the rest of the evening.
Abigail stood at the edge of the drawing room,
watching as the ladies brought forth embroidery,
walked by twos about the perimeter of the room,
and even read.

Then she saw that the duchess was alone, watching her. Abigail straightened, and to her surprise,
the duchess motioned her forward. It was at moments like this that she truly regretted the under-
handedness of her behavior.

The duchess graciously offered the seat beside
her on the sofa. "And how are you enjoying yourself thus far, Miss Shaw?" she asked, her faint
accent making her intriguing and different.

Was that one of the things her husband had seen
in her—that she was so different from the English-
women he'd known?

"Everything you have done for me has been so
gracious—Your Grace."

They exchanged smiles.

"Your home is warm and welcoming," Abigail continued. "How could I not be enjoying myself?"

"I know little about you, Miss Shaw, except that Lady Gwendolin said you are from Durham."

Abigail briefly—and nervously—recited the lies she'd created, about her life as a gentleman's daughter on the outskirts of the *ton*.

"So you have never met my son before?" the duchess asked, watching her too closely now.

"Only briefly, in Hyde Park, Your Grace." Abigail decided to be forthright. "He has been very kind and attentive. Has he always been that way toward a lost young lady? I had heard that in his youth he was far more bold and adventurous."

"Some would say wild," the duchess responded dryly.

"But those were simply rumors," Abigail hastened to say.

"With a basis in fact, Miss Shaw. You'll have your own children someday, and will understand that with youth can come rashness and a belief that nothing bad will ever happen."

A brief sorrow crossed the older woman's face, and Abigail wasn't even sure she would have seen it if had she not been paying such close attention.

"But he is a man full grown now, and so well respected," Abigail said. "It is obvious nothing bad *did* happen to him." She let her voice trail off, hoping subtly to encourage the duchess to continue speaking of her son.

When the duchess only smiled and shook her head, Abigail had a sudden revelation that something bad had happened to someone *else*. And the duke had been involved.

The story had not been written about in the newspapers. She had recently read all the articles that referred to the duke's family, back through his entire life. But perhaps it was so terrible a scandal that few knew. And that was perhaps the reason money changed hands.

The Ladies Swarthbeck and Greenwich approached, and Abigail used the interruption to curtsy and leave the duchess. Her mind swimming with thoughts, she found an unused table, withdrew from her reticule the notebook on the duke, identical to the notebook she kept on the ghost, and began to write. For several minutes she looked over her shoulder, but no one was paying her any heed.

Christopher stood in the corridor outside the drawing room, his shoulder braced against the doorframe, arms crossed over his chest. No one had spied him so far, and he was free to watch the unfolding tableau.

He had arrived in time to see Miss Shaw speaking with his mother, had seen the sorrow his mother couldn't hide. What had they discussed? Whatever it had been, it had inspired Miss Shaw to a frantic scribbling in her notebook. And it made him uneasy—uneasy enough to be curious about her writing.

Many men would not care about a woman's thoughts, but there was something about her need to put them into words that intrigued him—perhaps because he himself always felt the same way.

He walked purposefully into the drawing room, nodded to his mother, ignored the way the women seemed to preen their feathers in anticipation, and headed straight for Abigail. He was paying too much attention to her, he knew, even for their ruse, but he couldn't seem to stop himself. She was bent over the table, concentrating hard on what she was writing, so she didn't see his arrival—and obviously didn't realize what her position did to her décolletage. Her breasts almost overflowed the gown, as if with one deep breath she'd—

And then she looked up and saw him, her eyes going wide as she straightened. She closed the notebook and smiled up at him. "Your Grace."

"Would you care to walk with me, Miss Shaw?"

She blinked in surprise, then slid the notebook into her reticule as she rose to her feet. "Of course."

He gestured toward the great double doors at

the far end of the drawing room. "The night is beautiful. We can enjoy the moon."

Though she nodded, he saw the momentary look of confusion, the way she glanced at the other women.

"Do not worry," he said softly. "The doors will be open, and we'll remain in their sight."

"And you know they'll all be watching."

"True. But it will work in our favor, will it not?"

She showed not another qualm as she walked at his side. He felt the awareness of every female in the room.

Softly, Miss Shaw said, "You are making it look as if an evening of billiards with other gentlemen is not enough to keep you from my side."

"And that is how we want it to look—according to your plans."

Those plump lips turned up in a secretive smile that aroused him.

As the dimness of the torchlit terrace swallowed them, an evening breeze blew gently. Miss Shaw did not seem cold. She leaned on the stone balustrade and took a deep breath, tilting her head to the night sky and closing her eyes, her face awash in serenity. But again his gaze was drawn lower, to her breasts, full and creamy by moonlight, the deep vee between them a darkness that made his stomach tighten with lust.

To control himself, he said, "So how else do

you think two people playing a game of courtship should look?"

She slanted her eyes at him, batting them prettily. "You are much more experienced at such things than I, Your Grace."

"Then in my vast experience, I should be leaning too close."

He rested his hip against the balustrade, put his hand on the flat surface as he loomed over her. She didn't even look startled, although her gaze moved rapidly from his face to the hand beside her.

"Are you teasing me?" she asked, staring up at him. "I know you are still amused by my offer of help."

Amused? he thought with faint sarcasm. That wasn't all she made him feel. "I must admit to a certain enjoyment of the secret between us. Is that so very wrong?"

"No."

Was he imagining it, or was her voice a bit breathless? Some distant part of him set off a faint warning, but he didn't want to hear it.

"After all," he continued, "you are displaying a certain amount of flesh. How else am I supposed to act?"

Those intelligent eyes now narrowed in a frown. "How far do you mean to enjoy yourself?"

"How far would you like me to enjoy you?"

Abigail drew in a shocked breath, unable to believe that this sensual, flirting man was the same responsible, sober duke. It was as if, now that they shared a secret, he did not feel compelled to treat her as he would other ladies.

And she was not a lady—although he did not know that.

Or did he? Was she somehow behaving even more inappropriately than she thought?

But he was a man, not just a duke, and her mother had always warned her that a man could be more tempted than a woman. A woman had to act with sober judgment, for she was the one with the most to lose.

So although her stomach fluttered with nerves that seemed too pleasurable, Abigail forced herself to smile dispassionately.

"I think you are trying to test my determination, Your Grace."

He arched a dark brow, not giving her even room to breathe. And she was not about to back down, to step away as if his presence was too much for her.

"Your determination?" he echoed.

To her faint relief, she saw a curve of amusement on his lips, the lips she was paying far too much attention to. And that strengthened her resolve. He was not going to kiss her. She didn't want him to kiss her! He was *teasing* her, and she would have to show that he was having no effect.

"You are trying to see how firm my resolve is," she said, "and I assure you, your behavior will not change my mind about helping you. Though even now I am certain that your mother and sister are watching us, I will not disappoint you by retreating."

He did not even stiffen at the mention of his family, but she sensed his sudden remembrance of them. Though this was a game between the two of them, he would not want others to be hurt.

"You are far too clever, Miss Shaw."

Although he did not step away, he did straighten, allowing her room to breathe again.

"So what were you writing so furiously in your little notebook?"

She was impressed, wondering if he planned such a question after deliberately disorienting her. "You were watching me?"

"Am I not supposed to? We are trying to make this look real, after all."

"And I, too, am keeping this as real as possible. I was writing my theories about your ghost."

He arched a brow. "My ghost? The one I don't even believe in?"

"Your family's ghost, then. Gwen and Mr. Wesley are quite active in their pursuit of its history."

"Then I wish them luck."

He was still studying her closely, and she experienced a moment of doubt. Did he believe her? God forbid he should ask to read her notes. She had not brought her ghost notebook to dinner with her.

She tried not to appear hasty as she said, "I believe it is time to rejoin the guests, Your Grace. We have planted enough suspicion for one night."

He bowed and gestured her before him. She would have to be very careful not to rouse *his* suspicions.

The next morning, the men went off to shoot, and Abigail told herself it was good to be separated from the duke. She had constantly to remind herself that they were only using each other: He needed a female companion to hold his suitors at bay, and she needed information about him. A morning apart would clear her head and let her discover other things to use for her article.

While the ladies were sleeping, she had the breakfast room to herself, then the library. She found a book on family history that the ghost hunters had deemed unworthy of their interest. After perusing it, Abigail could see why. There was nothing about the ancient family; it was mainly about the duke's grandfather and how he almost lost his fortune only to regain it with intelligent decisions and carefully calculated risks.

Just before she was about to set it aside in frustration, she saw mention of the old duke's tutor, and it immediately started her thinking. The current duke must have had a tutor or a governess before he'd gone to Eton. Perhaps that person could give her insight into the wild escapades of the young duke.

Specifically, the one where someone was hurt, Abigail remembered with a shiver. Obviously he had suffered no lasting repercussions, nothing that had harmed his social status or that of his family.

And then she had another idea, something so wild and daring it froze her in place. She could search the duke's bedroom. The merest thought started a blush that she resolutely suppressed. She was a journalist, and she would do what she had to.

But not search his intimate rooms—at least not yet. She had other paths to explore.

To that end, she looked for the perfect opportunity to speak with his sister, and only found it during the cheerful confusion of the return of the shooting party. Lady Elizabeth planned a tour of the house itself. Standing in the high-ceilinged great hall, she'd sent for the other ladies, smiled distractedly at Abigail, and looked out the open door as the men walked across a distant field toward the house.

"Lady Elizabeth, you are handling such a large party with ease and experience," Abigail said.

The young woman beamed her delight. "It is all my mother's training, Miss Shaw. You know that this is my first chance to be the hostess for a house party."

"And I'm enjoying the entertaining theme you surprised us with. It is fascinating to research your family history. I was wondering if you knew of any recent employees who had seen the ghost, but who no longer live at Madingley Court. Say . . . tutors or governesses?"

Lady Elizabeth frowned. "I do not remember my governess ever mentioning such a thing. Madingley and I did have the same tutor, but my brother did not share any ghost stories with me."

"Do the governess and tutor still live nearby?"

"What an interesting angle of research," Lady Elizabeth said with admiration.

Frustrated, Abigail glanced at the men coming ever closer. She could make out the duke now.

"My governess died young, poor lady, but the tutor, Mr. Yates, still lives in Comberton, a nearby village. Though he has retired from private tutoring, he occasionally helps teach the village children."

"Ah, someone to interview!" Abigail said, not having to feign her excitement. "If it is not too presumptuous, might I ask you to please not share my interest in him with anyone else?"

Lady Elizabeth put a hand to her heart. "Of course not! You have my complete silence."

Together, they turned to watch the return of the men, as one by one the women gathered. At last, the men crowded the main entrance hall, bringing with them the crisp scent of the outdoors and the sound of masculine laughter. All of the women seemed to shine a little brighter in their presence, and Abigail admitted to herself that she was not immune. Mr. Wesley came searching for Gwen to discuss his latest ghost theories. Abigail had felt a little stillness grow inside her when the duke met her gaze. He nodded to her, before being distracted by Lord Swarthbeck.

Why did just a simple look from him make her relive the moments when they'd been far too close? She could only shiver when she remembered the moonlight glistening in his black hair as he'd so brazenly trapped her near the terrace balustrade. It had changed everything she thought about her reaction to men. She'd always assumed her work for the newspaper would be more important than any man, but apparently she'd been meeting the wrong men.

Not that the duke was the right man for her—he was just the first one to prove that she could be interested.

After a lively discussion of who shot the most birds, Abigail, Gwen, and Mr. Wesley followed at the rear as the large group tour began. Abigail saw the duke, a head taller than many of the gentlemen, near the front, walking at his sister's side. Lady Elizabeth asked her brother to discuss the history of the different wings of the house. He spoke with calm authority, reluctant though he'd initially been. Abigail looked on the sober, polite man, and felt a little thrill at what he was like underneath, the side he'd allowed only her to glimpse.

Next, Lady Elizabeth discussed the rooms where the ghost had been sighted: the library, the duke's study, the great hall, and the duke's dressing room—which they were not allowed to tour, of course.

"And those are the only places where the ghost has been seen?" Gwen asked.

"I had rather assumed that if only servants have reported a sighting," Mr. Wesley said, his face reddening as people turned to watch him, "then the ghost had been seen in the servants' quarters."

"No, not at all," Lady Elizabeth said brightly. "We, too, considered that unusual."

As the tour continued, Abigail found herself dwelling on this new ghost clue. The ghost had been espied only where the family frequented. That would make it most likely to be the ghost of an ancestor rather than of one of the servants or guests.

But she was not here to research a ghost, she told herself, suppressing her curiosity. She would tell Gwen her supposition and let her friend—and the vicar—work on it together. Abigail had a tutor to find.

After luncheon, when the guests had gathered to take a walk about the grounds, Christopher was trying to make a quiet exit to the privacy of his bedroom when the butler announced that the afternoon post had been delivered. Since he, too, was waiting for letters, he remained behind and watched the general air of excitement.

Miss Shaw received a letter that had been tucked into Lady Gwen's mail, and she seemed oddly confused and surprised as she stared at the envelope.

Christopher received several letters, most of which he already knew what the content would be. But there was one letter that surprised him. Michael Preston had written to him.

Christopher was so caught up with curiosity—and worry—that he didn't even think to retreat to his study. He unfolded the letter and quickly perused the contents. Michael wrote that he was worried about his sister's pursuing Christopher so openly and that he would do his best to control her. He was glad Christopher had left London before Madeleine could make a fool of herself on an even greater scale before Society. And then he actually apologized for her behavior, which twisted the longtime blade of guilt within Christopher's gut.

From the moment Madeleine had made clear that she felt entitled to be his duchess, Christopher had experienced a growing feeling of foreboding. He was not so worried about his own reputation as he was his mother's and sister's—especially

Elizabeth, who was making her debut. They didn't need for his youthful sins to surface once again.

He reminded himself that he had Michael on his side. Michael would be able to control his sister and make her realize that she was not going to have what she wanted. And perhaps the rumor of his courtship of Miss Shaw would play another role—dissuading Madeleine Preston. Miss Shaw was proving very convenient.

Seated on a sofa nearby, Abigail found herself watching the duke's expression. She'd been surprised when he hadn't used the mail as a convenient excuse to leave. Now, as he read one letter, he seemed thoughtful and concerned. She wished she knew what he read, but she could hardly research every aspect of the duke's life.

She slowly opened her own letter, feeling uneasy that her mother had written to her so soon. It had been sent to Gwen's residence, and the servants had forwarded it. Her confusion only increased as her mother went on to describe the further adventures of Mr. Wadsworth, the gentleman suitor her father seemed most fond of.

Why ever would Abigail's mother think she wanted to know which breakfast he'd attended, or how well he danced?

Did her mother press his suit because she and her father were even more concerned about their finances? Was this their way of trying to prepare her?

Abigail realized that she'd lost sight of the urgency of her mission. She was enjoying the duke's company more than she was following clues. She would have to find the tutor this afternoon, and the only way to do that was to leave the house, alone, as stealthily as possible.

Chapter 9

After luncheon, Miss Shaw seemed to disappear. As Christopher skirted a game of croquet, he saw that Miss Shaw was not among the players. He put her out of his mind as he headed for a meeting with the bailiff of the estate, only to see a bonneted, petite woman setting off by herself down the hedgerow-bordered lane that led to Comberton. He would recognize those curves anywhere, regardless of how Miss Shaw disguised them beneath a plain shawl.

With a houseful of people, she was going for a walk alone. Did she not understand the danger? Or was she going somewhere with a purpose, deliberately escaping a chaperone? He could only assume she was meeting someone.

Even as he hesitated, he remembered his appointment with the bailiff. At the horse barn where they were to discuss the breeding program, he rescheduled the meeting. And then he set off in search of Miss Shaw, walking instead of riding, since he didn't want to overtake her.

Though it was foolish, he still couldn't shake his instinctive feeling that something was . . . off about her. He could understand a friendly offer to help him, even if she didn't benefit. But she might actually suffer under the arrangement, and that was self-destructive.

By the time he caught sight of her again, she had put up a frilly parasol to protect her skin from the sun. It bobbed with each step she took, and even proved helpful as an advance signal when she was turning to look back over her shoulder. Christopher was able to duck behind a tree in time. He felt foolish that he was reduced to hiding on his own property, but his determination did not falter.

The lane rose and fell along the gentle hills, until at last, a mile away, he saw Comberton, a small village nestled along the confluence of two streams. Smoke rose from chimneys jutting from thatched roofs. Miss Shaw's pace picked up when she finally saw her destination, and he could only reluctantly admire her stamina.

Christopher didn't think he'd been to the village in almost a year. There was always something more important to do, and he'd been in London most of the time. But he'd been a boy here, treated as any other boy, not a duke's son. He'd been a foolish young man here, then a duke who took care of his people. The villagers did not treat him as if he were royalty but as one of their own. He never needed a carriage and grooms to visit, because they left him alone to go about his own business. If there was one place he could keep hidden, it was here.

And that was what he did as he watched Miss Shaw. She seemed to be walking with great purpose, going past the grocer, the little bookshop, and the draper. She didn't even browse the window displays.

Instead, she turned down another lane, walked up the pavement to a small cottage, and knocked. Christopher recognized the elderly man who answered the door, though it had been several years since he'd seen him. What business could Miss Shaw have with Mr. Yates, his childhood tutor? But Mr. Yates smiled at her as she spoke, then his eyes lit with understanding. He stepped back and invited her in.

Christopher slipped back into the alley, having seen enough. His curiosity about the woman was turning into an obsession. Maybe she simply knew Mr. Yates, or had heard of him. But if it were that simple, why not tell someone where she was going, or ask for a groom to accompany her?

He debated returning to Madingley Court, but it would be more difficult to question her surrounded by family and guests. And he didn't want to make her defensive by confronting her in the village. So he walked back the way they'd both come and waited past a rise in the road, where she would not see him until it was too late.

Not half an hour later, he saw the tip of her frilly parasol first. He quickly straightened up from the tree he'd been leaning against and walked toward her, as if he'd been out for a casual stroll.

When she saw him, she came up short, her expression surprised and wary, until she smoothed it away. His first thought was vindication; she was hiding something from him. And then came anger, although he nodded pleasantly. They met beneath the shade of a small copse of trees, by the bank of the stream that gurgled musically. He was in no mood to appreciate it.

Pleasantly, he said, "Miss Shaw, what a surprise."

"Good afternoon, Your Grace." She smiled at him as if nothing were wrong. "Out for a walk? I assumed dukes rode mighty horses to survey their property."

And now she was trying to put him on the defensive, as if he wasn't supposed to be here. The sheer arrogance of it was almost admirable.

"This duke enjoys an occasional invigorating stroll," he said. "And what were you about today?"

"I was meeting Gwen and Mr. Wesley at the parish church. He offered a tour." She blinked at him with innocent sweetness.

While inside his darker emotions churned. Now she was baldly lying to him. Even if she'd gone to the church after he'd seen her, she would have had at most a minute or two, not long enough for a tour.

What was she up to?

No one knew her but Lady Gwen, and how could he know if he could trust Lady Gwen's word after this? He longed to demand the truth, but that would only succeed in scaring Miss Shaw off. She had a purpose for everything she did here, and he was going to find out what it was.

"I hope you were impressed by the church," he said at last.

"Oh, I was, Your Grace."

This time she didn't quite meet his eyes.

"Where are Lady Gwen and Mr. Wesley?" he continued. "They left you to walk all alone?"

"They wished to take the carriage on the main road, but I wanted to walk on such a beautiful day."

He stepped closer, though he hadn't meant to. She had to look up even more to see him. Her bonnet shaded her eyes, and he could see the vague glint of gold in their dark depths.

"I am not certain it is so safe for you to be wandering alone," he said in a low voice. "Surely Mr. Wesley would have mentioned as much."

"He did," she answered without hesitation.

She could almost be an actress.

"But I did not see the harm during the day," she added. "Do you not keep us all safe?"

"But who keeps you safe from me?"

Her eyes widened, and her pink lips parted in shock. "Y—Your Grace?" she said uncertainly.

He took another step toward her, towering over her, but she did not back away, only lifted her chin. And desire swirled into his anger, making a dangerous mix.

"You're alone with me, aren't you? You don't even seem to be concerned about what could happen."

"Happen?" she echoed. "You would not threaten me."

"No, I would not." His gaze wandered down her face, lingering on plump lips that did not show a sign of trembling. The high-necked gown hid her well today, but the sight of the deep valley between her breasts still burned in his brain. "But others could be a threat. What if we are seen like this, as if we had gone off alone? You don't even seem concerned."

"I—I did not intend to meet you."

"Will anyone care? No." His voice was too stern, leaking the anger. "They would attempt to marry us off if they found us like this. Is that your intent?"

She flinched at his harsh words, but she had her voice under control. "I have already told you I do not wish to marry you. You are the one who accepted my idea to pretend to court me. Surely you must share the blame if people's perceptions are wrong about us."

He said nothing, not trusting himself to speak, knowing that it sounded irrational. It didn't matter that she was right. She was lying to him, and he desired her, and his dark confusion was twisting him up inside. He had a momentary thought that he should send her away—but he knew he wouldn't.

"We can end this now, Your Grace," she said firmly. "If you are suspicious of me, the plan will not work anyway."

"No, we aren't ending this," he said, trying to soften his voice. "I just—need you to understand the consequences of your actions."

"Believe me, I understand."

She was watching him now as if he were a cornered animal of which she had to be wary. And she was right. It had been many years since he'd felt so out of control. Surely it was because of the stress in his life—his worry about Madeleine, the project that would not reveal its secrets, and now the mystery of Miss Shaw. He wasn't sleeping well—was he even thinking correctly?

All he wanted was a kiss—one kiss. They were alone; no one would ever know. He reached out to her, then pulled back. It took everything in him to sound almost normal as he said, "Walk ahead of me, Miss Shaw. I will wait until it is obvious we were not together."

Her little bonnet trembled as she nodded. She passed by him and began to walk back toward Madingley Court with the speed of a woman who was used to walking. She wasn't lying about that.

When she disappeared over the next hill, Christopher pressed a hand against a tree. He bowed his head and tried to clear it of muddled thoughts. What was it about her that frustrated and infuriated him, all while he experienced a heady desire for her?

She was his opponent, he knew that now—in more ways than one.

Abigail's heart was still pounding from the close call as Madingley Court came into sight. She would have given anything to escape to her room and collapse in relief, but Lady Elizabeth had already spotted her from the croquet game spread across the smooth lawn near the east wing. The young woman waved, and Abigail waved back, knowing she could not rudely ignore her hostess.

Where was Gwen? Abigail wondered as she drew closer. She needed to alert her friend that she'd been forced to lie in her name. But she and the vicar had not yet returned. With Abigail's luck, they'd arrive just in time to face the duke's questions. And he had too many of them, due to her own stupidity. She had almost ruined everything with her mission to the village. He had not believed her, and she was still trying to grasp that fact. She had seen it in his dark eyes, which had fixed on her with intent. He had played it off as worry about being discovered alone together, but she knew it was not his main concern.

He was suspicious of her.

Would he end their pretend courtship? Deny her access to him, and thereby deny her the article? She couldn't let that happen! She would have to be more careful.

Looking over her shoulder, she saw that he was not yet in sight. Oh, if only Gwen would arrive before he did!

But Abigail was not so lucky, and soon the duke appeared from the house rather than the lane. He must have returned home a different way. Although he might be sparing her the censure of others, he was also sparing himself. Once again, they were using each other, twisting together in a tense rope of dependency. Where could it all lead?

And then her bad luck worsened, as Gwen and a lady's maid arrived in an open phaeton driven by Gwen herself. From across the lawn, the duke met Abigail's gaze, gave a small smile, then turned to greet them.

Her stomach plummeted to her toes. Gwen wouldn't know what to answer. Abigail could run to intercept them, but that would betray her just as much as Gwen's ignorance. Instead, she walked toward them sedately, letting the duke reach them first. Soon she could hear Gwen's trilling laugh.

"Oh, Your Grace, the village is so quaint and lovely! And your parish—why, you take wonderful care of it."

"Not just I, but all of its parishioners, Lady Gwen. You do not mind if I call you that, do you?"

Gwen only shook her head. "Of course not."

"I heard Miss Shaw use it, and I thought it endearing, more reflective of your personality."

He glanced over his shoulder at Abigail, but said to Gwen, "I see that Mr. Wesley did not return with you."

"He had to visit several ill parishioners today. He promised to return tonight."

In the bright sunlight, her faint blush was noticeable.

"Lady Gwen," he continued in a deceptively even voice, "did your friend, Miss Shaw, tour the church with you?"

Abigail could only widen her eyes at Gwen, who spoke without even hesitating.

"She did, Your Grace." To Abigail, Gwen said, "Mr. Wesley keeps such a clean church, doesn't he?"

It was an inane statement, but it gave Abigail the chance to say, "He does. And if I would have known he was not accompanying you back, I would have done so myself."

Gwen laughed and touched her arm fondly. "Oh you, I do not need time alone with Mr. Wesley. We are simply friends."

Abigail waited for the duke to say more, but all he did was smile and offer them both his arms. Each of them set a hand on a forearm as he escorted them back to the other guests.

Abigail's heart was beating so rapidly she almost felt light-headed. She'd won this skirmish, with further hope that she'd soothed his suspicions. Surely he could not believe that Gwen would lie to him.

Lady Gwen had lied to him, Christopher thought, taken aback by surprise and confusion.

After accompanying both women to the refreshment table, he stepped away and watched them help themselves to lemonade and iced cakes. Elizabeth approached to hear about what they'd done for the afternoon, but Christopher did not remain nearby. He moved through the crowd, nodding, saying a word here and there, but making it obvious that he had pressing business. He would attend his rescheduled meeting with the bailiff, then return to his room to stare at his work once more. He was beginning to see things in his dreams—when he wasn't seeing the provocative Miss Shaw.

She was intruding too much on his thoughts, and he didn't like it. He would not forget that Lady Gwen had lied for her, and he wondered if she truly knew Miss Shaw at all. What did Lady Gwen think her friend was up to?

Christopher would normally assume it was

another plot to rope him into marriage, but the involvement of his old tutor put a new spin on his usual suspicions.

He had to find out what was going on.

"He's gone," Gwen whispered.

Abigail gave a relieved sigh, and the two of them picked up their pace, walking away from the croquet game as if wandering a garden path on a lovely day. Abigail gladly set her glass and cake plate on a bench, convinced she'd gag if she had to pretend hunger for even another bite.

"What happened?" Gwen demanded. "I never even had the chance to ask you in private why you did not join the croquet game or Mr. Wesley and me. And to my astonishment, you did the latter!"

Abigail groaned. "It was horrible, Gwen. I went into the village to see the duke's old tutor, and on the way back, I met the duke himself. He claimed he was out for a walk, but really, at the time I couldn't believe it. Now I don't know what to think."

"What happened when you met him?" Gwen asked eagerly, her expression full of shock and excitement.

"I told him I had met you at the church, but that I wanted to walk back. Thank God you supported my story." She choked out a laugh. "What instincts do you possess that you knew how to answer his questions?"

"I simply looked at your face and took my best guess. And I was right?"

"You were. Now he can no longer suspect me."

"Why would he suspect you of anything other than walking down a country lane?"

"Unchaperoned," Abigail said solemnly.

"Oh dear."

"He was quite upset about it, as if I was unconcerned about our fate should someone discover us. I'm not certain I did our pretend courtship any favors today. I even said we could end it if he wished."

Gwen gasped. "You didn't!"

"I did. But he refused. Wasn't that strange?"

Her friend frowned thoughtfully, linking their arms together, and said nothing for several minutes. "It seems to me that he fears being alone with you."

"Fears?" Abigail gaped, then gave a rueful laugh. "You are wrong, Gwen. He was angry."

"But perhaps he was angry because when he is alone with you, he is thinking forbidden thoughts, and he's worried others will guess them."

Abigail remembered the way he'd stared at her mouth, and she'd simply assumed he could not mean to kiss her, that her weak feelings were her own. She felt confused and worried—and deep down, there was a sinful feeling of delight, for which she quickly scolded herself. She could not allow herself to think about him in any way other than as an assignment. And she had to discourage him from anything too personal. How was she to do that, when he seemed to enjoy this secret game between them?

Gwen was watching her with a knowing expression.

Abigail waved her hands in dismissal. "That cannot be so, Gwen. He has his choice of women, all of whom are more beautiful than I."

"Beauty is not everything, and if you had more experience with men, you would know that."

"And you have so much experience?" Abigail said with a friendly laugh.

Gwen smiled. "I have had every man of the *ton* paraded before me, and many of them were so handsome that a woman's knees should weaken. But not mine. Again, beauty is not everything."

"You just didn't like them because they were nobility, not a laborer championed by your father."

She giggled. "Oh, Abby, you are so silly. Forget that, and tell me what happened with the duke's tutor. And how did you even discover him?"

Abigail related her discussion with Lady Elizabeth. "And then I went to the village and met Mr. Yates."

"And he spoke to you?"

Abigail smiled ruefully. "He did, though he is becoming rather forgetful. But he spoke eloquently of the eccentric Cabot family and the challenges of teaching a boy as 'high-spirited' as the little marquess. Imagine having a title like that when you're born!" Then she rolled her eyes. "Well, of course you can imagine."

"And that wasn't even his birth title. He was the earl of Chesterton until his grandfather died." Gwen sighed. "So what else did he say?"

"He simply confirmed that Madingley was irrepressible as a youngster—along with his two male cousins. When they went off to Eton at eight years of age, Mr. Yates began to teach the young female cousins. I tried to hint about a scandal involving the duke, but every time I mentioned Madingley, the poor fellow was practically bursting with pride at what a good man he'd become."

"And does that imply he wasn't before?"

Abigail shrugged. "I couldn't tell. Oh Gwen, that was simply another disappointing interview."

"Do not let it frustrate you, my dear," she said kindly. "You are spending more time with the duke than any woman in my memory—except family, of course. That will lead somewhere."

"Maybe I should spend more time with Lady Elizabeth." Abigail's voice was glum. "Perhaps that will lead to a clue. She was good enough to alert me to the tutor."

"Be careful, Abby. The duke is very protective of his family. Probably more so than he is of himself."

Abigail nodded, knowing she could not afford to anger him further. She remembered the dark look in his eyes, the way he'd towered over her, the anger that seemed born of frustration. His words, *What will keep you safe from me?* still rang in her head. She had not worried he would physically harm her, oh no; she had worried about what she would *let* him do to her.

Chapter 10

❦

At dinner that night, Lady Elizabeth announced her intention to have a dance the following evening, but there was to be one stipulation: It was to be a costume dance in honor of the ghost. And she promised to guide them all to the attics tomorrow, where they could look through old trunks to find the perfect garments.

Excited, Abigail could only think that she was being given permission to explore the attics, when all along she had been prepared to sneak up there. Who knew what secret letters and journals she could uncover?

After dinner, when the men rejoined them in the drawing room, conversation was cheerful. Abigail sat conversing with Gwen in the corner, but really she was watching the duke—who was watching Lord Keane with Lady Elizabeth. Although Abigail thought the duke would be happy to see his sister surrounded by admiring men, there was something different about him this night, as if a pleasant expression was particularly difficult to wear.

He hadn't joined them for dinner, so she'd assumed he had had enough of them—of her—for one day. She'd been surprised when he'd entered the drawing room with the other men. His mere presence had lit the spark of her uncertainty, of her attraction, and it was difficult not to stare at him openly. Gwen had nudged her before she could appear the fool.

But the duke had had eyes for no one but his sister, who was giggling over something Lord Keane said. And Madingley's frown intensified. More than one guest was watching him and whispering to another.

At last he interrupted his sister and Lord Keane with great civility. There was fondness in his eyes when he looked at her, yet not even amusement when he looked at Lord Keane. He excused both himself and his lordship to discuss business, and Lady Elizabeth innocently moved on to the next small group of people conversing.

Abigail glanced at Gwen, who smiled, and whispered, "Just go."

Abigail waited a respectable amount of time and followed the two men out into the corridor. They were ahead of her, still walking, and she heard the duke's voice saying sternly, "You were standing too close."

She didn't hear Lord Keane's response, but it was obvious that the man soon realized that the duke was taking this more seriously than he was. Lord Keane apologized stiffly, and although the duke said something Abigail couldn't hear, his lordship gave a nod of agreement.

Lord Keane turned down a corridor, and before Abigail could retreat, the duke saw her.

"Good evening, Your Grace," she said, smiling, trying to pretend she was not following him. "I am in need of a new book to read and was going to the library. Do not let me keep you from your guests."

"My sister's guests," he said. "A new book sounds like a good idea."

She felt her smile go stiff as he waited for her to approach. She was forced to accompany him down another corridor, and when she reached the library, she opened both doors wide and stepped inside.

The duke closed them both.

She frowned. "That isn't wise of you."

He advanced on her, and the oil lamps scattered at different tables gave him several shadows. She didn't want him to think she was retreating, but with one step sideways, she put a sofa between them.

"I do not see why you objected to my accompanying you," he said, too mildly. "After all, you were following me."

She felt a jolt of worry. "Do not mistake my concern for your sister as *following* you."

He laughed softly, still moving forward until he stood on the other side of the sofa. There was something about him that seemed . . . tense tonight, as if he were being pushed too hard. There were lines of strain at the corners of his narrowed eyes.

He cocked his head. "And why are you concerned about my sister?"

"I saw the way you treated a man who'd shown interest in her. Is not socializing with men the point of this house party? Under your and your mother's supervision, of course. Or have you decided to reveal how controlling you are?"

"I am being protective."

"Your sister is behaving innocently. Let us look at this another way, shall we? I wonder if everyone thinks I should be protected from you?"

"Do you need protection?" He began to walk around the sofa.

How far was she going to take this? At her back were the double doors to the conservatory, but she wasn't going to run from him. What could he possibly do, here in his mother's house?

And why did she think the respectable duke of Madingley would do anything at all other than tease her?

"I must need protection," she said lightly, holding her ground as he approached. "You implied so this afternoon. I seem to recall you also saying that we should never be alone. Yet *you're* the one who closed the doors."

"So you *do* think you need protection from me."

His eyes lingered on her mouth again in the way that always made her breathing catch.

"I can take care of myself," she answered, lifting her chin.

"Really?"

She watched in bewilderment as he began to tug off his gloves one at a time. As he pulled on each finger, she felt an answering tremble inside.

"Then tell me what you'll do," he said quietly, "if I touch you like this."

She stood transfixed as he reached out with his bare finger and touched her bare arm, just above her glove. She thought she felt a shock; surely something had changed in the air around them. And then she found she couldn't breathe as he slid his finger slowly up her arm, toward her short, puffed sleeve. And always he watched her.

Just the small touch was far too warm, starting a tingling that raced from her arm throughout her whole body. She stared in shocked surprise from his hand back up to his face.

"So what will you do?" he asked again.

She swallowed. "I could slap you."

"If someone were watching, that might matter. But we're alone here."

"It's not right for you to tease me like this." She was trying to sound stern, but her breathlessness gave the lie to her tone. "I don't have to stand for it."

But she wasn't stopping him, and she didn't move away. What was wrong with her? He let the back of his finger caress her arm in little circles, and she gave a gasp as he slid his finger beneath the sleeve.

He smiled, and there was a wicked glint in his eye that made her realize he wasn't always the man he showed the world. But she'd already figured that out—wasn't that why she had chosen him?

"You don't have to stand for it?" he repeated. "Then you wish to end our arrangement?"

She opened her mouth but said nothing.

Though he did not release her arm, with his other hand he put a finger beneath her chin and slowly closed her mouth. She shuddered as he boldly caressed her lower lip with his thumb.

"Why are you doing this?" she demanded in a weak voice.

He stared down at her, eyes intense. "Tell me your secrets, Abigail."

Though he whispered those words, they struck her sharply, inducing a knot of true fear rather than just uncertainty. He was touching her, looming over her, his body giving off a heat that called to her even now. He wasn't trying to seduce her senses because he wanted her—he wanted information. And that rallied her defenses. She'd thought Gwen's lie had mollified him, but it obviously had not.

"My secrets?" she echoed. "You want to know a woman's heart? I've already told you why I'm here, why I offered my help."

He said nothing at first, just looked at her with measuring eyes. She jerked her head back, and he dropped his hand away from her face—only to take hold of her other arm. She realized he held her now, far too close, her skirts swirling about his legs.

His smile was almost grim. "Any woman I treated like this would flee the house—or demand marriage. What will you do?"

"Stand up to your bullying," she answered coldly, grasping her wits now that she knew the stakes were so high. *Secrets,* indeed. "I'm not leaving."

"No, I didn't think you would."

He released her, and she took a step back, trying to remember how to breathe.

"So are you going to toss me out?" she demanded.

"No. You are proving too interesting."

"Then do I have your permission to leave the room, or are you going to keep me here against my will?"

He stepped aside and motioned to the door. She stalked past him.

Just before she was going to fling the doors wide in an indignant manner, she heard him say, "You might want to be certain there is no one in the corridor."

She hesitated with her hand on the knob, and although she didn't look at him, she was very careful as she exited.

Christopher watched the door close softly behind her, and only then did he release his breath and sit down heavily in the nearest chair.

What had he done?

He'd stalked her, taunted her, and touched her, enough so that she threatened to slap him.

But her skin had been so soft . . .

It had been too long since he'd had a woman; that had to be the problem. Why had he thought that touching her might get him answers?

But no, she'd held up admirably. Even after he'd revealed himself—*Tell me your secrets.*

He was a fool. What had he hoped to gain? Her cooperation? The truth? Instead, he'd given her good reason to avoid him, to distrust him further.

But he didn't sense fear in her, and for that he was relieved.

And avoid him? From what he'd seen so far, she would not be doing that.

That night, Miss Bury came into Gwen's bedroom while the two young women sat side by side on the bed, slumped back against pillows.

Miss Bury was wearing a robe over her night-gown, with her hair pulled back in a single braid. She looked between Gwen and Abigail, a smile shining on her face. "My dear young girls, I saw such success tonight!"

"Success, Aunt Imogene?" Gwen said hesitantly.

"Why yes! Lady Swarthbeck, the old hen, told me I should keep a better eye on you, Miss Shaw."

"Why?" Abigail choked out, trying not to panic. Had the marchioness seen her and the duke alone in the library?

"She feels that you should be spending time with the vicar, a man more 'suited' to your circumstance in life."

A bit of her worry eased. "So . . . she thinks I'm spending too much time with the duke?"

"We can all see his attraction to you, my dear!" Miss Bury said, touching her shoulder.

Gwen sent a secret smile Abigail's way.

"Oh, he is simply being friendly," Abigail quickly demurred. But inside she felt a thrill of triumph. How could Madingley complain to her, when their false courtship was a success?

Miss Bury smiled. "So has he mentioned marriage, my dear?"

Abigail coughed to cover a laugh. "No, Miss Bury, of course not. Trust me, it will never be like that between us."

"But Miss Shaw—"

"Aunt Imogene," Gwen interrupted. "You are one to talk about men."

"What do you mean?" Miss Bury asked, although her wrinkled face suffused with a blush.

Gwen leaned forward conspiratorially. "You seem to be spending much time with Mr. Fitzwilliam."

"When he isn't dozing," Miss Bury said fondly. "Ah, there is much history between us. Such wild things we used to do when we were young."

Gwen and Abigail exchanged an incredulous look. They thought they'd hidden it well, until Miss Bury tsked.

"You girls can't believe we were always old and boring."

"Then why didn't you marry him?" Gwen asked.

Miss Bury's smile faded into one of sweet bitterness, the sort that had faded over time into quiet acceptance. "Because I didn't think I loved him. Sometimes I don't know what I was looking for. Sometimes I wish I'd been smarter. And sometimes," she said over her shoulder as she walked to the door, "I think I made the correct choice. My life has been a good one. But the future . . . ah, who can see what it holds . . . for any of us."

When she had gone, the two young women looked at each other in surprise.

Abigail mused, "I don't know whether to be sad for her or to feel envious of her peace of mind."

"At least she made her own decisions, and she can live with that. I have to rely on a *man* to come forward and show interest." Gwen pouted. "Oh, Abby, I don't know what to do! Mr. Wesley does not even notice me as a woman! I am simply a ghost-hunting companion."

"Gwen, I do not believe that. I have seen the way he looks at you, the way he blushes."

Her eyes lit with happiness. "Really?"

Abigail wasn't sure she wanted a man blushing when he looked at her. Smoldering eyes seemed so much more interesting . . . she caught herself too late. She was not going to think about smoldering Spanish eyes.

"Gwen, perhaps the costume dance tomorrow will help. He'll see you in a different light."

"Oh, that is a good plan. I cannot wait to see what is in the attics!"

"Nor I," Abigail said firmly.

Gwen cocked her head. "Ah, but you plan to look for more than a costume up there."

She shrugged. "We'll see . . ."

Christopher was in the breakfast room early with most of the other men before the fishing expedition he'd been coerced into attending. Dawn had just broken, and the men seemed to stumble wearily to the sideboard to make their selections.

He had just turned away with his own plate

when, like sudden sunshine, Abigail stepped into
the room and hesitated.

Her yellow dress was demure, clear up to the
lace collar at her neck, but it could not hide the
generous curves of her body. He'd been too close
to those curves just last night and come away with
nothing more than an innocent touch of skin. But
it had fueled a restless night full of fantasies, and
he was impatient with his susceptibility to her
when he had more important things to obsess over.
She was a young lady of Society, and he never let
himself have but a thought of temptation, quickly
discarded where a marriage-minded woman was
concerned. But the mystery of Abigail necessitated
a different approach. And a lying woman was not
an innocent miss.

She stood on her toes and peered as if she were
looking for someone in particular. Her eyes passed
over him, then sharply came back.

And even as she lifted her chin with defiance,
the sweetest blush came over her face.

Sweetest? Why was he allowing his thoughts to
soften toward her? It was one thing to woo her secrets from her, but he could not fall prey to his own
machinations.

She turned away in retreat, and he followed her
into the corridor.

"Feeling like a coward, Miss Shaw?" he called
softly.

She turned back to him, her hands laced before her. "Cowardly, Your Grace? I was looking for Lady Elizabeth and did not see her."

"My sister, awake this early?" He smiled. "You know most of the women are not. And why would you need to speak with her?"

Abigail arched a brow. "I cannot speak with my hostess without a motive? Did you not think a costume dance might inspire questions?"

"Perhaps you only came down so that someone would ask you to go fishing with us."

She blinked at him. "Do you now need my help against the men, Your Grace?"

He chuckled. It was difficult to remember that she was his opponent. "No, I think I can manage them."

She turned away with a nod, and he found himself calling, "So what historic costume will you wear tonight?"

She looked back at him over her shoulder, and now it was her turn to appear amused. "We have not yet searched the attics. Perhaps you know something I do not."

If he wasn't careful, his face was going to redden like a boy caught where he wasn't supposed to be. "I had forgotten. It is difficult to keep track of all my sister's little amusements."

"Good luck fishing," she said, before walking swiftly away.

Christopher watched her. It would take forever

to discover her motives simply by talking to her. More drastic action might be necessary.

As drastic as searching her room?

He was not that desperate yet.

When Christopher returned home later that morning, he went to his study, and there was the letter he'd been waiting for. He opened and read it, only to come away more confused than before. His friend, a matron who had made a study of Society in the north, did not recognize Abigail's last name.

Christopher sank into his chair and leaned his head back. He didn't like being lied to, perhaps betrayed—but was he supposed to ascribe the same words to Lady Gwen, whom he'd known since she'd made her debut? Her family was almost as old and respected as his. How could he believe that she was a willing participant in Abigail Shaw's misdeeds? Or perhaps Abigail was deceiving everyone?

He wandered to the drawing room and found the women gathering to ascend into the attics for dance costumes. Much to his dismay, Abigail was with his sister. They were laughing and chatting as if they were the oldest friends.

He didn't want Elizabeth growing fond of a woman who could not be trusted. What would happen when they returned to London? Christopher had no idea whether Abigail could harm his sister—or her reputation.

He couldn't let that happen. And he couldn't make Abigail leave, not until he knew what harm she could be to his family.

Furthermore, he didn't want her to go. The thrill of the chase was upon him; the old Christopher, the reckless one, was fighting to take over. She was a mystery of danger and desire, and he was caught in her web. But in the end, he would be the winner.

Chapter 11

❦

"Where have you been?" Abigail whispered to Gwen, who had finally joined the group of women at the bottom of the stairs to the attics. The men had all decided that their regular evening clothes would suffice as costumes, and had left the house for a shooting competition.

Lady May and Lady Theodosia were looking bored, as if every moment not involving the duke was unimportant. But they made sure to crowd ahead of Abigail at the stairs to get the best costumes. Abigail wasn't interested in luring a duke; she already had enough of his attention.

Just a couple days ago that would have thrilled her; she would have thought all her problems solved. But now she knew that she was on the edge of revealing too much to him, and he hadn't yet revealed enough to her. His suspicions worried her.

Gwen was still breathing unevenly. "Heavens, it is such a climb to get from the drawing room all the way up here. I do believe I am perspiring!"

Abigail rolled her eyes. "And it will only make you look lovelier. Now answer the question."

"Well, I was with the duke, of course," Gwen said loftily.

As Abigail's mouth dropped open, Gwen spoiled her image by softly giggling.

"Oh, Abby, it was so amusing!" she said behind her gloved hand. "He was questioning me about you!"

Abigail yanked on her friend's elbow until they were the last to go up the narrow stairs. "What did you say?"

"Your entire background, of course—the one we concocted," she added in a whisper.

Abigail felt despair wash over her. "Oh, Gwen, I hate that you are forced to lie!"

"I am not forced! I am glad to be helping you. Your family needs it. And besides, your family is not the only one benefiting from it."

"What do you mean?" Abigail asked with skepticism.

"The duke is a changed man. Everyone is saying so."

Shocked, she could think of nothing to say.

"He is usually so distant at these events, hardly even attends them," Gwen continued. "Yet with you here, he is . . . interested. His sister is thrilled at his attention to the party."

"She said as much to me," Abigail admitted.

"And he is taking an interest in a woman. His mother is surely happy that her ploy worked."

"But I am not the right woman for him to be interested in," Abigail hissed, as at last they started up the steep staircase.

Unfinished wood lined the walls, only illuminated by the shaking beam of an oil lamp held from above.

"I don't think who you are matters," Gwen said.

"It will to the duke."

And then they were at the top of the stairs and could no longer speak in private. Abigail had expected the attics to be dark and dusty, with a draping cobweb or two. This section *was* dark, for there were few windows, and little light leaked in between the curtains. But it was as meticulously clean as the rest of the house. Trunks lined the walls, along with stacked crates. In one corner an old standing mirror reflected strange shadows. Several pieces of unused furniture clustered in another corner. Surely the attics went on quite a distance, but the lamp did not have sufficient light.

"This is it!" Lady Elizabeth said with obvious excitement. "All the clothing trunks are stored in this area. Several maids will be bringing more lamps so that we can all see. You are welcome to use any garments you find, and the maids will be

ready with needle and thread to make things fit. It
will be so enjoyable to see the men's expressions
when we appear as women of another time."

Even Lady Swarthbeck and Lady Greenwich
seemed reluctantly interested in the costume idea
for the dance, for they were the first to open a
trunk and peer inside.

"The duchess does not object to this intrusion?"
Abigail called.

Lady Elizabeth laughed. "Believe me, she is
just as swept away as we are. She has a gown she
brought from Spain that she plans to wear, so that
is why she's chosen to rest before luncheon instead
of joining us."

That seemed to relieve the other women, and, as
the maids arrived with lamps, everyone spread out.
Abigail and Gwen found their own trunk, and as
they opened it, Abigail smelled a faint air of disuse.
She noticed that the garments were so old as to
have been worn long before the duke's birth. So
she temporarily let go of her investigation—since
she *did* need a costume for that night—and im-
mersed herself in the fun.

She and Gwen held up gowns before themselves,
displaying for each other's approval. They were
from the middle of the eighteenth century, needing hoops on both sides. The low square necklines
and bold colors would not do on just anyone. One
by one, Abigail held gowns up before her, and she
tried for something more demure, self-conscious

as she was about her plump figure. Gwen would frown and shake her head over and over again, until at last Abigail had to move on to the next trunk. With a frustrated groan, she held up another gown—and Gwen clasped her hands together with a cry of delight.

"That is it, Abby!"

More than one head turned their way, and Abigail tried not to blush as they critically examined the deep green gown.

"Green?" Abigail said skeptically.

"It will be perfect on you! And what about this one for me?"

She held up a gown that had once been white but had faded into pale ivory over time—or so Abigail estimated by lamplight.

"Gwen, you know every dress will look beautiful on you."

Gwen touched her arm. "You are too sweet. But I like this one, although it looks like it might have to be taken in a bit."

"And mine will have to be let out," Abigail said with a sigh, examining the bodice.

"Oh, what a problem to have!" She grinned.

"You wouldn't think so," Abigail muttered, knowing how much her comfort depended on the proper corset.

One by one, the other women had found what they were looking for and descended the stairs. By the time Abigail and Gwen finished, the only remaining person was Lady Elizabeth, and as they were admiring their gowns, they realized that she was waiting for them.

"Do you mind if we linger and explore the trunks?" Abigail asked. "I keep thinking I'll find a dress that suits me better."

Lady Elizabeth glanced at the stairs, then back with worry. "Are you certain? I wouldn't mind staying."

"Oh, no, please go on ahead," Gwen said, waving her away. "Dressmaking is so interesting! We are comparing the way gowns were designed in the eighteenth century and now. It is rather our hobby. We find that the stitching . . ."

And as Gwen went on, Lady Elizabeth's eyes seemed to lose focus. When Gwen took a breath, Lady Elizabeth shot to her feet.

"Then I'll leave you to it," she said quickly. "What an interesting hobby you have!"

And she was far too young to make that sound believable. When she'd gone, Gwen and Abigail exchanged an amused glance.

"You were excellent," Abigail said. "Wait a few minutes, then you go on ahead, too. You can take the gowns and find a maid to begin alterations. If yours is done quickly, tell her to just start letting out the bodice on mine. I shall be along eventually."

"Are you certain you won't mind being alone up here?" Gwen asked, glancing around uneasily.

Most of the lamps had been taken by women to guide their way down the stairs. There were only two left.

"I'll be fine," Abigail said with an enthusiasm she didn't have to pretend. "The worst that can happen is that I'll discover something for the ghost hunt from the ghost himself."

Gwen groaned more than laughed. "I'll leave you both lamps. The light at the bottom will do well enough to guide my way. Have fun!"

When she was alone, Abigail noticed that she could hear the wind outside much more clearly than in her room. A storm must be brewing. The windows rattled occasionally, and she felt the chill of a draft, but soon she didn't notice anything as she moved to a new group of trunks. She opened one and had to restrain herself from giggling with delight, for there were dozens of notebooks. Could there be a journal or a lady's diary? One by one she took each out, glancing through them quickly. To her dismay, they were household account books from fifty years ago. Eventually, she repacked that trunk and moved on to the next. These contained records of servants from the previous century. She even glanced through several to see if anything of a personal nature had been written, in case she stumbled on a ghost clue for Gwen and Mr. Wesley. Did no one save letters in this household? She grimly moved on to the next trunk, knowing that her time was running out. Luncheon would soon be served.

She needed to find something that would help her to understand the duke.

While Christopher was looking over the account books in his study, Elizabeth poked her head in.

"Wait until you see my gown!" she cried, her eyes alight with laughter.

"Everyone has a costume already?" He had been hoping for more time alone to work since he'd been so distracted the last few days.

"Well, almost everyone."

"And who cannot make up her mind?"

"Lady Gwendolin and Miss Shaw. I hated leaving them alone up there, but they insisted. Imagine, they actually enjoy historical clothing as a hobby!"

Christopher's suspicions flared back to life. "Isn't it almost time for luncheon?"

"It is, and I hate to delay. You know how Cook can be."

He stood up. "Then I'll go see what is keeping them."

Elizabeth grinned as if she thought she knew what his motives were and had deliberately given him an excuse to be with Abigail. But all she said was, "I do not wish to keep you from work . . ."

"Nonsense. I am happy to be of assistance."

"We entered the attics in the lady's wing. I imagine Mama will forgive you just this once for stepping foot there."

As if I haven't been in the lady's wing before, he thought dryly. His sister's naïveté reassured him. And, of course, he hadn't been there in many long years, once he'd realized that women of his own class did not make trustworthy—or scandal-free—bed partners.

He found the door to the attics still open and went up, prepared to find the two women giving a guilty start when they saw him. The attics were just as he remembered them when he used to explore on rainy days. He looked around and saw no one, although a lamp still gleamed beside him.

Had they forgotten to take it with them when they left?

And then he heard the sound of a trunk closing and stepped out of the shadow of light. He realized that across several rows of trunks and crates and old furniture, another lamp shone low to the floor. But he heard no voices. Surely, if Lady Gwen was still here, he would hear her "discussing" their supposed hobby. Or discussing something; she always had something to say.

Then was Abigail here alone?

Christopher did not call out, did not move carelessly. He wanted no squeaking board to announce his presence. He stopped feeling, stopped thinking, although some distant part of him warned that he was acting more like an animal on the prowl than a concerned host.

What was she doing up here alone? Surely not

still looking for a gown. Had she sent Lady Gwen away so that her friend wouldn't see what she was really up to?

When at last he moved past a sofa, he saw her headfirst in a trunk, displaying several petticoats beneath her gown. He hesitated, knowing he should alert her, but beneath the rising petticoats, he could see her slippered feet, dainty ankles, the long line of her stockinged calves, and hint of lace at the hem of her drawers.

He should be angry with her spying, indignant that he didn't know her true purpose in invading his family's home.

Instead, the lust hit him with unexpected power.

He was being driven to distraction with desire for her. It was a dark and sinful thing, this obsession that swept away his common sense, made him forget the rules he lived by, foremost of which was no affairs with women of his own class.

But it was as if she was outside the boundary somehow, all because she was keeping something from him, as if lies no longer made her a gentlewoman. He'd been lied to before, he reminded himself—but not like this. Not where he felt so personally threatened for his family.

Why did she make him feel this way? Her lie was nothing major, but added to her willingness to assist him at great cost to herself and the fact that no one had heard of her . . .

And she was here, alone in the dark, deep into a trunk, so vulnerable to him. He was so tempted to run his hands along her hips, to—

With great effort, he mastered himself. "Find anything interesting?"

With a cry, she straightened so quickly that the jostled trunk started to close. He jumped forward to grab the lid before it could hit her, but she caught it herself, then stared up at him in surprise and dismay.

He knew he should step back. Her head was at the level of his hips, making dark lustful thoughts burn hotter.

He put his hands behind his back to keep from reaching for her. "Miss Shaw, why are you alone up here? You could not find a gown?"

"Oh no, I found one long ago," she said, sitting back on her heels, her hand still resting on the edge of the trunk.

She had a smudge of dirt across her chin, and several curls had escaped her chignon to cling to her perspiring cheeks. And suddenly, he wanted to see her hair draped around her naked body. Her skin would glisten because of what he'd do to her, how he'd make her feel.

He stepped away, gritting his teeth, mastering his control. "If you found a gown," he said at last in a normal tone, "why are you still up here?"

She looked guiltily past him to the far staircase. "You caught me. I was trying to keep it a secret."

It could not be this easy. "What?"

"I didn't want anyone to know that I was looking for clues, perhaps in journals, about the ghost."

The ghost, he thought, blinking slowly as he tried to turn his mind around. Oh, she was good. The correct innocence on her face, the slightly guilty expression, as if she were being naughty, but not too naughty.

And he didn't believe her for a moment.

"The family journals are all in the library, as you've been made aware," he said pleasantly.

"But only the servants have ever seen the ghost, so wouldn't they be the ones to write about it?"

"Many of them can't write."

"I know, and it is such a shame," she said, smoothing her hand over a notebook. "They'll never know the pleasure and release of being able to write one's thoughts."

Though his addled mind wanted to take her use of the words "pleasure and release" another way, he calmed himself.

"You speak as one who writes often."

"Oh, I do," she said with enthusiasm. "And not just letters. I keep a journal, and write about everything that happens to me during the day. Not very exciting, I know," she added with a laugh.

He wondered what he could discover about her in such a journal. Would he be mentioned? Or was he just a means to an end, as he was with other women?

"You can learn so much about people from the way they write," she continued.

"And you thought to do so with the writing of servants?"

She shrugged and leaned back on both arms to look up at him, bringing the swell of breasts into prominence. How did she even expect him to think when she did something like that?

Or was that her intention?

"I had hopes," she said ruefully. "But you're right, there is nothing here from the servants, at least that I've been able to discover so far."

"You've been at this long?" he said, cocking his head.

"No, Gwen only left a short time ago. She felt the need to find a maid with the best sewing skills. There is much work to be done on our gowns."

A moment of silence stretched out, as she looked up at him, and he looked down at her. He wanted her to lie back, he wanted to come down on her . . .

"Did your governess teach you a love of writing?" he finally asked, to fill the charged atmosphere. His voice sounded far too rough, but she didn't appear to notice.

"And my father." She bit her lip and looked away.

"Am I not supposed to know that?"

She smiled and shook her head. "It is not that. Men simply are not usually the ones who keep the connections between distant family, but my father enjoyed that. He, too, kept a journal, and taught me how to write what my senses told me, to record my impressions of people."

He sat down on a crate. "So what are you writing about your time at Madingley Court?"

He thought he detected a blush, but it was hard to tell in this faint light. Yet her skin shown with luminescence, and her unusual eyes gleamed.

"My impressions of all the people of course. Lord Keane's arrogance and humor."

"You have him well mastered."

She grinned. "Lady Theodosia's class awareness, yet her uncertainty and desperation that she's not good enough."

"Ah, yes, I can see where you'd surmise that."

"Am I wrong?"

"No. What about Lady May?"

"Your other opponent in the marriage battle. Though she has backed down for now in the face of your apparent interest in me, I think she assumes good sense will win out on your part—and the fact that she believes me incredibly dull, plain, and beneath you."

And before he could help himself, he murmured, "Beneath me can be a rewarding place."

Chapter 12

Abigail knew at once that he was no longer referring to the difference in their classes, and the sensation that swept through her almost made her gasp. What was he saying? And why was he implying things no gentleman should?

Yet just those few words sent an answering heat through her and a curiosity no lady should feel.

But she wasn't a lady.

And she could admit that he made her feel . . . desired, beautiful. And that was too tempting by half. Why was he treating her so intimately? And what was she supposed to say?

Suddenly, they both heard footsteps on the stairs below. They stared at one another in shock, and she saw his eyes narrow. Being discovered alone together would ruin everything they had—every bit of trust that was already so damaged between them.

The duke leaned over and blew out the lamp, then sank down onto the floor at her side, so close that his shoulder brushed hers. The back of the old sofa rose high enough to block them from sight. They could see the bobbing light of another lamp rise higher into the gloom.

"Chris?"

It was Lady Elizabeth's voice, and Abigail was vastly disappointed that it was not Gwen. Gwen could be trusted, but Elizabeth . . .

To her shock, she felt the duke's mouth against her ear, and his warm, moist breath bathed her.

"Say nothing." The words were barely a whisper, but they were also a command.

What did he think she would do? she thought indignantly. Did he still believe every woman so desperate to marry him?

Then she felt a rush of sympathy. She understood the need to decide one's own fate. Wasn't that what she herself was fighting for?

"Chris?" Lady Elizabeth called one more time. "Someone left a lamp up here," she added crossly.

They could hear her heavy sigh as she turned and went back down the stairs. The light receded, the door at the bottom closed, and they were alone in the dark. The slits of light through the curtains only slightly relieved the gloom.

For a moment they were frozen, their arms brushing, their breathing almost timed together. Relief should be rushing through her, but instead she felt a rising tide of . . . of wildness, of reck-lessness. She was alone with him, this man she felt such a strange connection to. She didn't want it, she had to be objective—she had to leave.

She started to rise to her feet, but her skirts were trapped beneath him, and she fell heavily sideways into his shoulder. And then her world turned upside down as his arms caught her and spun her until she lay across his lap.

Stunned, she looked up at him, seeing only the gleam of his eyes in the near darkness. Her hands settled helplessly on his arms. He was so warm all around her.

And then he pulled her against his chest and kissed her, and she forgot everything else.

His lips were warm and moist as they moved on hers. She tentatively kissed him back, for she could do nothing else, wanted to be nowhere else. She had never been kissed before, and she was not disappointed by the surging feelings that swept over her, feelings that erased all sense of propriety and fear of discovery.

They'd already almost been discovered, and it had only made her heart pound more wildly. The near discovery had unleashed something long suppressed between them.

And then she felt his bold tongue lick along her bottom lip, and the rough wetness of it startled her. Then his tongue slipped inside her, her mouth forced wide against his, and she could only moan in wonder and amazement.

So *this* was what kissing was all about, she

thought to herself, even as she basked in his expertise. And then she stopped thinking and examining, and could only feel. His tongue dueled with hers, played along it, tasted it. And she was desperate to taste him back. She let her hands slide up over his shoulders, then she touched the soft thickness of his hair. She didn't want him to stop, found herself holding his head in her hands to keep him where he was.

He pulled her even tighter against him, her breasts flattened against his hard chest. And that made her moan. Though it was her mouth he took in a searing kiss, it was as if she felt it in the rest of her body. There was a heavy ache in her breasts that was only slightly eased by the pressure of his body. She wanted—no, she *needed* more.

One of his hands slid along her back, caressing the curve of her hip, molding against her backside. She arched into him, flooded by warmth between her thighs.

The new, strange feelings in her body were what finally made her remember who she was, what she was doing—and with whom she was doing it.

She pushed against his chest and broke the kiss, tipping her head back until it was stopped by his shoulder.

Now that her eyes were accustomed to the gloom, she could see the faint shadow of his face, the wetness of his mouth, the way his black eyes devoured her as if he would kiss her again.

And she wanted him to. She wanted to experience the pleasure she'd never imagined before.

And they still had all their clothing on! The rest of what went on between a man and a woman must be—

With a groan, she closed her eyes so she wouldn't have to look at him.

"You do not want my kiss?" His voice was deep and husky.

She shuddered. "I have already shown you that I do. But we must . . . stop."

"Why?"

For an insane moment, she couldn't think of one reason. His thighs were beneath her hips, his arms held her close in an embrace so hot she was surprised she couldn't see flames burning between them.

"It is . . . time for luncheon," she finally managed.

She felt the vibration of his chuckle all through her.

"Is that the only reason to stop?"

"You know there are so many more. I did not mean this to happen. I really only wanted to help you. I still do! And now you must think . . ."

He leaned closer, his lips just touching hers as he spoke against her mouth. "So now you know what I think? Then tell me, because I can remember nothing when I'm holding you like this."

Every movement of his lips against hers made

her tremble all the more. She hovered on the edge of giving up, of giving in and letting him do what he wished.

"You're thinking of . . . nothing?" she whispered, then regretted it, for she could feel his mouth so intimately.

His lips continued to brush hers. "I am thinking of licking a path down your throat, and dipping my tongue in the scented hollow at the base."

She gave a strangled moan as her imagination filled in the picture.

"You taste of sweet peaches, and I want to see if that continues."

For a moment, he kissed her lower lip, then sucked on it gently. She shivered even though he held her so tight she thought she'd never be cold again. But she couldn't stop her body's response.

"I noticed your bodice unbuttons down the front."

She held her breath in shock that he would mention such an intimate thing.

"I'm thinking of unbuttoning them one at a time, dipping my tongue between your sweet breasts, then popping them free from your corset, so that I—"

"Enough!" Her voice was a cry of pain and desire so mixed together that she felt lost. She didn't want to know what he would do with her nakedness. Nothing seemed to matter but this unfulfilled ache within her and the knowledge that he could make it right.

But this was a sin. And a lie—another lie between them.

"Let me go," she whispered.

For the barest moment, his hold tightened, her breasts were almost too painful against his chest.

And then his embrace eased, and she sat up, sliding to the attic floor and turning to rise onto her knees. Without thinking, she reached to steady herself against his shoulder, then realized that he was staring at her breasts, too close to his face. A wanton woman would lean into him, persuade him to make her feel so good she would never want to leave him.

But she was no wanton. She was a virgin, and she had invaded his home to deceive him. What a struggle it would be to remain objective after this!

She rose quickly to her feet, and he followed her lead. Though she could still hear the occasional spatter of rain on the roof, the curtains seemed to be letting in more light. She returned the books to the trunk, trying to pretend that he was not still watching her. It was embarrassing to lean over before him, and exciting, because she was half-afraid, half-hopeful that he would touch her. He didn't offer to help her, which only prolonged the moment. She was flushed by the time she straightened.

"Can you see well enough," he said, "or should I lead you?"

She couldn't bear the thought of what she might reveal if he touched her. "I shall manage."

And she was hurt that he sounded so normal, as if he did such things all the time.

Did he think the same of her?

She imagined him a much younger man, without the wisdom and experience to control his impulses. What had he done with such passion?

She walked before him to the stairs, fumbled for a moment until she found the rail, then descended carefully.

From behind, she heard, "I will remain here for several minutes until you have had a chance to reach your room. Is it far?"

"No, just a floor down."

As if he needed to know that, she thought, closing her eyes in dismay.

She had already learned her lesson where caution was concerned, so she leaned her ear against the door before opening it. When she heard nothing, she went through. As she turned to close the door, she found the duke holding on to the lintel over her head with both hands, leaning toward her.

Softly, he said, "My sister says your hobby is historical costumes?"

She looked frantically back and forth to see if anyone was coming. "It is," she hissed, "but what has that to do with anything?"

"So you like being in disguise?"

Her mouth fell open.

Wearing a wicked grin, he said, "Remember to wash the dirt from your face."

Gritting her teeth, she closed the door firmly in his face, then hurried to her room, determined to pretend that the kiss never happened. But why had he mentioned a disguise? she wondered in growing fear.

Though his rooms were in the next wing, Christopher made it a point to return to wash his own face. He used cold water, splashing it over and over as if he could splash some sense into himself.

What did he think he was doing?

He kept telling himself that Abigail had fallen right into his arms, that no sane man could have resisted those soft curves, that luscious mouth.

And she had tasted as incredible, as decadent as he'd *hoped* she would. It had taken everything in him not to seduce her, forgetting all his own rules for scandal-free conduct.

She hadn't resisted him, and the cynical part of him was not surprised.

He should send her away, but he knew he wouldn't. If he did, he would never get the answers he wanted. And he'd be left to the tender attentions of the Ladies May and Theodosia. He preferred Abigail to them, even if she *was* lying to him. What had he seen in her expression when he'd mentioned a disguise?

He wiped his face with a towel. Someone knocked at his door, and absently he called, "Come in."

Elizabeth leaned in. "So there you are! I thought you went to look for Miss Shaw and Lady Gwen. I found Lady Gwen."

"And I found Miss Shaw. We went for a walk."

Her grin widened with delight. "How wonderful."

He held up a hand. "You don't need to look like that. It was a walk. We talked about books we've read."

She shuddered. "How boring you've become."

"I like books," he said, trying not to feel indignant. How could anyone not like to read?

To his dismay, he saw their mother appear behind Elizabeth.

"Did I hear you say you went for a walk with Miss Shaw?" his mother asked.

Elizabeth giggled. "Maybe you should ask him what his intentions are." With a wave, she hurried out of the room.

The duchess came in and shut the door. She arched a black brow and simply looked at him in that way that had once cowed him, and made him confess everything. But he was not that young anymore.

"It's not what you think," he assured her.

"And what do I think?"

"That I am interested in her. I am not. We are simply friends."

"Friends?"

The doubt in her eyes made him realize that he wasn't ready to have his . . . relationship with Abigail taken apart in detail. But obviously he was doing a poor job of hiding what he felt. If he gave her some of the secret, perhaps that would satisfy her.

"She is helping me," he said at last.

"With the mystery of the ghost?" she countered in disbelief.

"No, helping me remain free of the cloying Ladies May and Theodosia."

The Spanish passion rose dangerously in her eyes. "The women you were considering as your bride? And how is she doing that?"

"Miss Shaw knows that I have to consider someone of much higher birth than her as my duchess, so she offered to allow a pretend courtship between us, leaving me some peace at this insufferable house party."

The duchess blinked. "There are so many responses I could make to everything you said that it's difficult to know where to begin. You told her that you need to marry a woman of higher birth? I did not think the son I raised would be so cruel."

It was his turn to blink. "*She* told me she thought I needed to marry such a woman. And she's right.

A duchess needs to be born to understand the role, raised to accept the duties and responsibilities."

"As I was?" she countered dryly.

"You are the rare exception, *Madre.* Most women could never be like you. Father found you, his perfect duchess, and now I have to find mine."

"And some poor woman has to live within your definitions or fail you?"

"It won't be like that. She will understand what our marriage will be."

"And love does not matter?"

"How can I trust in something as unpredictable as love?"

His mother's stare once had the power to reduce him to ash, but he'd long ago learned to stand against it. And now he saw the touch of sadness there, and he felt guilty for it. But he couldn't allow her feelings to sway him from what he knew was right.

"If by my actions I have not shown you the power of love," she said softly, "then there is nothing else I can say about it."

"*Madre,* don't act like—"

She put up a hand to stop him. "Then tell me this. You do not look as if you are uninterested in Miss Shaw, and I see you with the eyes of a woman who's known you your whole life."

He felt the first wrinkle of unease.

"Then I am a very good actor, am I not?"

"And she is not interested in marrying?"

"She says she wants to find a nice country squire. She's not interested in marrying me, and that's all I needed to hear."

"But I am not an innocent young lady, Christopher. I understand that there's more to what a man says, that love is not always a part of what a man is feeling for a woman."

He sighed and briefly closed his eyes. "I cannot believe we are discussing this. Yes, she is a lovely young lady, but I know my responsibilities, and I will marry the right person, and it's not Abigail— Miss Shaw."

Oh, that had been a mistake.

His mother's eyes narrowed. "I find it sad that you continue to be so rigid and unimaginative about your future. I sometimes feel like I have failed you."

He sighed. "*Madre*—"

"Know this," she interrupted. "Whatever game you think you are playing with this girl—or she thinks she's playing along with you—you have the power to hurt her terribly. And if I hear you do . . ."

"You will what?" he said mildly. "Turn me over your knee?"

She sighed. "It is not I who will punish you. No, Christopher, I believe you will punish yourself."

Chapter 13

"And you found nothing?" Gwen asked Abigail in disappointment, as they took turns looking at themselves in a mirror in Abigail's bedroom.

"Nothing." The logical place to search would have to be his bedroom. And she couldn't think about that right now.

The Madingley maid had done wonders with their gowns and proved herself even more valuable in dressing their hair, for their tresses were piled high in the Georgian style, laced with bows and flowers; Gwen even had a bird's nest perched on her head, and she confessed that she might have to steal the talented girl away with her when she returned to London.

"There was nothing but old clothing?" Gwen continued.

"Oh, I found plenty of ancient account books and notebooks dealing with the servants, but nothing of a personal nature. Although I hardly had time to look before—"

"Before what?" Gwen said.

Abigail shook her head, hardly imagining being able to tell her dearest friend how much she'd embarrassed herself and betrayed every standard of decency. "Before I had to come down to luncheon."

Gwen stomped her foot, and the fake bird in her bird's nest fluttered with realism. "Oh, please, Abby, do not think to hide the truth from me now!"

"I—I—" She put her face in her hands. "Oh Gwen, the duke came looking for me, and I let him kiss me."

She felt Gwen's arm around her shoulder. "It was only a kiss. Surely you have received many of them from daring young men."

Abigail shook her head, then raised damp eyes. "Never. I don't seem to appeal to most men in such a way."

"Or your father has sufficiently cowed the more daring suitors." Gwen smirked playfully. "It seems you appeal to the duke."

"Oh, no, I don't. He was sitting on my gown and I fell on him trying to stand up."

"Sitting on your gown? You were sitting side by side on the attic floor?"

Abigail waved her hand in dejection. "It was

only so that his sister wouldn't catch us alone. He didn't mean to do it."

"But he meant to kiss you."

She felt herself blushing hotly. "I'm sure he would have kissed any woman in such a situation. I was lying across his lap."

"*Lying* across his lap?" Gwen cried, then covered her mouth and glanced with guilt in the direction of the doorway. "So you think he would have kissed the snobbish Lady May, or the poised Lady Theodosia?"

Abigail opened her mouth—and said nothing for a moment. "Very well, he wouldn't have kissed them, but only because his wariness of entrapment is all-encompassing. With me he doesn't have to care."

"If you were discovered, he would be in the same predicament with you as if he'd kissed either of those others. So do not use such a silly excuse again. He kissed you because he wanted to, and in that moment he didn't care about the consequences."

"In that moment," Abigail echoed defensively. "Even you agree he wouldn't normally feel that way."

"I mean 'in that moment' he could no longer control himself from what he's feeling *all the time*."

Abigail stared in despair at Gwen, and finally felt real tears. "Oh, Gwen, do not say such a thing! He cannot feel anything for me. I'd rather it be a temporary desire than anything more. My guilt is bad enough as it is. If I truly hurt him deeper, hurt his family—"

"Stop. Stop it at once," Gwen said kindly. "You are becoming too close to your subject. Isn't there a rule about that?"

Abigail nodded forlornly.

"Then stop worrying. They do not need your concern. You should concentrate on your own troubles."

But he's become one of my troubles.

"Then what if I've ruined this pretend courtship?" Abigail asked. "How could he trust me now after I've allowed his kiss?"

"If he is any kind of a decent man, then he feels the blame for what he did with an innocent woman."

"Then he'll stop spending time with me. How will I learn what I need to know?"

"I didn't say he'd stop. Honestly, Abby, I don't think he *can* stop. You've intrigued him."

"That's because he senses I'm holding something back. But I've come too far to stop now. I may not have the truth about him yet, but it's hidden somewhere, I know it."

"That's the spirit!" Gwen said, hugging her.

Abigail took a deep breath. "Next, I'll try to become more friendly with his sister. She does not strike me as a young lady who's used to guarding her tongue yet."

"Give her a Season," Gwen said with sarcasm. "She'll learn quickly."

"Then it's a good thing I have her now." Abigail eyed herself in the mirror, critically examining the way her breasts mounded over the square neckline. "What if I sew more lace across the bodice?"

"Coward. Do you not want his eyes on you, to make him keep up this pretense? And if you alter the gown, it will lose its historic appeal."

Abigail couldn't help but laugh. "Oh Gwen, you are too good to me."

"It is so easy to do."

Abigail smiled, but inside she realized she was going to have to start lying to Gwen, who would have to seem clueless about Abigail's whereabouts when asked. Abigail could not tell her that tonight she planned to search the duke's rooms while he was attending the dance.

When Christopher entered the blue drawing room, he was glad that Elizabeth had seen reason and not used the second-floor ballroom. The party of fewer than twenty people would have seemed inconsequential in such a lofty space.

But in the drawing room, with the rugs rolled up and the chandeliers shining with thousands of candles, the atmosphere was intimate, yet festive.

To his amusement, several of the men had changed their minds about their costumes; they were wearing knee breeches and had powdered their hair. Their enthusiasm must have pleased his sister, whose face was alight with happiness.

He enjoyed the sight of the women, all dressed in gowns from the past century. They'd arranged their hair in elaborate ways that better suited a dessert concoction.

And then he saw Abigail. Although she, too, was hidden beneath a mound of hair, he could not miss those incredible breasts, nearly overflowing the gown.

He was not the only one taking notice. But he was the only one who'd had them pressed against his chest just that afternoon—who'd thought of little else but having them in his hands and mouth since he'd kissed her.

And now they were practically hanging there, ripe for the taking, and he could hardly stop looking at her.

But wasn't that the point? He was allowed to appear smitten, wasn't he?

So he approached where she stood with Lady Gwen and bowed low before them both. Abigail gave a graceful curtsy, which almost made him choke over the bounty she displayed.

"Miss Shaw," he said softly, when she arose. He remembered almost too late to say, "Lady Gwen."

Lady Gwen hid her amusement behind her fan. Abigail didn't bother to hide hers, as if she thought him endearing.

It was getting difficult to tell what was real and what was not. He hated admitting even silently that his mother had been right. He had to remind himself that Abigail was not what she seemed, that her costume was merely another disguise.

He smiled. "You both look quite delightful."

"Thank you, Your Grace," Abigail said.

"Is that a bird's nest, Lady Gwen?" he asked, and could not keep himself from laughing.

"Only an artificial one, Your Grace."

"Just as well," he responded. "Else you might be visited by unwelcome tiny companions, as I understand that most birds are rife with ticks and other creatures."

He noticed that more than one person had turned at the sound of his amusement, their expressions ranging from astonishment to calculation. So he was not in the habit of showing his emotions. Let them look; that was the point.

On a dais in the corner, the small orchestra began to play a quadrille, and Christopher turned to Abigail. "Would you care to dance?"

She seemed briefly surprised that he'd asked her. She must have experienced some trepidation after what had occurred between them in the attic.

Then she smiled and put her small, gloved hand in his. "I would enjoy it, Your Grace."

They lined up with the others, and since this was not a dance when she'd be long in his arms, he could not easily speak to her. They met up with others, bowing and performing intricate steps. But always they came back together. He saw her tension slowly dissipate; she was good at the dance. She did not seem to notice the way the other young men were watching her, as if she'd blossomed over the several days of the house party.

He was surprised by the uncomfortably tight way that made him feel. After only one kiss, he was already jealous of her future suitors? How preposterous.

When the dance ended, he offered to bring her some punch. He wound his way through the small crowd, speaking briefly to several people, forced to listen to Lord Swarthbeck, who'd decided to be bold as he proclaimed the merits of his daughter, Lady May. Christopher knew that an alliance between their families might be a suitable match. Lady May obviously understood what a noble marriage would mean, being the daughter of a marquess. But Christopher found himself watching Abigail all the while Lord Swarthbeck was talking. He liked the way she tilted up her face to speak to the taller Lady Gwen. Was that the shadow of a dimple in one cheek as she smiled? He hadn't even noticed before.

And then he saw Abigail greet his sister, who stopped to speak to the two friends. Soon they were talking and laughing, and Christopher found himself growing more and more uncomfortable.

Who knew what Abigail might expose her to? It was one thing for him to be involved with Abigail, another for his unsuspecting sister.

"Madingley?"

Christopher gave a start and realized that Swarthbeck had repeated his name more than once.

Gruffly, the marquess said, "Don't tell me that you, too, have begun to think incessantly about that ghost. I swear, my wife and daughter have lost all sense."

"No, it's not that," Christopher said. "I simply have too much on my mind. And I realized I offered to bring several people punch, and I'll never hear the end of it if I don't."

"Ladies," Swarthbeck said, shaking his head. "They can't forgive a man anything."

If that was true of the women in Swarthbeck's family, then perhaps Christopher should rule out Lady May.

By the time he approached the three young women—with punch for only two of them, since he wanted his sister to leave—they were all in a paroxysm of laughter.

"Then you really must learn to aim better," Abigail was saying, dabbing at her eyes. "Would you like me to teach you?"

Elizabeth shuddered as she tried to control herself. "The arrow just flies so randomly when I let it go."

"Obviously!" said Lady Gwen, and they all laughed again.

"But I would love a lesson with you, Miss Shaw!" Elizabeth said.

"Call me Abigail."

"What did I miss?" he interrupted, handing the punch to Lady Gwen and Abigail. He was trying to look pleasant when he was really gritting his teeth.

"Abigail is going to teach me archery," Elizabeth said, with a toss of her head as if she dared him to refuse.

"And which man will suffer an arrow wound because of it?"

Lady Gwen giggled. "We heard about some of her archery adventures. But Abigail is a very patient instructor."

And for some reason, even that made Christopher feel aroused.

"I have not seen you dancing, Chris," Elizabeth said, "but for one dance with Abigail. There are other young ladies here."

"And I will dance with them." He hated to leave the three women alone again. He caught a look of impatience from Abigail that made him wonder what she was thinking. "Save me the next waltz, Miss Shaw."

He saw Elizabeth's look of amusement, as if she enjoyed watching her brother make a fool of himself over a woman. Let her think what she would.

He gave the next dance to Lady Theodosia, and returned in time for a waltz with Abigail. He noticed as he took her in his arms that she tried to keep as far away as possible.

Softly, he said, "You cannot believe that I will allow this distance in a waltz. What will our audience think of our courtship?"

He pulled her closer. As he whirled her through a corner, he allowed his thigh to dip between hers and saw her shock. "Is something wrong?" he asked with innocence.

Her eyes narrowed, but she said nothing.

With Abigail in his arms, he was free to touch her, to feel the supple strength of her back, the delicateness of her hand in his. He wasn't sure he'd ever let his mind go to just enjoy the dance. Beneath her ridiculous hair, her brown eyes looked dark and forbidden, while the glitter within dared him to do more.

It was Abigail who remembered to stop when the music ended. He might have continued dancing like a fool. What was wrong with him?

She gave him a knowing smile. "There are other ladies who wish to dance with you, Your Grace, and you've had the proper two with me."

"Ah, Society rules can be so tiresome."

She almost pushed him away. "Go on with you before you make a scene."

It had been many years since he'd been the one to make a scene over anything. He almost laughed.

Instead, he bowed to her and went off to another room, where Lord Paul and Lord Gerald Delane, the younger sons of the duke of Sutterly, were waiting to discuss a bill their father would soon be championing in the House of Lords.

As Abigail watched the duke leave the drawing room, she knew that the time had finally come for her escape.

She heard, "May I have this dance?" behind her back.

She turned to find Mr. Wesley waiting politely for her answer. She glanced at the door through which Madingley had disappeared. Surely she had a few minutes before she needed to leave. How could she disappoint the vicar?

While they were dancing, she asked, "Did you dance with Lady Gwen? Isn't she graceful?"

To her amazement, he reddened. "No, it wouldn't be right."

"Right?" she echoed in bewilderment.

"Well, her station is so far above mine. The good people of my parish would want me to dance with you."

And then his eyes widened, as if he'd said the wrong thing.

Gently, she said, "I know that they all think I should confine myself to conversation with you rather than the other men. But am I doing that? No. I speak—and dance—with anyone. And Society will not crumble because I do so."

"But they're my parishioners, Miss Shaw," he said with patience, as if she were too foolish to understand.

"I know they are. And Lady Gwen is your friend. How can you not dance with her?"

Gwen was alone as they both glanced at her, and her lovely face seemed pale rather than happy.

"She looks like that . . . because of me?" he asked hesitantly.

"She does."

"Then . . . I would not wish her to be unhappy."

As the music ended, Abigail said, "Go dance with her," and gave him a little push on his way.

Then she turned and casually left the drawing room, as if she were looking for the small room set aside for the ladies' privacy. But she took a different corridor, then picked up speed as she hurried toward the family wing and to the duke's rooms.

Chapter 14

Christopher hadn't realized how long he was gone from the dance until he glanced at a mantel clock—only a quarter of an hour. But the Delanes were doing their best to convince Christopher to support Sutterly, and they'd had valid arguments.

When Christopher's reappearance was noticed, he decided to do his duty and dance several dances with the older ladies. Lady Gwen's aunt, Miss Bury, was particularly amusing, and she kept referring fondly to Mr. Fitzwilliam, who was dozing in a chair, as if the elderly gentleman were watching them.

And then Christopher surprised Lady Gwen by sweeping her into a waltz. She was energetic and athletic, and he enjoyed how well she kept up with him. It was a shame she didn't want to marry a duke, he thought. But then maybe that was a good thing, because he was realistic enough to admit to himself that he shouldn't marry a woman whose best friend was Abigail Shaw.

"So you have driven Miss Shaw away, Your Grace," Lady Gwen said.

Christopher frowned at her. "Your pardon?"

"Well, I had assumed she retired for a moment of privacy, but it has been quite a bit longer."

For a moment, he saw a strange emotion of realization come into her eyes. Then it was gone.

"Lady Gwen?"

"Well, I suddenly remembered that she wasn't feeling well. You know, we women are susceptible to such things."

And then she took her leave as if she couldn't wait to escape him.

Had she actually just hinted at female problems? Something was certainly going on if Lady Gwen felt the need to cover for Abigail. He felt unease begin to change into urgency. What was she doing?

He left the dance as quietly as possible. His first thought was that she'd gone to her own room, but he didn't believe it. He remembered her face when he'd mentioned a disguise. She was here under false pretenses, he already knew that. So what would she be trying to accomplish tonight, when everyone else was occupied? Certainly not ghost hunting.

The house was too big to search randomly. And he couldn't believe she would be in any of the public rooms, or else she could simply have remained in the drawing room. So that left rooms she wasn't supposed to be in.

And then he knew where she'd gone.

* * *

In awe, Abigail thought that the duke's bedroom was sumptuous—all dark wood with maroon curtains and counterpanes. To her surprise, one wall was comprised of bookshelves. Of course, the library was far away, she thought with the threat of a nervous giggle.

The fireplace was massive, with an intricately sculpted mantel. And the bed—huge bedposts held up a canopy draped in velvet bed curtains. She thought of lying on that bed with Madingley, letting him finish what they'd started this afternoon . . . and felt like a fool. That was never going to happen. She was at Madingley Court for one purpose—to get to know the duke and his past, but not intimately.

She went to his writing desk first and found herself hesitating. How could she go through his private things? She told herself she wasn't a thief, but she was trying to take a part of his life, wasn't she? Her hands were shaking as she opened the top drawer, only to find writing supplies. A lot of them, more quills than a man could possibly use.

She didn't want to do something so invasive to a man she'd come to appreciate. She liked him too much, from his sense of humor, to his sense of honor, to his acceptance of his responsibilities as head of the family. He tried to take good care of them, to be the best son, the best brother. And if that made him too overbearing, too in control, then he was to be pitied.

It was so obvious how hard he'd worked to achieve what he had. She wouldn't be tearing that down. She would make it obvious that he'd come a long way from . . . whatever the secret was.

And he was the one who'd committed the deed. She had done nothing wrong, and yet she was about to lose her freedom if she had to marry, her future, if she could no longer write for the paper.

Gritting her teeth, she opened the next drawer and the next. She found an account book, and although she only glanced inside to make sure what it was, she gasped aloud at the sums involved. She felt . . . dirty, and quickly put the book away. She didn't find anything that resembled a notebook at all, although, in the bottom drawer, she did find a sheaf of paper bound with a ribbon. She was just about to take it out when she heard something in the corridor that sounded like footsteps.

Oh God. She swiftly closed the drawer, grabbed up her gloves, and turned toward the draperies.

"Abigail."

She froze. Very slowly, she turned toward the duke, trying not to twist the gloves in her hand. Wiping away all expression, she raised her eyes to his angry face and waited. She would take her clue from his response.

And he was more than angry; he was livid. His dark eyes blazed with it beneath lowered brows.

"What do you think you're doing?" he demanded harshly.

He caught her by the arms and she let him, knowing she deserved it. And then inspiration struck, although it was a dangerous one. Softly she murmured, "I'm waiting for you."

He pulled her closer, up against the heat of his body. She could feel the passion of his fury overwhelm her . . . but she could also feel her own traitorous reaction to his touch. She wasn't afraid of him; she thought she knew him well enough to know he would never physically hurt her. He could send her away, perhaps even humiliate her, but she had to take the risk.

She let her memory of his kiss show on her face, so close to the surface that she could almost taste it—taste him—again.

And something in his expression changed, growing harsher, but not with fury. There was a struggle inside him, and she knew suddenly, powerfully, that he really was susceptible to her, that he wasn't just toying with her. She felt at once ebullient, then deeply afraid, for she knew she felt the same way.

"I am not trying to change our arrangement," she quickly said. And although he still gripped her upper arms, she let her hands touch his waist beneath his black evening coat, then slowly began to slide them up his chest. "But that kiss we shared made me realize how little I know about men. It probably was very obvious to you that you're the first man I've ever kissed. I thought that since we had to be together, and I was helping you, that perhaps you could help me, so that when I found the perfect man, I would know what to do, how to begin."

His hot gaze dropped to her mouth, his hands pulled her closer. Now her breasts touched his chest, and she found a sigh of relief and expectation slipping between her lips. Good lord, he could make her feel such wonders with just a touch.

But inside he must be fighting a battle, for although he drew her flush against him, pulled her right up onto her toes, he didn't kiss her.

"I have a friend who knows all of Society," he said mockingly. "She has never heard of your family. Even your accent doesn't speak of the northern part of the country."

She blinked at him, hiding her vulnerability. He was already suspicious enough to look into her family. How much longer could she keep this up? And yet she had not discovered the truth of his past.

She tried to smile. "And it bothers you that my family is reclusive? I already told you that they never come to London. Even the city of Durham itself is too populous for them. And forgive me if my governess insisted I speak proper English."

She could almost see his brain trying to work. Was she supposed to rub herself against him to distract him? But that might work too well. She didn't want to find herself beneath him on that big bed, seduced and compromised.

But the thought of his long body covering hers—

"I think you have a hidden purpose here, Abigail."

"I don't."

"I saw you talking to my tutor."

"You followed me?" she cried, horrified. Had he heard her questioning the old man?

"And now what am I supposed to think when I find you in my bedroom? That you're only here to be kissed?"

"Teach me," she whispered, licking her lips as she'd seen another woman do when a man was looking at her.

And it seemed to work, for his eyes focused on her mouth and seemed to blaze even hotter with dark passion.

"I can learn so much from you," she added quickly. "Mama was too shy to speak of such things to me"—that wasn't true, for she knew too well what the hard length she was feeling against her stomach was—"and you are the first man I've trusted to show me."

"You trust me?" he said with a harsh laugh. "I don't trust *you*. And you want me to show you everything?"

She gasped. "Oh no, not—you know I cannot mean—relations!"

"Be quiet. I'll give you what you want. For now."

And then he kissed her, and it was full of wildness and fury and passion. She kissed him back, meeting his tongue, darting into his mouth with her own wicked curiosity. His hands had slid from her arms down her back, and were pressing her hips against his. She moaned into his mouth, letting her hands explore the hardness of his arms beneath his clothing, the powerful width of his chest.

He broke the kiss. "If you can touch me, then I can touch you."

She didn't understand what he meant—because of course they were already touching—but then he put his hands on her shoulders and slipped the capped sleeve and undergarment straps down her arm. The release of some support for her breasts made her suddenly feel very vulnerable, as if she'd lost control of her purpose.

"But—"

His clever hands slipped lower, and suddenly her breasts popped free of gown, corset, and chemise all at once. The expression of admiration in his eyes made her burn with pleasure, but she knew where this could lead. She used her arms to cover herself from him.

"No you don't," he said in a voice that rumbled deeply. "You wanted my help, my tutoring."

"But no man would dare to—"

"All a man has to do is look at you so revealed in this gown, and this is what he's thinking of. Didn't you want me to look, Abigail?"

She bit her lip, and he gave a tight laugh.

"You wanted me to look at you in this gown. Here's your first lesson. When you display yourself before men, this is what you're inviting them to do."

Although she struggled, he took one arm at a time away from her chest, twisting them very gently, but firmly, behind her. She was mortified to be so revealed to him. But she had pretended to offer herself by coming to his room, and now he was accepting.

She found herself slowly bent backward, felt the first heavy curl slip free from her head and glide down her shoulder. He moaned and pressed his face against that lone curl, inhaling deeply. He let his mouth follow the trail of her collarbone, then travel lower, pressing openmouthed kisses as he went.

She couldn't seem to breathe, didn't know what she was supposed to do as she hung against him, so vulnerable. She felt the roughness of his whiskers against her breasts when his chin touched her. It was awkward to keep watching him when her head wanted to fall back, but she had to see what he was doing.

"Madingley, please—"

"Christopher," he breathed against her breast as he followed the curve to the peak. "Chris."

And then he took her nipple deep into his mouth, and she convulsed in a shudder against him.

"Oh, Chris, oh—"

But she had nothing coherent to say, could hardly remember her own name, so deep did the pleasure of his mouth pull at her, tugging at intimate parts of her body that were slowly awakening. Though helpless and trapped, she needed to move, found herself pushing against him, rubbing, and all the while he did the most incredible things to her breasts. He took turns between them, alternatively licking at the peaks, then suckling her. Her legs could no longer support her, but her hands were suddenly free to grip his shoulders, to hold herself against him. He cupped her hips in his hands, lifted her so much that one foot came off the floor.

And that was when she knew there were even more wonders to come, for he pressed himself between her thighs, and though her petticoats and gown muffled some of the effect, just the pressure of him was enough to enflame an ache of longing in the depths of her belly. Then she realized he was moving quite deliberately, pressing and retreating, his body teasing her, his mouth encouraging her, all together lifting her higher and higher, shuddering against him—

And she was so afraid of giving in that she violently broke away from him and fell back on the edge of the bed. She scrambled to her feet, turning her back, trying desperately to push her overflowing breasts back into her tight clothes, but she could not.

She must have made a sound of distress, because he stepped nearer, and she could not help cringing away from him.

"You know I won't hurt you," he said in a low voice that ached with the same frustration now boiling through her veins. She'd been so close to knowing the pleasure that a man could give a woman.

But he wasn't her husband—would never be her husband. And he didn't deserve the honor of her innocence.

Even though she'd taunted him with it. Oh God, she despised herself, she thought, almost bruising her sensitive flesh trying to hide her breasts.

And then she felt him tugging on the back of her gown. She stiffened.

"I'm only loosening your garments so you can repair yourself," he said shortly.

She had no choice but to believe him.

Christopher swore at his shaking hands, forcing them to obey him. Each hook on the old-fashioned gown slowly came undone to her waist, then he was able to loosen her corset strings.

She was still trembling as she waited, with all the temerity of a frightened fawn. By the devil, he'd almost ravished her, seduced her, taken her innocence—he was positive she *was* innocent.

She wouldn't be innocent for long if she kept throwing herself at men.

If her inexperience was obvious, her delight in the new ways he'd pleasured her was transparent. Her breasts had been like the sweetest berries to him, her nipples as pink as new rose blossoms. And he'd pressed himself between her thighs, aching for the release she could give him. Even fully clothed he'd almost forgotten himself in his passionate delight of her.

Until she'd stopped herself—stopped him—from making the worst mistake imaginable: seducing a virginal young lady.

She was shaking before him, covering her marvelous breasts.

"Shall I lace you up?" he asked, feeling as if he almost didn't remember how to speak.

She glanced over her shoulder, eyes downcast, not quite meeting his gaze. Her cheeks were rosy with passion, and several more curls had fallen to lie artfully across her bare shoulders. After a shy hesitation, she nodded.

He pulled on her corset laces and started to tie them up.

"Please, tighter," she said in a quiet voice.

"Tighter?" He was doubtful.

"I need . . . they require . . ."

And then he understood. "More support?" His tone was dry, stiff, as stiff as his control. The breasts he'd just held in his hands must need a great deal of support.

She gave a quick nod, and he tied tighter, then

hooked her all the way up. When she would have stepped away, he put his hands on her shoulders, where the skin was bare above her tiny sleeves. His fingers spanned to her neck, and he felt the flutter of her pulse. With his fingertips, he caressed her softly, slowly, feeling the trembling that spread throughout her body.

"Lust has not addled me into forgetfulness." He kept his voice low, with just a touch of threat. "You were here without my permission, and I don't believe the reasons you gave."

"How strange," she said with growing firmness, "for you acted as if you did."

"I took what was offered. I am a man, not a saint. Unless you had tried to kill me, I would want you regardless of what you've done. So end it, and tell me what is going on. Because you have not convinced me to forgive you with this performance. I guard my privacy too well."

"I've told you the truth," she said.

And now she really was giving a masterful performance. He heard nothing but bewilderment and a trace of anger in her voice.

"Offended by my accusations?"

She said nothing, but as he leaned over her shoulder, he saw the stubborn set of her mouth.

"Then be offended—and take my warnings to heart. Stay away from my sister, for I don't want her hurt by whatever happens between us."

"I would not hurt her! And I cannot rebuff my

hostess. Why do you not tell me to leave and be done with it?"

She knew he wasn't going to do that, the little minx. She was getting too confident by half.

"I don't want to hurt Lady Gwen," he said, trying to hide his frustration—and his amusement. "I don't think she knows what you're doing, but she seems to love you dearly."

All the stiffness went out of her then, and her head drooped with dejection. Whatever she was up to, it seemed to be costing her her peace of mind, and for that alone, his temper at last faded. But not his determination to unmask her.

Surprising him, she said hotly, "I think you aren't making me leave because you think that—I will let you seduce me. I will not! I would shame my parents, and you'd feel honor-bound to marry me, and neither of us wants that kind of life."

"You think I would marry you if I didn't want to?" he scoffed.

"I think honor is so important that you've let it rule your life."

"Not always." The words slipped out without thought, and he realized he was letting her see too much of him. He was standing behind her, his hands still on her shoulders, and he didn't want her to turn around.

But she'd stopped moving, almost stopped breathing, and he knew she was listening intently.

"You are a duke," she said with disbelief in her

voice. "You have been reared with nothing but honor, and you love your family. I do not believe you've ever had a moment of weakness, not like the rest of us mortals."

And for a moment, he wanted to unburden himself to her, as if she could somehow absolve him of his guilt.

Did he think her that powerful in his life—already?

"Go back to the dance, Abigail. Or perhaps you should go to your room to repair yourself further."

He spun her about and set one finger on the upper curve of her right breast. "I think I marked you with my mouth."

She stared up at him, her pink lips slightly parted, her eyes searching his. And he didn't see bewilderment and fear there, but dawning curiosity.

"Go." His voice was too harsh.

She turned and fled, leaving him alone. His hands were fisted as he got himself back under control. And then he performed a methodical search of his bedroom, the dressing room, and the bathroom. Nothing was missing, which did not surprise him; she wasn't a thief.

But it was time to send a man to London to investigate her, for he was having trouble finding the answers he needed. She was too distracting. Although an investigation would certainly last longer than her visit, he wanted to know all about her.

Until then, he would have to continue on his own, even though there was a risk of others discovering something amiss. He would inspect the mail every day, to see if she was regularly corresponding with someone. He would remain close to her, their pretend courtship intact, not give her the chance to be away from him. She would eventually reveal something.

Or he would, he thought with a slight wince. But he was determined to be the stronger one.

Chapter 15

The next morning, after looking through the outgoing post and finding nothing for Abigail, Christopher chose not to stop Elizabeth's archery lesson. At the last minute, he backed out of a hunting trip with the men, so that Abigail wouldn't know he was still nearby. He watched surreptitiously from the house as the women followed the gardeners, who were setting up targets on the lawn—far from the house. Even the gardeners knew that Elizabeth couldn't be trusted with a sharp object.

Christopher had decided that turnabout was fair play. If Abigail could search his room, he could search hers. But just when he reached her door, Miss Bury opened hers.

"Your Grace!" she cried enthusiastically.

Christopher stiffened, glad he had not already put his hand on the doorknob.

"Miss Shaw is not here," Miss Bury said, lowering her voice and looking about. "Although I must admit, it is rather daring of you to look for her in the ladies' wing. But it *is* your house!" She grinned.

Christopher gave her a chagrined smile. "Foolish, I know, but I simply had a question about the ghost—"

Miss Bury burst into laughter, then covered her mouth. "The ghost. Oh, that is too dear of you."

"I beg your pardon?" he asked as if he were confused.

"It is no secret that you favor Miss Shaw, and she you," Miss Bury said in a lowered voice that still seemed to carry down the corridor.

"I am trying not to favor any one woman."

"And it isn't working, my dear boy—if I may call a duke that!"

The kind old lady looked so hopeful that he found it difficult to lie to her. "Miss Bury, I do not wish you to imagine secret plots where there are none. Miss Shaw and I are forced together this week, but as for a match, that wouldn't suit either of our needs."

Her expression grew confused, then sad. "Your Grace, I did not think to find you such a snob. You did not seem like all the other foolish young men chasing titles."

For a moment, he didn't know how to answer. *Was* he a snob? Did trying to find the right woman—for both himself and his family—make him seem too exclusive to outsiders?

But no, only a woman born to a life of privilege and nobility could possibly understand. How could he burden anyone else?

"Miss Bury, you have given me much to think on. But you know that a duchess's lot is not an easy one. Should I not consider carefully what woman could best be happy with it?"

"Is not love your first consideration, Your Grace?" she asked in almost a motherly tone.

"No, it cannot be," he said simply.

"Ah, then you are proving yourself to be like so many of the others. Perhaps a worthy woman— a woman in love—would put up with everything that goes along with being your duchess, all for the sake of having your love."

He wasn't going to win this one; in fact, her words unsettled him to a degree he didn't want to think about. And he had to hurry, or the archery lesson might be over too quickly.

He bowed. "Thank you for your advice, Miss Bury."

Her smile returned. "If anyone can accept and act on it, it is you, Your Grace."

And then she walked away, leaving him bemused.

When she'd turned the corner, he slipped inside Abigail's room and shut the door behind him. He searched quickly through the wardrobe and chest of drawers, finding only clothing. Lying atop the desk he found the notebook she'd been writing in the other night. And as she had said, it was all about the ghost hunting—and her curiosity about Lady Gwen's and Mr. Wesley's budding relationship.

Was Abigail really what she said she was? Was he being a fool?

But when he finished going through the desk, he found another notebook, identical to the first. In a neat hand, with no ladylike frills, she had written a date almost a fortnight previous, then the first line: *The Duke of Madingley is not what I expected.* And the next paragraph was all about her impressions of him.

Something inside him tightened.

And then he heard voices in the corridor. Without thinking about the consequences, he stepped behind the draperies, still holding the damning notebook.

When the door opened, he held his breath at the feminine laughter, and it only took a minute before he recognized three voices merrily discussing where an errant arrow had landed: Abigail, Lady Gwen, and Elizabeth.

If he was discovered like this, with so many witnesses . . .

But no, he was adept at talking his way around everyone from politicians to the Prince Consort. If necessary, he could make his behavior a joke, or a mistake. He was so busy planning various strategies that he barely noticed when the door shut again, and there was nothing but the swish of skirts as a woman walked about the room.

Was she alone?

He waited another minute, but no one spoke. Without breathing, he carefully peered out from behind the drapery and saw Abigail alone, not a step away, her back to him, reaching behind her neck as she undid the hooks of her gown. He followed her fingers as a line of smooth skin was revealed, then saw the pure white lace of her chemise.

He was instantly aroused, would have forgotten everything if he'd not been holding the incriminating notebook in his hand. When she groaned in frustration and took a step toward the bell-pull, he emerged from hiding and slid his hand over her mouth.

As she stiffened, he said into her ear, "Shall I help you unhook your gown?"

Though her shoulders sagged with obvious relief, she tried to yank at his hand with both of hers. He made her wait a moment, taking satisfaction in her frustration for all the trouble she'd caused him.

At last he let her whirl about and face him, those brown eyes alive with anger—and worry. She could no longer hide her emotions so easily from him.

He refused to believe she could read him as easily.

"What are you doing here?" she demanded in a furious undertone. "If you had been caught, all of your plans would have been ruined!"

He held up the notebook. "Perhaps you wouldn't have cared. Since you seem to have a fascination for me."

Her face paled, but all she did was roll her eyes. "I don't know how much you read, but of course I was interested in you! If you noticed the first page, it was the date I saw you in Hyde Park. I'd just been told by Gwen that I was to visit your home. I had never met anyone as . . ." Her voice faded away, and she looked him up and down. Her paleness was replaced by a splotchy blush.

"Handsome?" he supplied coolly. "Hardly original on your part."

Her stare cooled. "I was going to say someone as exalted, but I meant in consequence. Of course you wouldn't have taken it that way!"

She started to snatch the notebook, but he held it away from her.

"What else will I find in here?"

"You already know, I am sure, and simply want to torment me about it." And then she really looked at him. "But you don't know yet, do you. Did your silly pride and blue blood not permit you to read a woman's private thoughts?"

He arched a brow but did not answer. He would have read it had he not been interrupted, and he didn't feel one bit of guilt.

"I wanted you to teach me about men," she said very slowly, with exaggerated patience. "Is this not more proof that I am telling you the truth? I have chosen you, after much deliberation. What other man could I trust to end our relationship when I wish it?"

"Chosen me? How far do you intend to carry this little game between us?"

A knock sounded on the door, and although he saw her stiffen, she did not look afraid, only proud and firm in her convictions.

Could everything he found so suspicious about her really lead back to a virgin's deciding it was time to lose her innocence?

Did she really not understand the consequences? Or was she counting on the lust that had taken hold of his thoughts where she was concerned?

A woman's voice called, "Your bath has arrived, miss."

Here was the perfect opportunity to prove she was lying.

"Go ahead and bring in your bath," he whispered. "If you want me to teach you, then this is the perfect opportunity, for what man can resist a naked woman in her bathing tub? And a woman who means to learn carnal secrets can have no virginal misgivings."

Once again he stepped behind the draperies, knowing that his reputation was in her hands. If she revealed him to his servants, a new scandal would be created, and she would be ruined.

But he'd spent many years reading the faces of his opponents. No, she would not cause a scandal—because she wanted something from him, something that meant more to her than the seduction of a duke.

And she was willing to risk everything to achieve her goal.

When Christopher disappeared, Abigail stood frozen, knowing her careful plans were spiraling further out of control. How could she avoid offering herself to the duke after everything she'd implied?

And did she want to?

She called for the maid's entrance, then stood back and watched a parade of footmen bring in a bathing tub and buckets of steaming water. After the maid finished unhooking her gown, Abigail claimed she had a headache and wished to be alone. Certainly she was giving herself a headache in panic that Christopher might sneeze and reveal himself. He would despise her for trapping him, even though he was the one taking the risk by being there.

As the footmen gathered their buckets, and the maid left towels and soap, Abigail could barely keep herself from looking at the window where Christopher hid. She had the wicked thought that if she were no longer a virgin, her father couldn't force her into marriage, not without lying to the groom. And if she weren't married, she could prove to her parents that she could support herself, once her article about the scandalous duke went to press.

But no, she would not give herself to a man, then betray him for the world to see. Even she wasn't that desperate for a story. She would keep her wits about her.

When the servants were gone, she stood holding her gown up at her shoulders. Should she call for him?

But he stepped out from hiding and looked at her.

Shouldn't it be dark instead of broad daylight? How could the duke—Christopher—stare at her as if night had come, and his disguise of goodness had fallen away?

She lifted her chin. "Just because I want you to teach me about a man's kisses, and what a man expects, does not mean I intend to bathe in front of you, Your Grace."

"I told you my name." He walked slowly toward her, then around her. "What a shame. The maid already loosened your corset. And I was so looking forward to doing that."

She closed her eyes for a moment, trying not to shudder with the heat that swirled inside her with his wicked words. "Stop taunting me. It makes me think I have made a terrible mistake in trusting you."

"Trusting me?"

He laughed behind her, and she felt his warm breath on her neck.

"You do not trust me," he said. "And I don't trust you. But that doesn't mean we can't enjoy one another."

She had to remember her purpose here, even as she held up her clothing. "Do you do this often . . . Chris? Tease women of your class? Shouldn't this be reserved for your mistress?"

"I don't have a mistress."

She felt his fingers threading through her hair, removing pins, until curls began to fall around her shoulders.

No mistress? From everything she'd heard, was that not unusual?

"I don't trust you, so I certainly wouldn't trust other women like you." He slid her hair slowly to one side, then pressed his mouth to her shoulder.

She shivered and closed her eyes. Her determination was fast fading as her traitorous mind groped for reasons to let him finish what he was starting.

"Then do noblemen like you remain . . . celibate until your marriage?" she whispered, as he pulled her back against his body.

He chuckled in her ear, even as he licked along the edge of it. "Celibate? Sadly for women, they are held to a much stricter moral code than men."

"And you do not follow such a strict moral code? You, a duke? But you said you have no mistress. Then am I to assume you meant right at this moment?"

"No, I've never had a mistress," he murmured absently.

She felt his hands separating her bodice farther, the corset loosening. Both were slowly being tugged down her body, leaving only her chemise, not much protection against him. Thank goodness for the petticoats, which clustered at her waist. Then he was loosening those, as well, one at a time.

She gathered her thoughts and looked over her shoulder at him, asking with deliberate innocence, "Then you are a virgin, too?"

He laughed and turned her about so that he could look down her body. The chemise was some coverage, but not much, especially when with just his focused gaze, her breasts tingled and hardened against the thin material, betraying her desire for him.

His smile faded, and he looked like a man about to feast. "I have not been a virgin since I was sixteen."

She winced. "So young?"

His smile returned, and it was crooked. "Not so young. I was very eager to become a man. And it was not difficult to succeed with such a mission when one lives at school."

"And when one is a marquess."

He shrugged. "A woman such as that understands coins more than a title."

"You *paid* for the experience?"

She thought of the unfortunate women who made their living on the streets, the articles about them in her newspaper.

But those desperate women were not the same as the beautiful women who would earn their living from the nobility. Mistresses could make a fine living, with their own households and servants, and even be seen in public with their men—under certain circumstances.

But he said he'd never had a mistress.

"Many lads 'paid for the experience.'" He slid the sleeve of her chemise off her shoulder. "But after that, I never paid again. Many women outside of Society enjoy a night of passion that will have no lasting commitment." He met her eyes again. "Just like you and me."

She grasped hold of her convenient lie. "But I *am* of Society." And what would happen if he found out she was not? Would his rules no longer matter?

He was looking down her body again. He sat down on her bed, leaning back on his hands. "Perhaps I should make an exception. It's time to remove your chemise and enjoy your bath."

"No." She crossed her arms over her chest. It took everything in her to refuse, but she had reached her limit on what she'd do for a story—

on what she would allow herself to experience with him while she was being dishonest. There seemed to be nothing scandalous in his past that concerned a woman—or at least nothing that bothered him. That was enough investigating for now.

He looked up at her, smiling with such promise. "No? I thought I was to teach you."

With all sincerity, she whispered, "I can't trust myself to resist you."

His smile faded, the playfulness went out of him. "Do you think I won't be able to stop when you ask me to? I always stop."

"But would you be angry? Do you have a temper I don't know anything about?"

She saw the hesitation in his eyes before he masked it. He had a temper. It no longer controlled him, but it must have once. What had he done when he was angry? And to whom?

He rose to his feet, and she did not allow herself to back away.

"My compliments," he said. "You have already learned the art of resistance. Many women would use that to lure a man even further." He cupped her cheek, raised her face to look at him. "But with you I don't sense that."

They looked into each other's eyes for that moment, and it would have been so easy to be lost there in the mystery of him, in the very maleness of him.

"A kiss to remember me by," he murmured, and lowered his mouth to hers.

No gentle kiss was this, but hot and full of frustration—and his obvious need to show her what she was missing. She gladly melted into his embrace, let his arms hold her tight to him. Somehow, she trusted him to respect her wishes.

Wearing only a thin garment, she could feel the heat of his muscles, the arousal as he pressed his hips into hers. And then her will began to fade as need surged to take its place.

He backed away, wiping his mouth, not even looking at her as he strode to the door. He listened intently, opened it a crack to peer out, then left, silently closing it behind him.

With a groan, she sank back on the bed and covered her trembling lips with her hands. How much more would she have to do to discover his secrets?

Or would she betray all of hers if she weren't careful?

Chapter 16

At luncheon, Abigail had to listen to Elizabeth praise her archery skills to everyone in attendance, and before she knew it, the men had decided to plan a tournament for the following morning. They were deep into their discussion of the rules when Elizabeth suggested to the ladies an outing to visit the village shops. Abigail would have rather avoided the afternoon—she really did have an aching head after the stress of dealing with Christopher—but Gwen squeezed her arm with such excitement.

"Perhaps I can see Mr. Wesley!" Gwen whispered into her ear. "He mentioned he was visiting an ill parishioner today. I would so love to see him minister."

Abigail hid a smile.

She felt Christopher's gaze briefly linger on her, but she did not meet it. She was certain a riotous blush would betray her thoughts of him and what had just—almost—happened between them.

And how close she'd come to being discovered. The fact that he hadn't insisted on reading her notebook was a true miracle. How much longer could she hold his suspicions at bay?

In Comberton, Abigail and Gwen strolled arm in arm past the little shops until the Cabot guests had dispersed.

At last, Gwen craned her neck. "I don't think anyone is watching. Are you certain you don't mind if I leave you? Mr. Wesley told me he would be at Rose Cottage with an elderly couple today, and he thought they would enjoy my company. I am so looking forward to helping him!"

"Go," Abigail said, shaking her head. "I'll come to find you before we leave."

Gwen kissed her cheek. "You are a dear!"

After spending an hour browsing in the bookshop—and looking for anything on Madingley Court—Abigail was startled when she heard her name.

Elizabeth was coming in the open door. "Miss Shaw—Abigail," she amended quickly, smiling. "You will never believe what just happened! Our little ghost party is garnering notice."

"Notice? I'm certain the villagers think we're amusing, but—"

"No, no, not the villagers, a journalist. And from London, at that!"

The stuffy little shop took on a sudden chill, and

Abigail had to force away a concerned frown. "A journalist?"

"Yes, and from the *Times,* no less! His editor heard about our local ghost and our effort to find it. He sent his writer to interview us, so that he can write an 'amusing article for the womenfolk,' or so he said."

Though Abigail wanted to believe that, the fact that she was investigating the duke led her to believe that she was no longer alone in her pursuit. What had happened?

"Elizabeth, are you certain he is not simply intending to amuse his readers at our expense?"

"I cannot believe that—and if so, we will simply look like we are having a silly, amusing time. I invited him to join us at the house tomorrow morning!"

Abigail wanted to ask if she'd thought of her brother's reaction, then decided against it. It was already too late, and she didn't want to upset Elizabeth needlessly. Abigail had a feeling that Christopher's reaction would do that.

"Do you know where Lady Gwen is?" Elizabeth continued, looking past Abigail as if they might be together. "The carriages have returned for us."

"I'll find her. She is visiting parishioners with Mr. Wesley."

Elizabeth grinned. "Who would have thought an earl's daughter and a vicar would make a match?

And to think I invited her because I thought she was interested in being a duchess!"

Abigail put a finger to her lips. "They are not a match yet, so please do not speak to others of it. I promise I will let you know what happens!"

At Rose Cottage, Abigail found beautiful Gwen, an earl's daughter, sitting at the bedside of a sick, elderly woman. Instead of reading from a book at a distance, she was bathing the woman's brow from a basin of water. Abigail remained silent for a moment, looking at the sweet tableau—from Mr. Wesley's wondrous and dazed smile, to the old man's gratitude, to the sick woman's look of peace. Perhaps Gwen really did understand—and appreciate—the lot of a vicar's wife. Now if only Mr. Wesley appreciated Gwen enough to do something about it!

As they walked back to join the others at the carriage, Gwen chattered on about how good it felt to be helpful. And then she proceeded right from that into analyzing the vicar's response and if they could have a future together. Abigail's head was spinning from all the speculation.

"Oh, that reminds me!" Gwen suddenly interrupted herself. "Mr. Wesley and I were speaking about the ghost stories, and putting together the exact number of times the ghost was seen in each place, and do you know what we discovered?"

Abigail shook her head.

"He was seen the most in the duke's dressing room! Perhaps he was a servant to a duke—or a duke himself. Fascinating, isn't it?"

"You're bound to win the prize, Gwen," Abigail said, but found it difficult to concentrate on the game when her mind wouldn't stay off the other journalist. She could not let someone else steal her article idea—and treat the family far worse than she would.

After dinner that evening, instead of Christopher's stealing Abigail away to the terrace, his sister had the honor. Although Christopher was being polite, Abigail thought he was not as solicitous toward her as usual, which was encouraging the Ladies May and Theodosia. And the duchess was looking between Abigail and her son in confusion. Abigail was glad to escape.

Clouds covered the moon, and if not for the lit torches, they would have had a difficult time seeing.

"The sky threatens rain," Elizabeth mused, as they walked arm in arm.

Abigail nodded, saying nothing, hoping to encourage the girl to reveal her thoughts. When Elizabeth didn't speak, Abigail eventually asked, "What did the duke think about the journalist's arriving tomorrow?"

"I did not tell him."

Abigail gave her a skeptical look.

"He will not be here," Elizabeth insisted. "Of course he doesn't care for publicity of any kind, but it's just an amusing story about the ghost."

"Perhaps he does not want to turn Madingley Court into a destination for ghost hunters."

"I had not thought of that. I will make very sure that Mr. Walton understands that we are just having fun. There's certainly no real proof of a ghost."

Abigail was doubtful, and she knew that if Elizabeth wasn't going to say anything to Christopher, she would have to. Besides his need for privacy, she had her own need to see that *she* was the only one writing a story on the duke.

"Oh, you will think me silly," Elizabeth said, after they'd walked a few more minutes, "but I could not help seeing how . . . close you and my brother have become."

Abigail reminded herself that Christopher's sister was innocent—more innocent than Abigail felt lately. "We are friends," she said with caution.

Elizabeth chuckled. "That is quite an accomplishment where my brother is concerned. He is a very private man."

"And yet you and your mother are so very open," Abigail said. "Why is your brother different?"

"Well, he is the duke, of course, and he has always taken that responsibility seriously."

"As I've been able to tell, from what he's told me about his search for a duchess."

Elizabeth gaped at her. "He talked to you about that?"

"Well . . . yes. I think he felt comfortable doing so, because we both know I am not someone he will be considering."

"But . . . he has made it seem as if . . . why—" Elizabeth threw up her hands. "Oh, I do not want to hurt your feelings!"

"You are not." Abigail hesitated, but if she wanted Elizabeth to trust her, she needed to know some of the truth. And she liked Elizabeth, and wanted to lie as little as possible to her. "The duke and I have come to an understanding that has made us friends. Perhaps it . . . helped keep him free of several of your other . . . female guests."

Elizabeth covered her mouth. "Oh, I feel so foolish. I was positive that you . . . that he . . . that you both might have had feelings for each other."

Abigail was surprised to feel a tension that was almost pain at the thought of a future that could never be. "Friendship only, and I already treasure that. But I do not understand why he finds it so difficult to relax around others."

"You really do not know, do you?" Elizabeth said hesitantly. "But then you and I were far too young to remember."

Abigail felt as if the world suddenly grew very

still, and even her breathing would disturb too much. "Remember what?" she asked carefully.

"The terrible tragedy that Chris was a part of when he was a young man." Elizabeth's voice was soft and sad. "It is in the past, of course, and the two men are now friends."

"When you first said 'tragedy,' I thought someone must have died." Abigail put a hand to her throat as if relieved.

"Oh, no, thankfully not. But it changed Chris forever."

"Elizabeth?" called a man's voice.

The girl gasped. "Oh, it is my brother. Please do not tell him I was speaking of him!"

Abigail could only nod, even as her frustration mounted. She'd been so close. It sounded as if he'd been involved in an illegal duel!

"Miss Shaw," Christopher said, nodding to her. "Elizabeth, you look to be stealing her away from the other guests with a secret purpose."

"Perhaps ghost hunting?" Elizabeth said, then laughed at his skeptical expression. "Excuse me, I will leave you to the stealing away of our female guests."

She walked away, a spring of purpose in her step.

Abigail stopped at the edge of the balustrade and leaned against it, looking out into the cool darkness. "It feels like rain."

"Do not start with a discussion on the weather," he said impassively. "It is beneath you."

"What else do you want me to discuss? How even though we are at odds with one another, I find you still using me to keep the other women at bay?"

His smile was grim. "You are useful that way."

She gave a heavy sigh.

"And useful in other ways that I keep trying to forget," he said in a lower voice.

His sleeve brushed hers. He stood too close, but she didn't stop him.

"Useful," she murmured. "How romantic a notion."

"Surely I am useful to you," he said. "At least that's what you've told me."

"So we are using each other."

"Then again I must ask you to please not include my sister in this . . . relationship between us. She will only be hurt when I do not pursue you in marriage."

Abigail felt a pang of sorrow and worried that Elizabeth would not be the only one to be hurt. "As I've already told you, your sister is my hostess. I am doing my best to keep her at a distance, but she is so friendly."

"I have said my piece."

He linked his hands behind his back as he looked out on the land that was his.

She finally said, "You might want to be here in the morning to see me defeat all your guests in archery."

"And why would I wish to do that when I have business in Cambridge?" He bent his head. "Of course I imagine your form is rather fine as you compete."

But his teasing almost seemed by rote, as if he sensed more to her words. Did they understand each other so well?

"Because not only will you see a fine competition, you'll see the journalist who has come from London because he heard of the ghost hunt. He asked for Elizabeth's permission."

He put his hands very carefully on the balustrade. "A journalist."

"I thought it curious myself. Why would the *Times* care about ghost rumors? But of course, you are a duke. Is there another reason he would come?"

He glanced at her, and his faint smile was reluctantly approving. "You are too clever, Abigail. You know there is always something a duke doesn't want publicized. Thank you for the warning. Shall we return to the other guests? I hear a fascinating game of charades is about to start."

"Your favorite."

"What a shame I have to retire for the evening."

She did not know if he meant to plant the thought of his early bedtime in her mind, but it was there now, and she despaired of her weakness for him. Would he come to her again, continue her lessons?

But he did not, and she was left awake long into the night, considering her own plan for the journalist.

The writer from the *Times* arrived promptly after breakfast, and although Christopher was tempted to throw him bodily out the gates, he knew better than to create even more of a scene for the man to write about. Mr. Walton was nearing middle age, yet still trim and fit, and filled with a restless energy that made him seem as if he were always looking for something.

And of course, he must be, but Christopher had no way to discover what it was. He certainly wasn't going to talk to the man, and although he was polite, he rebuffed every attempt, claiming he was not involved in the ghost hunt.

"But it's your family, Your Grace," said Walton, as they stood outside and watched the guests examine the archery tournament schedule. The man had made it a point to remain near Christopher since he'd arrived just a half hour before, and he couldn't seem to refrain from making pointed little comments, as if he were deliberately trying to arouse a response.

How soon could Christopher politely ask him to leave?

"My sister is a fanciful young woman who came up with an amusing theme for a house party," Christopher said placidly. "I am not sure why this is news."

Walton glanced at him briefly, with a touch of skepticism that made Christopher know at once that the ghost hunt was only an excuse. There could be any number of reasons Walton was here, for Christopher was involved in many projects in London. But when the *Times* wanted information on any of those, they knew to see his secretary first. Walton had to be looking for something else.

Christopher left him, deciding to read the competition schedule himself. To his relief, he did not find his own name.

"Are you wishing you had agreed to participate?" Abigail said softly at his side.

He looked down at her. "Competitive, Miss Shaw? Is it so important that you defeat me?"

"I would like to defeat you at something, Your Grace," she said through sweetly smiling lips.

He studied her. "I think you did that yesterday."

She arched an eyebrow and waited with patience he couldn't help but admire. His own patience had taken so long to cultivate, but it was threatening to rip apart at the seams.

"You successfully distracted me from reading your notebook, did you not?" he said, then lowered his voice even more. "And still, you managed to make sure I did not see you in your bath. You've kept me off-balance, made me desire you rather than pursuing my suspicions."

"I've *made* you desire me?" she shot back, then looked about her furtively. "I did nothing of the sort."

"So you are claiming innocence, then?"

"And who are you to talk about innocence, Your Grace?"

She spoke his title with faint sarcasm—and even that aroused him. But he saw the journalist watching them.

Abigail followed the direction of his gaze. "You let him stay?"

"Elizabeth invited him. But he will be leaving soon."

"I do not hear him discussing the ghost much."

Christopher frowned. "No, I noticed that."

Elizabeth called for everyone's attention, and the tournament began. As the warm summer sun beat down through the morning, Christopher noticed that most of the women retreated to a parasol's shade—but not Abigail. She was focused on the competition, and to his surprise, he thought she was making private evaluations of each man in case she competed against him. When it was her turn to shoot, he saw why.

She was very good, and she easily defeated her opponent, Mr. Tilden.

And when she wasn't setting arrow to string, she was talking with the journalist. Christopher let her have her head, but when he overheard snatches of their conversation, he realized it was mostly about

Elizabeth, and that annoyed him. Did she want to bring his sister to the attention of the world? Why would she be doing so?

When they paused for lemonade, he cornered Abigail to discover her purpose.

She gave him a faint smile. "Did you not notice how focused he is on you? He is discussing *you* rather than the ghost with everyone he can. I decided to distract him."

"My knight in shining armor."

She grinned.

"Feeling guilty?"

Her grin faded just a bit. "Aren't *you?*"

They looked into each other's eyes. Damn, but if she wasn't making him feel guilty. *She* was the one who was lying.

She was the first to look away, taking a sip of her lemonade, then speaking quietly. "Did you notice that Mr. Walton almost seems to be . . . antagonizing you?"

He shot a glance at the journalist, who was trying to speak to his mother. The duchess's look was polite, but cool, and Christopher found his buried temper beginning to simmer.

"And I think it's working," Abigail added.

How could she think she knew him so well? "Your next opponent is waiting, Miss Shaw. Shall I give you some pointers, show you just how to stand? I could demonstrate from behind you, my hands on your hands as you held the bow."

Her eyes widened, her lips parted, and for a moment, they were thinking about other things. The color rose in her face, and he thought about standing so close behind her that his chest touched her back, that his hips nestled against her backside.

"Ooh, that is unfair," she said. "Are you trying to make me lose?"

She handed him her lemonade so quickly that some spilled onto his hand. He barely withheld a chuckle. Why was it so easy for her to make him laugh, even when he could not afford to lose his concentration?

Then she had the audacity to look so cool and composed under broad daylight, as she next defeated the earl of Greenwich, who did not take his loss to a young lady well. He stomped back to his wife, muttering.

The other women of the party applauded enthusiastically, and Christopher realized that Abigail was the last woman still in the competition. Only when she faced Keane in the final match did she lose, and not by much. Keane held her by the hand, displaying her to everyone while they applauded, and Christopher felt the stirrings of jealousy.

A picnic luncheon was set up in the park, and Christopher calmly approached the journalist, and said, "Walton, you may enjoy the meal, but afterward, you will make your excuses to my sister and leave. I am certain you have enough for your little ghost story."

"One can never have enough research, Your Grace. Perhaps I don't wish to leave."

Christopher studied him with interest. Why was the man deliberately trying to provoke him? "That is what a duke has footmen for. I will be happy to have you escorted from the property. Now do enjoy your luncheon."

He walked away. He kept his mother company and amused the older guests. Only sometime later, when he glanced around to see what Walton was up to, did he realize that the man was missing.

He could not believe that he would leave so easily—and early, at that. Christopher excused himself and wandered through the crowd, but could not find him.

And Abigail was missing, too.

Damn her, he thought, trying not to pick up his pace too obviously. Was she again attempting to protect him? Or was she taking it upon herself to discover the man's true purpose?

He thought of where Abigail might take him and remembered her fascination with the castle ruins. He casually headed that way, even hid on the path to make sure no one was following him. If he had to escort Walton out, he didn't need an audience.

He expected to find them speaking calmly, for Abigail was not one to lose her composure. Instead, he heard them before he saw them, and the angry tone of their voices made him instinctively remain hidden behind a curve of the path.

"Don't bother lying," Walton was saying. "I thought I recognized you the moment I arrived, but I assumed it was only because you were of Society. I finally realized that you're as much of Society as I am."

"I do not know what you're talking about," Abigail said coldly.

But Christopher recognized a faint thread of fear in her voice. And his instinct was to go to her, to protect her.

But he'd suspected her for several days now. Could Walton know more than he did?

"You're Lawrence Shaw's daughter. What did your father do, send you to work on a story that only a woman might be able to get from a duke?"

Work on a story? Christopher thought to himself in disbelief. Lawrence Shaw? And his brain, usually so analytical, suddenly put the clues together: Lawrence Shaw was the owner and publisher of the *Morning Journal*.

"I am not—" Abigail began.

"Do not deny it," Walton interrupted. "Are you here investigating the same story I am?"

"What story?" she demanded.

But Christopher heard the urgency in her voice, and at last, he could no longer deny the truth. Abigail was here under false pretenses, intending to write a story, the same as Walton was.

And since she'd come up with every way possible—including temptation—to stay close to

Christopher, he knew *he* had to be the focus of her interest. And to think, only a moment ago, he had thought she was trying to protect him. No, she'd been protecting her story all along.

"I am not confiding anything in *you*," Walton said coolly. "We'll see who comes out the winner in this contest."

Christopher barely got off the path in time, sliding between tall shrubberies as Walton hurried back toward the house.

For a moment, Christopher felt overcome by the sickening blow of her betrayal. It had taken him his entire life to win respectability, to know people were looking at him as a force in business and politics, rather than the cause of the next foolish scandal in his family's long line of them.

And Abigail wanted to expose everything. From the beginning, she hadn't fitted in, with her self-confidence, her certainty and intelligence. She was a woman who knew what she was, and what she wanted.

What had she discovered already?

He heard her walking past him at a brisk pace, and he emerged only to grab her arm and drag her back into the cool darkness of the overgrown plants.

Chapter 17

A bigail almost screamed as a hand gripped her hard. But as she was drawn through the shrubbery, feeling a long scratch across her arm and leaves brushing her cheeks, she saw the dark, angry face of the duke.

And she knew that he'd heard everything.

She hadn't imagined the pain would hurt so, but she found her eyes stinging as she looked up at him. He grabbed her hard by both arms now, staring down so contemptuously at her. She couldn't allow herself to fall apart, to regret what she'd done. Even knowing her lies would someday be revealed, she'd made her choice to investigate him.

She'd just foolishly assumed she wouldn't see his face when he found out. She'd been wrong about everything.

"You're a journalist," he said coldly, leaning down into her face.

She didn't cringe although she wanted to.

"Do not bother to deny it," he commanded before she could answer. "I heard everything. Lawrence Shaw's daughter, are you?"

Her mouth was so dry with fear that she had to lick her lips even to speak. And that seemed to incite him, for he gave her a little shake.

"Do not try your seduction on me! It will not work anymore."

Baffled, she said, "I am not trying to seduce you! That has never been my intent. And you can attest to how many times I have stopped our—our private moments from going too far."

"You're only proving yourself a flirt and a tease. Now tell me the truth! Try to explain how you've used me for your own selfish gain."

"Not for my own gain!" she shot back, indignation fighting her feelings of humiliation and despair.

"Then you admit you're using me."

"I—" How could she lie to him anymore when he'd discovered the truth? It was too late—and she owed him that much. "Yes," she finally breathed, feeling as if she wilted in his grip.

If he released her, she might fall in sudden exhaustion. How long had the secret been eating her up inside? From the beginning?

"You flirted with me to get what you wanted, invented a story to stay near me. And I'm sure when I acted the besotted fool you counted yourself lucky."

"No, no I didn't mean it to be that way," she protested. "I didn't expect—I didn't think we'd—"

"What?"

Now he drew her up hard against him, and she knew she was supposed to feel intimidated by his height and muscle—and she was. And she felt so dreadfully sad. She had not realized how much she'd enjoyed his friendship—but it had never been a real friendship, not with her lies. And how could she admit she had any tender feelings for him? He would despise her even more.

Her voice quavering, she said, "I had thought that you were used to articles about you and your family. I didn't think I could hurt you. And I'm sorry that—"

He let her go so suddenly she almost fell.

"Don't you dare apologize now! That means nothing to me. Only the truth matters. What have you been investigating me for? Why is Walton here?"

"If you heard us talk, then you know I know nothing of his purposes. He wouldn't tell me."

"Then tell me about you, *Miss Shaw*."

His tone oozed ugly sarcasm, and she flinched.

"I am not a journalist for my father's newspaper—not yet. I have been the literary and drama critic, anonymously, but this was my chance to prove that I could investigate a news story and write as well as any man."

He was staring at her so hard, she knew he was trying to read the truth in her eyes.

"Then why the hell did you choose me?" he demanded.

She wouldn't tell him about the rumors of illegality; she didn't even know if she could believe such a thing about this man. Though he was a duke, she knew that he would never consider himself above the law. But had his family done something on his behalf?

"The public seemed to relish any story of the Cabots," she said. "And because out of all of your family, you are the only one who seemed without scandal."

For just a moment, she thought he was the one who flinched, but she couldn't believe he would lose such control.

She continued, "I thought finding a scandal about you would be so sensational that my father would be forced to publish it." She was too embarrassed to reveal the state of the newspaper and her parents' finances. It didn't matter after all, and it was her own private humiliation. "But as you can see, I'm still here. I didn't find out your secrets."

"Not for lack of trying," he said hoarsely. "And as if I could believe anything you say! You worked your wiles on everyone, from my mother to my sister—hell, to my tutor."

Her mouth dropped open. "You really did follow me that day."

"I knew you'd lied about touring the church, knew you'd somehow coerced Lady Gwen into lying for you."

Abigail briefly closed her eyes and shuddered. "And that was one of the worst things I had to do. It was not fair to use her, and she so innocent." She prayed he wouldn't ask more about Gwen; she didn't want to keep lying to him, but she didn't want her actions to affect her dearest friend.

"*That* was the worst thing you had to do?" he demanded. "What about deceiving my family about your motives here?"

She nodded tightly.

"What about searching my room, pretending you wanted to learn how to behave with a man?"

He grabbed her again, hauling her up against him, and she gasped out her response. "You'd startled me! I was desperate for some sort of story you might believe, and since women throw themselves at you—"

"You thought you'd do the same. I could have bedded you right there."

His breath was hot on her face, and to her mortification, even though she was frightened, she felt something for him; her body still came to life at the touch of his.

"Would you have given your virginity for a story, Abigail?" he said harshly.

She blanched and shook her head.

"No? Maybe you're so used to lying that you're even lying to yourself now."

"No, I—" She shut her mouth. How could she say that she was drawn to him, that she couldn't help what she felt for him? He'd laugh in her face.

"Are you even innocent?"

She bit her lip, trying not to cry, trying to remember that she wanted to compete in a man's world, and she had to accept the consequences of her actions. Christopher would have thrown Walton out but was treating her differently. Not just because she was a woman, but because she'd hurt him, betrayed him.

Whispering, blushing, she said, "I've never . . . been with a man."

For a moment, he said nothing. He held her so hard against him that she could not miss the hardness of his arousal. Her wide eyes met his, and he pushed her away again.

"You're leaving, right now," he ground out, his look full of disdain.

Christopher was losing control of himself, of this argument—and he knew that Abigail recognized it. And now she knew how little he could control his own body where she was concerned.

He waited for her response. Surely she'd try to blackmail him by claiming she'd write lies about him; or she'd threaten to expose herself and whatever she'd already learned about him.

But she said nothing, only hugged herself with such a look of sad despair that he was taken aback. She didn't cry, she didn't beg. She waited for his sentence.

And then he realized that if he forced her to leave, he couldn't control what she did—whom she saw. She could join forces with Walton against him; although even as he thought it, he knew she wouldn't do that. She had wanted to accomplish this alone, to prove something to her father, and perhaps to herself.

He knew nothing about her except that he desired her, had thought her amusing and intelligent, and that she'd somehow given him back a feeling of being alive, even when he suspected her.

He couldn't let her write her article and publish it. He had to know the truth about her, to find out what she really knew about him. He had to control her—and this terrible attraction to her that overcame all his good sense.

"No, you're not leaving," he finally told her.

Her eyes widened in shock, but she said nothing.

"You owe me. I want to know what you know. I could damn well hide you away where no one could find you, force you to write nothing about me, but that won't help me stop Walton, and whatever he's uncovering. No, *you're* going to help me stop him. And in exchange I won't tell Lady Gwen—and everyone else—what you've been up to. For now. You do know that if I reveal you, everyone will assume your dearest friend was also involved."

She inhaled sharply, and now he could see the fear in her eyes.

"No, please, she's innocent. I used her, just as I used you. She thinks this is simply a lark, having me here. You know her and her family—she thinks she's only proving that the social classes are equal."

"I'll try to remember that, whenever I feel like despising her for bringing you here."

She hurried to say, "As for Mr. Walton . . . what can I possibly do? You heard him refuse to tell me what story he is working on. Why would he change his mind?"

"I don't know, and I don't care. It is your task to discover a way. When you're ready to confront him, I'll remain nearby, listening. You're a woman wise in the ways of the world; figure out a way to accomplish this new assignment."

He started to leave the little clearing, and she grabbed his coat sleeve.

"And if I can't?" she cried.

With his eyes, he gave her the cold look he reserved for enemies. "You'll wish you'd never come here."

Somehow, Abigail managed to return to the picnic. For a moment, she met Mr. Walton's cool gaze, but he only shrugged and turned his back to continue talking to Mr. Tilden. His look said that he considered this a contest between them, and he fully believed in his own ability to triumph. Well, at least he wasn't going to reveal her deception, not right now. She would have to be very careful as she decided how to handle him.

It took everything in her to smile at Gwen, to speak with Elizabeth about her success at archery, to avoid even looking at the duke. Abigail pretended she was a normal woman enjoying a lovely day.

But she saw Christopher staring at her, and knew that he despised her even more for her ability to pretend that everything was all right.

How good a liar she was, he must be thinking. And how much he must want to keep her away from his family.

But he was the one using his threats to ensure that she remained here. And it was going to work; she couldn't leave—wouldn't. Regardless of how much she'd grown to hate what she was doing to him, she was trapped not only by his threats, but also by her need to help her father's newspaper. How could she give up?

How she would accomplish these contradictory tasks, she didn't know, but for the moment, she concentrated on getting through luncheon—and trying not to think how much Christopher despised her. He had no qualms with controlling her through fear, and though she deserved it, she could not help noticing how he always made sure he got what he wanted.

Yet inside her an ache burned. She didn't want him to hate her. But how else had she expected their relationship to end?

Her first concern had to be protecting Gwen, who would never recover her standing in Society if she were linked to Abigail's schemes. Much as Gwen thought there should be no divisions between classes, she would be terribly hurt to be on the outside, shunned by her family and friends.

And Abigail could not live with herself.

She watched the picnic as if from a distance, saw Elizabeth and her mother giving Christopher strange looks as he flirted with the Ladies May and Theodosia. Abigail had always known that some-day he would have to return to the women of his world, as if he'd decided against courting her. She had understood that she might be humiliated—hadn't really even cared, so focused had she been on her story.

But it hurt, like a burning knife in a deep wound. He would never again look at her with amusement and interest in his dark eyes. She hadn't thought she'd become used to his presence, to his deep voice.

And now it was all gone, and all she had left was his contempt.

And his threats. She had no choice but to do

what he had commanded of her, and she might as well begin immediately.

She placed a small selection of cheesecakes on a plate and took it to Mr. Walton, who for the moment was standing alone.

He looked down at the plate, his thin lips quirked up on one side in amusement. "What is this?"

"A peace offering," she said softly. "I don't see why we both can't have what we want."

"Do not even try to suggest we work together on this."

She shot him an amused glance. "Believe me, I can be just as competitive as any man. But I certainly wouldn't want to share this with you, even the story of the decade. After all, I've been here for days; I'm already close to his family—to him. Just remember that."

She left him curious, and would return to him that afternoon in hopes that he'd thought through his options.

But for a while, she needed to retire to her room and be alone. But when at last she closed her door, Christopher pushed it open, then closed it by leaning back.

And for the first time, Abigail felt almost frightened of him because his face was so expressionless.

"You were supposed to wait to approach Walton until I could overhear," Christopher said coldly. "I am hardly going to trust what you tell me."

She sighed and sat down heavily in a chair near the bare hearth. "We discussed nothing new about you. But I had to begin to ease my way into his confidence. I think he's curious now about what I know."

"You cannot delay this. I won't have him in my house beyond today."

She nodded, feeling so weary and alone. "I understand. I will try this afternoon. Is there someplace you can hide if I bring him to your study? It seems to be the only place I can guarantee others will not be."

He watched her with narrowed eyes, then finally nodded. "There is a bathroom off the study. I will wait in there. What time?"

"I am letting him debate joining forces with me. Let us give him an hour, then I'll go find him while the ladies are resting and the gentlemen are playing billiards."

"I'll be there." After listening at the door, he left without another word.

And she wanted to cry. Her throat was so tight she felt she couldn't swallow. But she held it all in, knowing that if she appeared before Mr. Walton with a red, splotchy face, he would suspect something.

Just then Gwen came in, her expression full of confusion. "Did I just see the duke in our corridor?"

Abigail's tears let loose, and she quickly used a handkerchief to staunch them.

Gwen rushed forward, putting her arm around Abigail. "My dear, what happened? Goodness, you even have a scratch on your arm!"

Abigail stared at the faint line of blood that had already dried. "I'm not crying about that. Oh, I am such a fool!" Trying to keep herself under control, Abigail told Gwen about the duke's discovery of her true identity. "I truly never imagined what it would feel like to be so revealed to him. I knew I was betraying him, had justified it in my mind, but the look on his face . . . his fury . . ."

They were sitting side by side on Abigail's bed, with Gwen's arm giving her support.

"Abby, perhaps he was furious because he cares for you."

Abigail rolled her eyes. "He *liked* me." *He desired me, and that was worse for him.* "And now he despises me."

Gwen took a fortifying breath. "Then we are leaving? I can pack quickly."

"We are not leaving," Abigail said grimly. "And he thinks that I misled you, and we will keep it that way."

"But, Abby—"

"No! I insist. I could not live with myself if you suffered for what I've done."

"I won't suffer." Gwen's voice softened, and she leaned her head against Abigail's. "But he is not making you leave?"

"No." Abigail winced at how weak and unsteady

she sounded. "He insists that I must help him discover the story that Mr. Walton is investigating.
And he's right; I do owe him that much. Then . . . I
don't know. But I don't want to leave. I'm so close
to finding out the old scandal!"

"With his open knowledge of your intentions?"
Gwen said doubtfully.

"I know, I know. But I have to do something,
Gwen! My father will lose everything, after all he's
done to help people. If I fail, there won't be a newspaper for me to inherit. Oh, I know, it's foolish of
me secretly to wish that I could be the one in my
father's place someday."

"No, Abby, it's not!"

Abigail whispered, "And the worst thing is, now
that I've . . . kissed Chris, I am so afraid that in my
father's haste to secure my future, he'll try to make
me marry someone I don't love." Now that she
knew something of passion, she could not imagine
being so intimate with someone she didn't care for.
For the rest of her life. It made her shudder with
despair. At last, she stood up, and Gwen's arm
fell away. "I have to go. Chris—the duke—will be
waiting for Mr. Walton and me."

She barely heard Gwen's whisper of "good
luck." It was time to fulfill her end of this dreadful
bargain—and hope that she could use it to sway
the duke.

Chapter 18

⌒⌒

For Christopher, the hour seemed to pass with excruciating slowness. He remained with the men in the billiards room, not concentrating when he played, losing badly. Walton was not here, and he imagined the man watching Abigail, wondering what she was up to.

Just as Christopher was.

At last, the wondering got to be too much for him, and he excused himself and went to hide in his study. Would she be able to succeed in bringing the suspicious journalist there?

Of course she would—it was the duke's study, after all. Christopher made certain that his desk contained only minor papers pertaining to the estate. He didn't want to look like it had been cleared deliberately. And then he closeted himself within the bathroom, steadying the washstand as he bumped it. There was no window, and he could not risk lighting a candle.

He left the door very slightly ajar and tried to

ease the tension within him. This was almost over. He would survive this close call and be more cautious with strangers in the future.

How much more cautious could he be, he thought wryly, without barricading himself inside a house and never leaving?

When he heard a distant knock on the study door, he stiffened.

After a moment, Abigail said, "Your Grace? Is anyone here?"

There was movement, then a door closing.

"Impressive," said Walton. "I did not think it would be so easy to breach the duke's private study."

"It is not easy," she said, "but the staff knows me after almost a week here."

Christopher winced at how light and playful Abigail sounded, as if it were all a game to her. He could not forget the sadness and defeat in her eyes when he'd last seen her. Which was the real Abigail?

"Why bring me here?" Walton continued. "Surely you are not planning to allow me to investigate the duke's papers."

"Of course not. I just wanted a place where we wouldn't be disturbed. Would you like a glass of brandy? Only the finest in the Cabot household."

Christopher thought he heard the faintest hint of tension in her voice, and he gritted his teeth. She had to make this work.

He heard nothing for several minutes except the clink of glass.

Walton said, "Ah, that is good. Join me?"

That wouldn't be a smart idea.

"It *is* good," Abigail soon breathed.

They said nothing, and Christopher imagined them drinking together, looking at each other, conspirators alone in a forbidden house. When he realized his fists were clenched, he forced himself to relax. It was no longer his concern who looked at Abigail—it had *never* been his concern, only he'd been too blinded by lust to see that.

"So have *you* explored this study?" Walton asked Abigail.

"No. I am at Madingley Court to talk, and to listen, and that's what I've been doing."

There was another long silence, and Christopher imagined them sipping his brandy, loosening their tongues.

"And what have you heard?" Walton continued—without subtlety.

Abigail gave a low laugh. "What have *you* heard?"

"So that is how it is to be? We play this game with each other?"

She giggled. "I am not playing a game, believe me. How I handle this chance to prove my worth to my father will chart the course for the rest of my life."

"It is unusual for a woman to want to be a journalist."

She made a little "hmm" sound, and Christopher could imagine just how she'd shrug her shoulders, her head tilted to one side. She should keep up the delaying tactic, give the brandy a chance to loosen Walton's tongue.

"I loved that what my father wrote affected people, changing the course of their lives. Stories in the *Morning Journal* were debated in Parliament, made factory owners change their working conditions out of shame, made women sigh with amusement at the end of a long day. A newspaper matters."

Though Christopher told himself he could not believe anything she said, part of him felt that he was seeing into her soul, seeing why writing was so important to her. Her love of the craft called to him on some level, even as he regretted it.

Dryly, Walton said, "You have a foolish view of a simple means of employment. I am good at writing, and I am good at getting people to talk about what they don't wish to."

"And you came here, thinking you could coerce the *duke* into speaking?" she asked, incredulity in her voice.

Walton chuckled. "More to see what he'd do with my presence. I already have people willing to talk."

Christopher's tension increased, even as he held his breath so that he'd miss nothing.

"Who has something bad to say about Madingley?" she said, with an air of bitterness. "You'd think he was a saint, the way his family and friends praise him."

"You're talking to the wrong people. More brandy?"

"Please."

They did not speak although Christopher thought he heard another giggle from Abigail. She could hardly have much experience with brandy—could she?

"I've spoken to other people," Abigail continued. "I am very careful with my research. But even my sources in Parliament have nothing but praise for him."

"Yet we're both searching for a story," Walton mused.

And Walton was trying to get it from Abigail. Didn't she see that?

"*I* am searching," Abigail said thoughtfully. "But you already know something. Why else would you be provoking the duke?"

"He has a temper. Don't you know that?"

Walton's voice had gone soft. Christopher's fists were clenched again, head bent as if he could will his hearing to sharpen. What was Abigail doing?

"A temper?"

She sounded a bit too relaxed now. The brandy was doing *her* more harm than it was doing to Walton. What had she expected?

"I haven't seen a temper," she continued as if baffled. "And believe me, with the way these single-minded ladies pursue him, I would have seen signs of it."

"Then what signs are you looking for?"

"I—" She broke off, and a moment later, Christopher heard her rich laugh. "Very good, Mr. Walton. But even this brandy will not loosen my tongue."

In a moment of silence, Christopher thought he heard footsteps. A glass was set down.

"Mr. Walton—"

"You look as pretty as peach pie," he said, his voice slightly slurred. "What about a taste? Perhaps we could loosen each other's tongues?"

Christopher's hand was on the doorknob.

Then he heard the faintest sound from her, and he thought it was, "Oh, Chris . . ." Barely a moment passed before she breathed, "If he finds out . . ."

"Chris?" Walton said. "The duke? You call him by his Christian name?"

Christopher slammed open the door to see Walton jumping away from Abigail. She was leaning back against the desk, hands braced behind her, as if she were trying to get away from the man.

And Christopher's blood boiled.

"I always find out what is going on in my own home," he said coldly. "Walton, leave the grounds immediately, and if I find you still here—"

Walton put his hands on his hips, the liquor making him bold. "What would you do, Madingley?"

"Deprive you of the employment you think you're good at."

"You can't—"

Giving in to a dark impulse, Christopher caught his arm and twisted it behind his back. "You need this arm to write with, do you not?"

"Nice temper, Madingley," Walton sputtered, then stopped struggling as Christopher pulled his arm a little higher.

Abigail straightened, but did not release her grip on the desk. "Your Grace! You must not—"

But he ignored her, hustling Walton toward the door. Christopher reached around and flung it open, startling two footmen who were talking near the business entrance.

"See that this man leaves the grounds immediately," Christopher ordered.

He pushed Walton, who stumbled, reeling, until the two servants caught his arms.

Walton looked over his shoulder and grinned. "Nicely done, Madingley. You'll see the results soon enough in the newspaper."

Christopher didn't wait to see him removed from the house. He turned around, saw Abigail standing shocked in the doorway, and caught her arm to drag her back inside the study.

When he'd shut the door, she groaned and covered her face. "I didn't get the information you wanted."

He stared at her, barely withholding his uncertain emotions. "Don't you mean the information *you* wanted?" Then he pointed to the empty brandy glasses. "What did you mean to accomplish with that? Other than get yourself ravished."

"He was talking," she said defensively, hugging herself. "I thought if he was a bit inebriated—"

"That he'd try to kiss you?"

"No, I—"

He advanced on her. "Or is that your usual investigative technique?"

He saw her wince, knew he was losing control over himself, but couldn't stop it all from happening. Inside, he felt angry and confused and furious that she was about to let that man—almost old enough to be her father!—kiss her.

"Nice idea, by the way."

She stared at him in confusion.

"When you said my name, then you quickly pretended that you were concerned I would find you."

Her face turned a riotous shade of red. "I . . . I was trying to get your attention, since I wasn't succeeding with him."

"Get my attention?" It was his turn to make her back up against the desk. "Oh, I don't think so."

He towered over her now, and her head tipped back as she looked up at him defiantly—helplessly. He could see the shadowy depths of her cleavage in the gown she'd chosen to wear—for Walton. Something in Christopher seemed to snap.

"You weren't trying to get my attention," he said harshly. He watched with disbelief as his hand curved around her waist, pulled her against him. And then he felt the warmth of those curves. "You were thinking of me. After all of your teasing and your kisses, if anyone is going to bed you, it's going to be me."

All she had time for was a gasp as he took her mouth with his. And then she moaned, and her trembling hand touched his chest, and Christopher was lost in a need he'd been resisting so much it felt like a lifetime of denial. Her brandy-flavored mouth succored him, lured him, made him forget who he'd worked so hard to be—and who she was. As his world began to crumble, none of it seemed to matter anymore.

Abigail reeled in shock and passion so potent she had no strength against it—no will to resist. Christopher's fury and desire merged into a hot kiss that invaded her mouth, invaded her senses. For a moment, she forgot what she wanted in life. She existed only as his, and she would have done anything to crawl into his skin and be part of him.

Had she so lost herself?

She pushed away, and breathing hard, demanded, "Do you think I'm desperate enough to give myself to you so you'll keep my secrets?"

Possessively, his hand molded over her hip, then up over her breast, making her mind reel with sinful pleasure.

He lowered his head and whispered against her mouth. "Aren't you?"

The confidence in his tone made tears flood her eyes. She pushed past him and raced out the door, not thinking of caution until she was already in the corridor. If anyone had seen her . . . she thought, slowing to a brisk walk even as she shuddered with fear. She angrily dashed her tears away. Christopher had no concern for her. She knew he would let her suffer all manner of shame were they caught together.

Because she wasn't of his class, he didn't have to care what others thought.

Hadn't he said he only slept with women not of Society? Was that why he'd propositioned her?

Even when she should have hated him for how he treated her, she could not, knowing his anger at her betrayal was driving his emotions, driving his revenge.

For a man who prided himself on control, she was making him lose it, and she hadn't realized how sad that would make her feel.

In her room, Gwen was still waiting for her, and Abigail knew that she could not reveal everything.

Numbly, she said she'd failed, that Christopher had tossed Walton off the property. But she could not confess what had happened between her and Christopher afterward.

"So did the duke say what would happen now?" Gwen asked hesitantly.

Abigail shook her head. "I don't know. He made me promise to help him, but I failed. He might . . . do anything." Though she worried about his promise to expose her, something made her pause. She could not believe that he would deliberately harm Gwen, much as he might have threatened to. No, this was all about punishing Abigail herself.

"I'll stay by your side," Gwen vowed. "He won't dare—"

"No, you can't! Remember, he knows nothing of your involvement. It will only make him realize that I've . . . lied to him about you."

"You shouldn't have done that, Abby."

"I wanted to. You mean so much to me, Gwen. I want, no I *need* to protect you."

"But I'm the one who suggested you come here! He should blame me!"

"I blame myself!" Abigail cried, then lowered her voice. "In the end, it is I who must pay for what I've done."

"So you have given up? You are not going to write this story?"

"I don't have a story to write! There is something here, and I don't know what it is, but it has hurt him deeply. How can I add to that? And yet . . . I still want to discover his secrets. But I don't know if I can cause him any more pain," she added in a whisper.

Gwen was studying her with worry. "Oh, Abby, your feelings for him will only get you hurt."

Abigail shrugged and tried to smile. "Then so be it. Right now, I am at his mercy."

He was undone by her, Christopher thought morosely, staring into the mirror in his dressing room. He could not stop wanting her, could not stop his fury with her. Two journalists were ready to write a story about him, making him wonder if something new had happened. And all these emotions seemed roiled together in a way designed to make peace a distant memory.

At one time words had been his friends; he could write his thoughts, working them out with pen and paper. But even that was denied him.

And he could not stop thinking that Abigail was no longer bound to Society—or the rules he'd created for himself to keep women, and scandal, at bay.

Or had he simply given up trying to be perfect?

At dinner that evening, Abigail appeared in a plain gown that seemed designed to hide the magnificence of her figure, but it didn't succeed. And he couldn't stop looking at her, the focus of all his turmoil. But she wasn't the source of his problems in the past; he was. She simply wanted to uncover them.

Some part of him had thought she might flee, had even set up well-hidden observers just in case under the pretext of their watching for Walton to return. Wasn't she off to write her precious story, like Walton was? Christopher would have stopped her, of course, but his precautions had been unnecessary. She hadn't tried to leave.

And why hadn't she been frightened away by Christopher's conduct, his rash proposition? He didn't know what to make of her behavior—and his own confused thoughts. He kept hearing the sweetness of her voice when she had told Walton what writing for the newspaper meant to her. Words were important to her, and Christopher could not forget that, nor did he like how much he understood it.

He also found himself suspicious of the reason she'd given for the crazy idea of hiding her identity, thus exposing Lady Gwen to risk. All because she wanted to prove herself to her father? Her look of despair when he'd discovered her betrayal had seemed about something deeper than that. But he'd been too furious to question anything. He had her at his mercy, could do as he wished with her.

Could even take her to his bed.

He remembered her moan when he'd kissed her, the gentle trembling of her hand on his chest, as if she could barely restrain herself. As if she felt the same things he did.

He wiped one hand down his face in confusion.

Abigail did her best not to watch Christopher, but she couldn't help stealing the occasional glance at him, knowing that the others expected it of her. . She kept waiting for him to look smug, as if he knew he had her trapped in his power. But he didn't. He seemed . . . distracted, and of course she knew he was worried about Walton.

He didn't have to worry about her. She'd seen the footmen following her at a distance when she moved through the house and the others stationed about the grounds. On Christopher's orders, of course. He was not going to allow her to write her story. And she didn't have the heart to write it, regardless of what it meant to her future—to the future of her father's newspaper. She would have to start all over, find a new idea.

Why didn't he just put her out of her misery and reveal her? She'd failed her part of the bargain, after all. If this agonized waiting was her punishment, it was a good one. As the women went into the drawing room, leaving the men to their cigars and brandy, Abigail risked one last look at him. Would he tell the men of her foolishness? Ways to answer him and yet protect Gwen kept crowding her mind. He seemed to be leaving her to simmer in fear and worry, for he didn't even meet her gaze.

Did he think her turmoil would somehow help

him? She could not forget his words, *If anyone is going to bed you, it's going to be me*. As she settled onto a small chair near the hearth, she ignored the ladies' animated discussion about the coming end to their ghost hunt and who might win. Such thoughts seemed so trivial when a man like Christopher had blatantly said he wanted to take her to bed.

She remembered the woman she was trying to become—an independent woman who didn't need a husband to support her.

And an independent woman could take a lover—discreetly, of course.

She turned her face away from the chattering women as if afraid what they might see in her expression.

Why was she considering sleeping with him? He desired her against his own best judgment and seemed angry with himself for it. Although that hadn't stopped him from coming to her rescue when the pursuit of Walton had gotten away from her.

But if she agreed to his proposition, he'd think the worst of her—that she was trying to buy his silence. Somehow, her ruse to have him teach her about men had become a goal she couldn't put aside.

And then the men joined them. Christopher was smiling boldly at something Lord Keane was saying, and in that moment, he met her gaze.

What she saw there both frightened and fascinated her. And in another moment, it was gone as
he turned away from her. There had been fire in
his eyes as he beheld her, as if he remembered their
kisses as well as she did.

Chapter 19

A bigail was not asleep when she heard her door open late that night. She did not even think of being afraid. The moon streamed in her open windows, and Christopher walked into the pale light. He looked boldly down on her, and she wondered how she looked to him, her nightgown covered by only a sheet in the summer warmth, her hair pulled back in a simple braid.

He was dressed in only trousers and shirt-sleeves, with his collar open to reveal the lines of his throat. His dark hair was mussed as if he'd run his hands through it. Even his bare feet made her shudder.

He stared down at her with eyes that had lost their cool, composed expression. "I've come to fulfill the bargain we made," he said in a low voice.

She sat up slowly, wanting to catch the sheet as it fell into her lap but at the last second deciding against it. Her nightgown was plain and covered her almost to her throat, but the knowledge that it was all that stood between them made it seem like nothing.

"Which bargain?" she whispered.

"The one where we agreed that I would show you what it was like to be with a man."

He started to unbutton his shirt, and she stared hotly as his chest was revealed to her, taut flesh covered with a scattering of dark hair.

She almost couldn't swallow, could barely remember her own name. "But why—"

"Don't speak." He spread his shirt wide, shrugged it from his shoulders, and she caught a shuddering breath at the beauty of his sleekly muscled torso. "I don't want to talk, I don't want to think."

He began to unbutton his trousers, and some distant part of her screamed that he was still angry, that she shouldn't want him like this, that they were both confused about what was between them. They would be using each other for the pleasure that would distract them from everything else going wrong in their lives.

And she didn't care. She could only stare in rising tension as she realized that the hair on his chest narrowed and continued on down.

And then he started speaking in a low, taut voice that was full of hunger. "From the moment I saw you sitting in that carriage in Hyde Park, you captured my attention."

She clenched the sheets in her fists to keep from reaching for him. And then she knew she didn't want to stop herself. She slid the sheet from her legs and turned to face him, sitting on the edge of the bed. She didn't care anymore about who she was or what she was supposed to do. Here in the dark of the night, she only wanted to be his lover.

"You were against every rule I set for myself," he murmured, "which only made me want you more."

As he undid the last button on his trousers, she let loose her hair, and he froze, watching her, his dark eyes gleaming out of the shadowed sockets. And then she began to unbutton the bodice of her nightgown. Though her fingers trembled, she didn't stop. When she could go no further, she let the sleeves fall from her shoulders. The gown separated at her breasts, baring her to him. For a moment, a spell trapped them in infinite awareness of each other and what they were about to do.

His voice was as guttural and dark as night. "I held myself back from seducing you. But I no longer care about why I shouldn't."

And then he dropped his trousers and stepped out of them. His body glistened as if it were a work of art, dark muscles highlighted by moonlight. The hair that had narrowed beneath his trousers circled his erect penis. Instead of being afraid of the very differentness of his body, she felt awed and somehow proud that she had inspired his arousal.

And then he dropped to his knees and pulled her to the edge of the bed, his arms about her waist. His body parted her thighs, making her nightgown ride up. She bent her head for his kiss, but instead he lifted her breasts in both hands as if to feast on them. Her head fell back in deep pleasure as his lips and tongue tormented her. She clasped her legs about his back, held him hard against her, felt his flesh against the intimacy of her womanhood. Then his mouth moved lower, tracing down her stomach, dipping into her navel, even as his shoulders broke the hold of her legs. She fell back on her elbows, had no time for even a moment of embarrassment, for with a groan he spread her legs wide and kissed her where she hadn't even imagined a man touching her.

But it wasn't just a kiss; he suckled her, caressed her with his tongue, even dipping inside her until she cried out with the pleasure of it. Heat and desire swirled inside her, making her tremble. Inside her rose a need so powerful, she didn't understand it, didn't know toward what he could be guiding her.

And then he rose, and without even climbing onto the bed, he grasped her hips in his hands and entered her with one swift thrust. The momentary pain made her gasp, and he held still, watching her. He felt so large, so foreign inside her. She stared at him with wide eyes.

He leaned over her, hands braced on each side of her, and began to move. She groaned, and her body responded by again finding that fever pitch, that rising urgency that made her arch against him, lifting her hips. Everything he did felt so good. His face was harsh with concentration, half-shadowed by the pale light. She wanted to touch him, please him, but she didn't know what he wanted her to do. At last she reached to touch his chest, his neck, the damp heat of his shoulders.

Then he bent farther and took her nipple into his mouth, and she hugged his head to her. The spark of that made her strain against him, seeking the elusive culmination of this passion that soared between.

And then it seemed to explode inside her body, breaking over her in shuddering ripples of pleasure. She lost awareness of everything but how they were joined as one, moving together through this wondrous sensation. He groaned deep in his throat, thrusting into her ever more slowly.

She reached for him, wanting to touch him, to share the drowsy feeling of contentment their love-making had inspired in her. But he levered himself to his feet, almost as if he were unsteady. Passion had drained her of will and the energy to move, but when he left her body and reached for his clothing, she brought her trembling legs together and sat up. He didn't look at her as he pulled up his trousers and fastened them. Her feeling of peace began to fade beneath mounting tension.

"Chris?" She hated how tentative her voice sounded—almost frightened.

Still keeping his eyes averted, he buttoned his shirt. "The bargain is met."

She frowned in confusion. "But—what does this mean? What will you do?" *Am I supposed to leave your home now? After this?* But she couldn't speak the words aloud, was afraid of the answer.

She suddenly realized that her nightgown was still bunched at her waist. Pulling at it in embarrassment, she felt the urgent need to cover herself.

He hadn't even kissed her, not once.

Although he'd kissed her body. She thought she should feel ashamed of that, but she wasn't. She'd wanted him, and she could not blame him for that.

He turned toward the door, then stopped, his back to her. "I don't know," he said in a low voice. "I don't know anything anymore."

And then he left her, not even taking the precaution of making sure the corridor was empty.

She sat still as a sense of numbness crept over her. Her nightgown felt suddenly . . . damp. At last she made herself get up in the darkness, and she hid the garment in a back corner of the wardrobe, not wanting the maid to see it. Abigail had been told enough about lovemaking to know there might be evidence of what she'd done. She would dispose of it later.

As she washed and drew on a fresh nightgown, her body felt not her own, as if it had changed. Everything had changed, she reminded herself with a sigh. She didn't know what her purpose was anymore, except the growing feeling that regardless of how coolly Christopher had just treated her, she was more and more convinced that she could not write about him. She would not be able to live with herself.

Was she going to be allowed to return to London? Even after what they'd just shared, it galled her to know he had that kind of control over her. He'd said he never had a mistress, so she must be the sort of woman he enjoyed for a night, then left, with no commitment between them.

That's what she wanted, wasn't it?

Yet she would see him at the breakfast table in the morning, would have to pretend that nothing had changed. And although part of her wanted to cry, she was mostly angry. She was not meekly going to creep away. He didn't trust her, and didn't want her to write the article. So she would see how he treated her.

And try not to watch him with calf's eyes, revealing the sentiments that would never be returned.

Christopher didn't come to breakfast, and Abigail's frustration warred with her relief. She was sitting alone, absently eating a piece of toast, hoping she wouldn't soon be ordered to pack, when Lady

May and Lady Theodosia, carrying full plates, sat down on either side of her. They never arose this early.

Abigail looked between them thoughtfully. "Good morning."

"Good morning!" they both said, almost in unison.

They exchanged a laugh, as if they'd somehow become friends. Well, of course, since they opposed the duke's interest in Abigail, that put them on the same team: Abigail's opponents.

"It is a lovely day," Lady May almost chirped.

Abigail arched a brow. "It rained early this morning, so I imagine it's still a bit damp."

"Ah, it rained hard enough to awaken you?" Lady Theodosia asked in her quiet tones.

"I didn't sleep well," Abigail admitted.

"Then what you need is an invigorating walk," Lady May said.

Lady Theodosia smiled. "You can come with us. We planned to walk the woods on the western edge of Madingley Court."

Abigail almost refused, but the thought of lounging about the house, dreading Christopher's appearance and her own reaction to it, was suddenly not so appealing. "Very well, thank you for the invitation. I'll join you."

The two ladies shared a grin, then turned to finish eating.

Abigail glanced between them, and her curiosity came to life. "I'm sure Lady Gwendolin will awaken soon."

"Oh, we do not have time to wait," Lady May cut in quickly. "We have plans later in the morning. I do believe several of the gentlemen are going to fence. How exciting!"

Abigail simply nodded, feeling suspicious about why they just wanted it to be the three of them.

And an hour later, she knew why. Somehow, when she'd been admiring a lovely patch of violet columbine, they'd abandoned her, their skirts not even making a sound against the undergrowth. And for a woman with intelligence and an excellent education, Abigail had an appalling sense of direction.

She was soon lost, as they'd obviously meant her to be.

Christopher had been in his study since before dawn, trying to use hard work to make him forget Abigail. It wasn't working.

He, who prided himself on his ability to resist temptation, to make the correct choices, had been unable to resist his overpowering desire for a woman who'd come to his home planning to betray him. He'd gone to bed last night with her on his mind, and while he'd lain awake, the scent of her, the feel of her soft skin, had woven through his mind, wiping away every rational thought. And then he'd gone to her.

How was he supposed to resist the sight of Abigail by moonlight? She'd looked at him so solemnly, knowing why he was there, and accepting it. And that was all his traitorous body had needed.

He'd told himself she was just another lover he'd taken for a night's pleasure.

But she'd been a virgin, and he hadn't even kissed her. Had it been lovemaking? Or some kind of punishment? Oh, he'd given her pleasure, but he'd barely spoken to her afterward.

And although a tiny voice inside him still protested that she deserved no better treatment, most of him was ashamed. He'd been raised not to treat a lady so abominably.

But she wasn't a lady.

He leaned back in his chair and gave a low groan. What was he supposed to do now? He couldn't send her away, not until he was convinced she would not write an article. Then again, another article was already being written, he thought cynically.

Or perhaps he was only lying to himself. She had to stay, because already the night was calling to him, and he wanted her again. Whether it was his anger with her or not, the sex had been . . . intense, overwhelming, satisfying in a way that had shaken him to the core.

How was he supposed to pretend nothing had happened between them when next they met? He had avoided breakfast like a coward, and only when a footman interrupted to tell him about the men planning a fencing display did he realize he had to confront his confusion directly.

As he passed by the morning room, he heard his mother call his name.

He stepped just inside, leaning against the door-frame as he smiled at her. She was sitting at her desk, menus spread out before her.

"Good morning, *Madre.*"

Instead of a smile, she gave him a frown. "I did not see you earlier."

"I have been working."

"I am sure your absence confused Lady May and Lady Theodosia, to whom you gave hope with your outrageous flirting yesterday."

His smile started to feel a bit forced. "I have to converse with every young lady, don't I? Wasn't that your plan for this week?"

She sighed. "Do not put your behavior on me. You gave them hope again, when it was already obvious to me that you have stopped thinking of them as potential duchesses. You have renewed their rivalry with Miss Shaw, and the three of them went off together this morning."

Christopher straightened. "Off where?"

She threw up a hand. "I do not know! But just a few minutes ago, they returned without her. I was about to send for you."

"Surely she is outside enjoying the day," Christopher said placidly.

"Is she? Then why did those two ladies seem so pleased with themselves?"

"You can't be accusing them of something underhanded."

"There are many things that women can do to one another that might not break the queen's laws but can wound just the same. I suggest you find Miss Shaw. Unless you're punishing her?" she added dryly.

Was he about to break into a blush, which she'd often inspired in him when he was a boy? "I am not punishing her," he said with conviction. "I will speak to the ladies."

"That would be pointless. They will not admit anything."

"Then I will go to see if Miss Shaw needs assistance. She is probably at the ruins."

His mother only arched a brow, then returned to her menu planning.

Abigail wasn't at the ruins.

After speaking to several gardeners, he at last discovered that the three ladies had gone into the woods. When he took the path in, the sunlight dappled overhead beneath the spreading branches of the oaks as they grew ever closer together. This woodland had once been part of a king's royal hunting ground, and many of the trees were ancient.

He started calling Abigail's name, walking ever deeper. Several paths left the main one, and he had no idea which one she might have used. Or if she were even here.

At last he heard the echo of his own name, and with several more shouts, they found each other. Across a clearing, they stopped and stared. For a dark moment, all he could think was that they were alone, that no one would know what they did in these remote woods. He imagined pressing her up against a tree, lifting her hips to his, finding the slit in her drawers and—

He came back to himself, stunned. Abigail wore a blush, as if his expression had given away his lustful thoughts, and she was no longer meeting his eyes.

"Can you not even look at me?" he asked hoarsely.

Her gaze shot to his. "It is difficult, because when I do, I remember where you put your mouth."

His mouth went completely dry, and he knew his gaze moved hotly over her. "Abigail—"

"No, you didn't let me speak last night, but I will now. I'm not Lady May or Lady Theodosia, the women you're accustomed to. I won't scream public hysterics because of what we did together. I am a grown woman who made a choice to be your lover for a night. But I have plans for my life, and they don't include you. I am a journalist, and I will take care of myself and remain independent."

He cocked a brow, trying to hide his irrational

amusement. Was his anger toward her fading so easily? He didn't want to admire her, not after everything she'd done. But he was not above his own sins, and he'd had to beg forgiveness more than once in his life.

"I don't even know if I wish to marry," she continued, crossing her arms over her chest. "I think men have their uses, but allowing one to have total say over my life? I think not."

"We have our uses?" he choked out, pretending to smother a cough. "As in rescuing damsels in distress in the forbidding forest?"

She lifted her chin. "As must be apparent, I am London-born and -raised. I have no idea of the countryside. Except for a city park, I think I drove through a woodland once as a child."

"So you weren't raised in Durham." He tilted his head, finding that it wasn't difficult to wear a faint smile when he was around Abigail.

She met his gaze, looking speculative, as if she wondered at his mood. At last, she gave a shy smile. "No. But I did not think it would be so difficult to find my way back. These paths wind about together, don't they?"

"So you came out here alone and lost your way?"

She hesitated. "Yes."

And though it was a lie, it was the kind of lie that was an attempt not to bring trouble down on two misguided young women. "Funny, my mother claims she saw you leaving with the Ladies May and Theodosia."

Her eyes widened, and with all seriousness, she said, "Your mother must have been lying."

He almost wanted to laugh. "My mother doesn't do that. Does yours?"

He approached her, and she turned and walked at his side.

"No, my mother is the soul of honesty. My father, too. I imagine they would be quite appalled if they knew what I was doing here."

There were so many ways to interpret that statement. He wanted to understand her, and how she'd come to a decision to manipulate him.

"Do your parents know you write?"

"Yes, because of course every young lady writes. I was very fond of writing in my journal."

"I was fond of writing, too," he found himself saying, then regretted it when she glanced at him with surprised interest. He didn't want to reveal more about himself to a woman who was trying to uncover his secrets. But he wanted to know about her.

"You write."

Her voice was so full of obvious doubt that he could have been offended. "Every gentleman is trained to do so."

"Not only gentlemen," she said dryly. "You may be surprised to hear it, but we of the lower classes can also be well educated."

"You sound very defensive. Have I ever spoken of different classes of society with any arrogance?"

"No. But when one has grown up reading the newspaper, seeing how peers can treat those they consider their inferiors—"

"And so you grouped me with others of the *ton*, and that's what made it easy to come here to deceive me."

She walked slowly, hands clasped behind her back, her gaze straight down the path. "It was never easy," she said in a low voice. "I was simply desperate."

"Make me understand why. Because I can't fathom your behavior."

She left the path and headed for the soft embankment of a stream. Water tumbled over small rocks, and the sound seemed to soothe her, for the sadness in her expression faded to determination.

"From childhood, I saw that the *Morning Journal* changed lives, even helped all of society. When gossip and scandal seemed to become more important than news, my father did not follow the trend. Consequently, the paper's circulation began to slip. While I was writing reviews, the managing editor finally told me that the paper was foundering."

Money, he thought, and protecting her father. Those at least were better reasons for what she'd done.

"I knew what was selling," she continued, "and I decided to write about a family that seemed to draw London's interest like no other."

"The Cabots."

She glanced at him and shrugged. "You were the only one with not a hint of scandal."

"And you didn't believe it?"

She spread her hands wide. "I didn't want to. I needed there to be a great mystery about you. I thought that then my father would be forced to use the article, even though I was the one who'd written it."

"You did not want to trust your father to solve his own problems?"

"I would have, but part of his solution was forcing me into marriage, with a gentleman, of course, so that I could better our family connections. And a large dowry is necessary for that," she added cynically. "I guess he was worried about losing the dowry. I know he thought he was doing what was best for me, but forcing me into something I don't want is appalling. He did the same thing to my mother, although it took me many years to see it. She was the daughter of a simple tailor, and he insisted that she make new friends among his business acquaintances and leave her old friends behind. And she did it. I do not plan to be so accommodating, not when my writing is so important to me. What gentleman husband would allow me to work for a living?" she added with bitterness.

And she was not wrong with that conclusion, he knew, understanding more of her desperation. It would be a scandal of no small proportion for a wife to have a career.

"And what will you do now?" he asked.

She bent to pluck a blue flower from the ground and contemplated it sadly. "With my life? I don't know."

"Then with my life."

She gave him a faint smile. "As I already told you, I did not learn anything about you that would ever be termed a scandal. Although I did hear clues." She regarded him curiously.

He said nothing.

"Even if I knew something about your past, I could not write it." Her voice was solemn. "I have become too fond of . . . your family, and I regret that I thought it would be so easy to deliberately hurt them. When I first had this idea, I had convinced myself that what I was doing was fine because I didn't think someone as wealthy and powerful as you could be hurt by a scandalous action you'd committed. After all, you seem to have a charmed life—but for the pesky noble-women chasing you."

Abigail let relief ease through her at last as she watched Christopher's slow smile. Her decision to tell him the truth had been the correct one. He did not trust her—and she didn't blame him—but after last night, he'd been willing to hear her out. And she was grateful.

"So what will you do?" he asked again.

"I just said—"

"I mean for your future? For your father?"

An arrow of sorrow and fear lanced her. "I don't know. I'm not certain I can be the dutiful daughter he wants. But if I find a man who attracts me physically as you did, then perhaps I shall reconsider."

"You know I can't let you leave, not yet."

She sighed. "Because of Mr. Walton and his article. You cannot trust that I would not be tempted to join forces with him."

"I can't trust that he won't force you to tell him what you might have learned here."

"So you're protecting me." Though she tried for a bitter tone, it ended up only as faintly amused. "My, how things have changed. Yesterday it was blackmail and intimidation, now today everything you force on me is for my own good."

"You make it sound like I'm your father."

"Oh believe me, I don't think that."

"Well, that's good." He glanced down her body again.

She somehow had to combat this ability of his to make her forget herself. "If you had *asked* for my help with Walton, I would have granted it, even if only out of guilt, although it would have truly been for more reasons than that."

"I wasn't in the right mind to be polite."

She leaned back against a tree and regarded him coolly. "But that didn't matter last night, did it?"

He stiffened but did not come to her. "No, it didn't. As I already told you, nothing mattered but what I wanted from you."

"And now that you have taken it, you can ignore me yet keep me here until you deem it safe."

"No, I only wish that were true." Those dark eyes still smoldered, even in dappled sunlight. "I won't be able to ignore you, Abigail, for one taste was not enough."

Heat flared in her, conflicting with worry and even satisfaction. "Are you asking me to be your mistress?"

"I've never taken a mistress, and I don't intend to start."

Boldly she countered, "But you want me."

He took a step closer. "I do."

Her breath tightened in her chest, but she was determined to ignore his effect on her. "Is that not a contradiction for you?"

"I haven't given it enough thought."

She moved toward him, knew he tensed. "Think all you want, Your Grace. I am going to watch the fencing." She paused at his side. "Are you participating?"

He hesitated, and she prepared herself to be disappointed.

"Yes."

She eyed him with interest. "Perhaps I'll have to place a wager."

Chapter 20

Abigail tried not to gape as she watched Christopher, in his shirtsleeves, fence against Lord Paul on the terrace. They wore no fencing masks or chest protection, but their sword points were covered with safety tips. The Lords Greenwich and Swarthbeck acted as judges to interpret what constituted a hit. Both competitors, speckled with perspiration, ignored the cheers by the various spectators seated on benches and chairs out of harm's way. They were intent on winning, using their muscles to thrust forward and jerk back to dodge a well-placed counter.

Abigail felt so overheated at the masculine display that she could have fanned herself. She felt as if everyone could see the way her eyes were glued to Christopher. She had to keep reminding herself that she'd volunteered to help him keep the ladies at bay, that she was *allowed* to gaze worshipfully at him. But enough was enough. To master her control, she turned to Gwen, expecting her friend to say something witty to distract her.

But Gwen was biting her thumbnail, looking off into the park rather than at the contestants.

"Gwen?" Abigail murmured.

The woman gave a start, then a quick smile when she met Abigail's eyes. "Yes? Who won?"

"It isn't over yet."

Gwen glanced at the competitors and blushed. "Oh."

"What's wrong?"

She looked around to see who could overhear them, then leaned forward. "Oh, Abby, the party is almost over."

"Yes," Abigail said slowly, even though her own stomach knotted at the thought. "You knew we would return to London eventually." Abigail would have to leave Christopher and return home to her parents' renewed pressure to marry. And if the newspaper failed, could she really deny them her security? Watching Christopher's absolute devotion to his family, regardless of the sacrifices to himself, was making her wonder if she wasn't being selfish, wanting to prove she could survive on her own. She was too confused.

"But Mr. Wesley doesn't come to London often!" Gwen was saying.

"Ah."

"And he would never try to court me, thinking my father would be against the match."

"He doesn't know your father well."

"And he'll never even meet him, given the hesitant way he's treating me now. Oh, Abby, how can I persuade him to propose to me? And what if he doesn't even want to? He might be content in his small parish, and you know my father would expect us to see some relatives and friends during the Season."

"Wait, wait!" Abigail said, trying to slow down Gwen's frantic pace. "If Mr. Wesley has not spoken of this to you, then you don't know his thoughts."

Gwen pouted. "No."

"Then you must speak to him about it."

"Bring up marriage?" she cried, aghast. "He will think me so forward!"

"Better that than you never coming to an understanding that you both might have wanted."

"Abby, sometimes you are too modern," she sighed, "even when you're right. But . . ."

"But what?"

Gwen's shoulders slumped. "What if I have misread my father all these years? What if . . . although he may talk of a utopian England someday, maybe he doesn't mean it for his own daughter? It would be quite unthinkable in most families for an earl's daughter to marry a poor vicar."

Abigail thought it would be the same outrage— and scandal—for a duke to marry a commoner. It was a good thing she was not foolish enough to wish for marriage, she told herself. She glanced at

Christopher again, at the way his body moved so precisely, and thought about going to bed with him every night. To distract herself, she turned back to her glum friend.

"Gwen, you cannot know what your father is thinking. You will have to talk to him, too."

"But surely I would need Mr. Wesley to help with that. And he's not even talking to *me* about marriage!" She moaned and closed her eyes, then took a deep breath. "But you're right, I must initiate a discussion. Perhaps I can come at the conversation from a different angle, try to get Mr. Wesley's thoughts without his realizing I'm talking about the two of us."

"Maybe that will even make him really think about you as a wife."

"And scare him off," she said forlornly.

"Is he coming for dinner? Perhaps you can speak then, or just after."

Gwen patted her knees. "I will be brave like you, Abby."

And I will try to be as brave as you think I am, Abigail thought with determination.

While everyone was distracted with the fencing tournament, it was surprisingly easy to sneak into the duke's bedchamber. Listening to Gwen's dilemma about marriage to a commoner made Abigail want to reassure Christopher that she had no such thing in mind.

But she could use another demonstration about how to behave with men, she thought, shivering with anticipation. He could refuse her, since they still circled each other so warily, but she thought they had improved things between them this morning. And it had been far too amusing to tell the Ladies May and Theodosia that they needn't have worried about her after she "accidentally" wandered away from them. When she said that the duke had rescued her, their faces had turned almost green with envy—and frustration.

It was ill of her, she knew. One of those women could very well be the one he chose.

But she didn't think so. It would be some other woman. Hopefully one she never met, so she wouldn't have to imagine . . .

To distract herself from foolish jealousy, she thought of the conversation they'd had, where he'd revealed that he liked to write. It had been strange, yet enjoyable, to hear a man say such a thing. It explained all the quills in his desk—

And the bound sheaf of papers in the bottom drawer?

She focused on the same drawer, and when she saw that it was partially open, her gaze quickly lifted to the desktop itself.

The stack of papers was there. Hesitantly, she came to her feet and moved until she could see Christopher's bold handwriting lining a sheet, top to bottom. Had he written this? It seemed like his penmanship, from what she'd seen in his study.

Not thinking about right or wrong, heeding only her curiosity, she examined the first page, realizing it was in the format of a play, and began to read. Fearing to be interrupted, she skimmed it quickly, reading in wonder the story of a poor but noble man, taken from his own country, forced to survive, then learning to thrive in a land hostile to him. She couldn't read all the details, but she grasped that Christopher had a wonderful imagination, that his dialogue sounded so real. But somehow, for some strange reason, the story struck a chord within her that she could not identify.

It ended abruptly—too abruptly, with a half-empty page and the hero fighting for his life. She didn't know if he would live or die. Maybe Christopher didn't either.

The kinship she felt for him warmed her inside. Was this one of the secrets he guarded so protectively? He wanted to write, just like she did. And Society had been telling each of them that their dreams were not suitable.

His name wasn't on the manuscript. Did he plan to do anything with it, or was it just something he felt compelled to write? She put the pages back the way she'd found them. He would think she planned to use this secret against him if she told him of her discovery. It would be just another reason he couldn't trust her. She didn't want that; she wanted him to tell her the truth himself.

She might as well be asking for the moon, she thought, leaving his room and creeping down the servants' stairs to another floor.

Reaching her own room, she realized that she'd come full circle. She wanted to know how he felt about his work, whether he would brave an attempt at publishing it. She knew what it was like to have words that demanded to be written, and the wish that someone would read them and give meaning to one's dreams.

But would a man who wouldn't even kiss her during their lovemaking want to share something so intimate?

Christopher was in the drawing room before dinner with their gathering guests, speaking to his mother, when the butler announced the arrival of Miss Madeleine Preston.

His mother gave him a sharp glance and murmured, "Christopher, you would not have invited her here after telling her you would not marry her."

"No, I would not have," he replied dryly.

When he'd last seen Madeleine, she'd promised he would pay for not marrying her. Had she come to make a scene? She had to know that she couldn't change his mind just by embarrassing herself before his mother and friends.

Madeleine approached him, and he met her in the center of the room, knowing they had everyone's attention. She was a beautiful woman, whose brown hair gleamed like the richest chocolate, whose face possessed strong beauty. But she had never learned to hide the haughtiness in her eyes, the way she always seemed to be looking for more than she deserved. Now those eyes gleamed with satisfaction, and he knew something more was about to happen.

"Your Grace!" she cried, holding out both hands to him, making sure all in the drawing room saw her. "Thank you so much for inviting me to join your little party."

He bowed over her hands and gave her a brief smile, not surprised by her cleverness. She was getting bolder. Had his search for a duchess finally made her too nervous? He brought her to his mother, where Madeleine curtsied with elegance and humility.

"Miss Preston," the duchess said civilly. "So you decided to join us."

Christopher heard his mother's emphasis on the word "decided," but Madeleine ignored such subtlety.

"And I thank you so kindly, Your Grace." Her cat's eyes slid to Christopher. "My brother Michael sends his regards."

"Yes, I recently received a letter from him," Christopher said.

Now she flushed but only lifted her chin higher. "Poor man, letters are the only way he can communicate with the world."

Christopher stiffened, his smile disappearing with the gibe.

His mother briefly touched his arm. "Do introduce Miss Preston to our other guests, Madingley."

Abigail watched the unfolding tableau with open curiosity. Christopher was obviously uneasy, the woman triumphant, and although the duchess looked polite, Abigail sensed an undercurrent of tension. Neither Christopher nor his mother liked the woman, but she didn't seem to care.

Elizabeth was more openly troubled, but she smiled when Christopher brought the woman over to her to be introduced to those she didn't know.

"That is Miss Madeleine Preston," Gwen murmured.

Abigail glanced over her shoulder at her friend. "That name is familiar to me. She claims the duke invited her. Does his expression look that way to you?"

"No, it doesn't. And I cannot blame him. I told you about her when we first arrived."

"Oh, the woman who boasted that the duke was courting her," Abigail said with new interest. "Shall we see what Elizabeth has to say?"

When they motioned to Christopher's sister, she

seemed glad to leave the older noblewomen to join them.

"We hope we aren't being rude," Gwen said, "but is Miss Preston a late arrival to your party?"

Elizabeth's smile was faint and distracted. "She claims to have been invited, but I would never do that."

"Why?" Abigail asked.

Elizabeth gave her a searching glance, then whispered, "Because she wishes to marry my brother, and he would not have her attempts at manipulation."

"Ooh," Abigail and Gwen said together, as if hearing all of this for the first time.

"Would she be here to cause trouble?" Abigail asked.

Elizabeth shrugged. "I hope she would not embarrass herself so. And her brother is such a wonderful fellow; although when he was young, he was more like his sister." She pressed her lips tightly together, as if she regretted what she'd said.

But Abigail understood. Was Miss Preston part of the tragedy that haunted Christopher's past? To look at the duke, he seemed in command, but she knew he'd done something he regretted, and if this Miss Preston thought to capitalize on his pain . . . well, Abigail could not allow that to happen. She felt protective of Christopher, and although he would never agree, he needed her help.

So Abigail excused herself from Elizabeth, took Gwen's arm, and steered her toward the Ladies May and Theodosia, who stood together, fuming. They warily watched Abigail approach.

"Ladies," Abigail said pleasantly, "it seems we have more competition."

"This is so unfair," said Lady Theodosia in her contained manner.

"I suggest we all make sure that His Grace has little time to devote to Miss Preston."

"We can take care of that," Lady May sniffed, sweeping past Abigail and Gwen. "You need not bother."

When the two women had gone, Gwen said musingly, "We're the competition, too, of course."

But the two ladies performed admirably, stealing Christopher away, leaving Miss Preston to be leered at by Lord Keane.

Yet the woman was not going to be dissuaded. After dinner, when Elizabeth gathered everyone together to discuss the end of the ghost hunt two days hence, Abigail could only watch in helpless frustration as Miss Preston led Christopher out of the room.

Christopher knew that Madeleine would use any tactic she could for them to be alone together. She was not above making it appear she'd been compromised, so he did not plan to be in an enclosed room with her. He took her to the great hall, where several servants were lighting oil lamps. They hurried away when he nodded at them, and he almost wished they could remain as chaperones, but the large public room would have to do. He led Madeleine into a secluded corner, where two chairs faced a sofa. On the wall above were numerous battered shields used by his ancestors long ago, which now gleamed menacingly in the lamplight. She gave the décor a quaint smile. He indicated the sofa, and she sat down, leaving room for him beside her. He took the chair opposite her.

Madeleine frowned. "Afraid of me, Madingley?"

"Cautious, Miss Preston. And since I have not changed my mind, what could you possibly have to say to me that made you intrude on my sister's party?"

"I've decided to give you another chance," she said, sitting so straight, her hands folded delicately on her knee.

"Another chance?"

"To reconsider marriage. Our families have been close for many years and it seems—"

"Madeleine, this is a waste of your time." He knew he should speak gently with her, but they'd already had this conversation. He was getting frustrated by her inability to accept the facts. "Our families have not been close. I am friends with your brother, and that is the sum of it."

She cocked her head. "You owe him so much."

The guilty part inside him never went away—he didn't need her to remind him. "I know that. And I have made amends to Michael's satisfaction." He tried to gentle his voice. "He would not want you here."

Her smile finally faded, and the cold light in her eyes shone. "It is none of his business."

"Yet you are *using* him and his situation, are you not? Madeleine, you need to stop this foolishness and get on with your life. There are plenty of men who—"

"But they are not dukes!" she hissed. "Do you not see how perfect a wife I could be for you?"

He said nothing; he didn't want to hurt her or further inflame their conversation.

At last she stood up and leaned over him, gripping her skirt in her fists. "You will regret this, Madingley."

"You've already said that." He kept his voice mild. "Do you need a ride back to London?"

"I understand that a writer from the *Times* recently visited you."

He frowned as the first feeling of unease swept through him. "You obviously know about it."

"I do. I have had the pleasure of many discussions with Mr. Walton."

Of course. She was a woman who needed revenge against imagined wrongs, and she'd found the perfect way to make him suffer.

"Madeleine, then I guess you will not be happy

to hear that he went away without anything to report."

"I know you had him thrown from the property," she said, tsking softly. "What a temper you have, Madingley. But don't worry, he did not need anything from you. I gave him everything he could wish for, including witnesses to your behavior."

"Your brother didn't talk to him," Christopher said with certainty.

Distaste and frustration flashed in her eyes. "No, he didn't. But he wasn't necessary, was he? You will so enjoy the article. I am positive it will make the front page. 'The Scandalous Duke of Madingley.' It has quite the ring to it." She leaned toward him. "Now are you certain you don't wish to change your answer?"

He stood up, towering over her. "No. You will leave first thing in the morning."

"But I only just arrived!"

"Uninvited. And if you press this, I will tell them all so. Remember, you've already told me that all my secrets are about to erupt. Why should I care what you'd say tonight?"

"I won't stay another moment under your roof," she said in a low, deadly voice.

"I'll lend you some footmen for extra security on the dark roads."

Gripping her skirts, she whirled around and fled the great hall.

Abigail appeared in one of the arched doorways. Pausing, she looked from one to the other of them. To Christopher, she was like spring after a harsh winter, and something inside him eased just looking at her. Then his worry rushed back. So many people would be hurt if Madeleine went through with her plan. There wasn't any way to stop her, short of sacrificing himself. And that he wouldn't do.

"He's all yours," Madeleine said grimly to Abigail. "You won't enjoy him for long. After tomorrow—"

Christopher interrupted. "Just go, Madeleine!"

When they were alone, Abigail raised a brow. "How kind of her to grant me her permission."

"We have that kind of relationship," Christopher said dryly.

"I came to see if you needed to be rescued."

"And I appreciate the thought."

"We're all to give our final effort in the ghost hunt, and since Gwen wished to have some time with Mr. Wesley, I am alone. I have a lead to follow. Would you like to accompany me?"

"I would welcome the distraction," he said, approaching her.

"Well, you really must be upset if the ghost and a dozen people carrying candles about your immense home can intrigue you."

He shrugged.

"And it *will* intrigue you. Mr. Wesley, Gwen,

and I have figured out where the ghost appears the most. Would you like to explore that room with me?"

Alone in a room with Abigail. He was flirting with danger, and knew he needed the distraction. Unless he gave in to blackmail, his orderly world was about to come apart, and there was nothing he could do about it. His past had returned to haunt him. A brief liaison with Abigail was the least of his problems.

"Lead on," he said, feeling the old thrill of danger taking over him.

She glanced at him with narrowed eyes, and he thought he could see the pulse in her neck—where he wanted to press his lips.

She cleared her throat. "We're going to the family wing. Do you know a more indirect route, known to few?"

"And to think I was going to enjoy the sway of your hips as I followed you. But yes, I know a better way."

Abigail found herself watching Christopher's hips, now that he'd given her the idea. She admired the width of his back, the way his body tapered in such a masculine way. He picked up a candleholder and lit the taper from a lamp. As she followed him into a servants' corridor, narrow and dimly lit, she forced herself to forget her questions about Miss Preston. Now was not the time.

After several flights of stairs, and surprising a

few servants, Christopher said over his shoulder, "Where in the family wing?"

"Your dressing room."

He came to a stop on a step above her and blinked. "You're hunting for a ghost there."

"Thanks to Gwen's research, we realized that the ghost appeared the most in your dressing room. There has to be a reason, don't you think?"

"You're persistent, even with a party game."

She shrugged. "Let us simply call it curious. And have I distracted you?"

His gaze dropped to her breasts. "Oh, yes."

She gave him a push. "Go, Your Grace."

Eventually, they left the servants' corridor right next to his chambers, but instead of using the main door to his room, he went beyond and entered what had to be the dressing room, lit by a single lamp. It was decorated in a far more subdued manner, papered walls and simple draperies, but there was plenty of light. A standing mirror stood ready for him, and through another doorway, she caught a glimpse of his own private bathing tub. She sighed with the decadence of it.

The dressing room held several wardrobes, some appearing far older than others, as well as chests of drawers. She eyed the differences in the furniture with curiosity.

Christopher closed the door and leaned back against it. "I appreciate how much you want to be alone with me."

She gave a start and glanced at him. "But I also promised Gwen I would search this room. I cannot disappoint her after she's worked so hard on the mystery of your ghost."

"My ghost."

"Your servants' ghost. And it appeared here the most. Don't you wonder why?"

"Not really," he said, coming toward her. "I don't believe in those stories."

"But there are such similarities in every encounter!" She was backing away from him now, feeling excited and eager and almost afraid. There was no anger in him tonight—what would it be like to experience him? And how much more difficult would it be to give it—him—up?

She came up hard against a wardrobe, felt its smooth carving with her trembling fingers. "Now this is an old piece," she said breathlessly.

"It is." He put his hands on either side of her head, trapping her. "Sixteenth century, according to my father. It is the oldest item in the room."

She tried not to look at his mouth. "And you still use it?"

"Folded shirts cannot be harmed by old wood."

She ducked beneath his arm and whirled to examine the wardrobe even more carefully. "Perhaps it is as old as the ghost! May I look inside?"

Without waiting for a response, she gently opened both doors wide. On the left, some garments were hung on hangers, but on the right were layers of shelving. Guided by some instinct she couldn't name, she moved a stack of shirts, then one of trousers, handing Christopher a third stack, all so that she could reach inside and feel every wall.

"What do you think you're doing?" he asked in an amused voice, as several shirts fell off the pile in his hands.

"Looking for a clue. Perhaps the ghost comes here because of this."

"Because of a piece of furniture," he said doubtfully.

"Or something that is in it. They say the ghost seems upset. Perhaps he is missing something—or wants something found."

When he rolled his eyes, she turned away from him and bent over, reaching in the lowest shelf as far as she could.

In a tight voice, he said, "Your hips are far too tempting, Abigail."

"They're too big," she said distractedly, wincing when a sliver of wood pierced her thumb.

"Too big? Surely a woman said that, because a man never would. You're just the right size to—"

She put another stack of clothes in his arms, and they fell against his face. He grudgingly remained silent as she searched the entire inside of the wardrobe but found nothing.

"Are you satisfied?" he asked, as she took the last stack of clothing from him and returned it.

"No." She got down on her hands and knees and peered beneath, at the scrolled legs that held up the wardrobe. She ran her hands over each of them, then began to feel the bottom of the wardrobe itself. "Chris, this is strange. Part of this is lower than the rest."

"Surely it was only repaired that way."

"I didn't feel anything that needed to be repaired on the inside." She lay down on her back on the carpeted floor and used her heels to slide her upper body beneath.

"You're going to get filthy."

"Perhaps a lady would care," she answered primly. "But—"

"You're not a lady. I know."

"I need a candle to see. Would you hand it to me?"

He knelt and placed the candleholder beneath the wardrobe at her side, where it illuminated the bottom. The wood was unpainted, though still fitted together skillfully. There was even a mark burned into the wood, perhaps the emblem of the carpenter.

She felt his hands on her ankles. "No, don't drag me out!"

"I wouldn't think of it."

So while Christopher slowly lifted her skirt, even tickled beneath her garters, she did her best to examine the underside of the wardrobe.

She'd been right—one spot was lower than the

rest, and made of a different wood. She put her fingertips into a crack and tried to pull but could not budge it. And she didn't want to break the priceless antique.

He succeeded in attracting her notice again when he separated her legs.

"Chris! Stop it! I found something. Lie down beside me."

"I thought you'd never ask."

But instead of teasing her, he lay back and slid beneath until their heads touched.

"There's a hidden space here," she said, "but I am afraid to damage it. Pulling on it does no good. Do you have an idea?"

He explored it with the same competent hands that had explored her just last night, and she almost forgot her purpose here.

And then, instead of pulling, he pushed the wood sideways, and it began to move.

"Careful!" she urged.

Dust fell on their faces, and she didn't turn away in time. Several sneezes later, she opened her eyes to see Christopher lowering a piece of wood roughly two of her hands in length.

"There's something heavy resting on it," he said, finally sounding just as intrigued as she was.

He set it on his chest, where they saw that it was some sort of wrapped package. Without speaking, they both slid out and sat up. He put the item between them.

She brought the candle closer. "Open it!" she whispered with reverence and excitement.

"It's your discovery."

"It's your ghost!"

Without lifting it, he widened the drawstring on the leather-bound package. He hesitated, and their eyes met for a moment's anticipation.

He looked inside, wearing a frown, then reached in and slid the item out. It was a bound sheaf of papers, yellowed with age.

She squealed with delight when she saw the writing on it. "Oh, you had an ancestor who was a writer, just like you!"

And then she saw his excitement fade and his wary mistrust return. She realized her error too late.

"What are you talking about?" he demanded.

Chapter 21

Christopher watched the blood drain from Abigail's face. She winced without trying to hide it. The yellowed papers were like a chasm between them.

"Abigail, answer me. What do you mean, a writer just like me?"

He saw moisture gather in her eyes.

"I . . . came to see you this afternoon, meaning to wait when you weren't here. I could not stop thinking about last night, and I wanted you to show me . . . but that doesn't matter."

Her voice trembled, and he almost couldn't hear her.

"You'd left your manuscript on your desk. I . . . saw your penmanship . . . and then I couldn't help myself."

A tear slipped from the corner of her eye, but he was unmoved.

"You read my private papers," he said coldly. He couldn't stand just sitting on the floor next to her, so he rose to his feet, pulling her up with him. "Are you so determined to make sure I never trust you? How are you going to use *this* in your article?"

She briefly closed her eyes as she moaned. "I told you that I will not write an article about you! You can keep me here as long as you wish until I can prove myself to you. And this"—she pointed at the papers—"is hardly a scandal. So, you're a writer!"

"And how do you think it would look to everyone who respects my accomplishments if they discover that I write common plays? At some theaters, *prostitutes* work the saloons! There are many respectable people who won't even attend *Shakespeare* because of that. I have to be above this sort of thing, a serious man doing serious work." He remembered the stories of the difficulties his own father had, proving himself and his reputation after marrying improperly.

"Even if you have to uphold your image, I can't believe you think you have to deny yourself something you love, something that gives you joy. It's *good,* Chris," she said softly, touching his arm. "I didn't have time to really read it all, and I noticed you haven't finished it, but I *like* it. The characters seem so real to me and their conflicts important."

He hesitated, torn between keeping his secrets as he always had—and at last having someone to confide in. He looked down at Abigail, whose face shone with excitement and admiration.

And suddenly the words wouldn't remain unspoken. "There is a company willing to produce it if the ending is suitable." Words he'd written— characters he'd created—would at last become reality. When he'd first heard the news, he had felt the same pride as anything else he'd done that others might consider more worthy.

She gasped, then grabbed his arms. "Your play will be on the stage! Your family will be so proud!"

"No, no one knows, no one but you. And it has to stay that way." Writing had been the release he'd needed, and he didn't care that no one else knew. He had been a disappointment to his father, had given Society another reason to disparage his mother, and had seemed likely to be the most scandalous of all the Cabots—and that was saying something.

Her expression clouded over with confusion, then came a calm look of serenity. And he realized how it sounded, that she would be the only one to know. She would think he trusted her, after everything. And that trust shocked him. But he couldn't take it back.

Perhaps he didn't even want to take it back, he thought, looking down into her brown eyes, so alive with a light of their own.

"It is the scandal, isn't it?" she asked softly, putting a hand on his chest. "You are worried that a city that could praise your good deeds could taint them just as easily."

"Everything I've worked so hard for would matter little if they could use me in their cartoons as the duke compelled to write tawdry plays."

"It wasn't tawdry!" she insisted.

He felt a smile twist one corner of his mouth. "It wasn't tawdry?"

"No! It was well-done. Perhaps you inherited your writing ability from an ancestor." She looked down at the old manuscript they'd left sitting on the floor. "The ghost was known to carry a quill and look anxious. And he appeared here, near this manuscript! Perhaps he was never able to finish it."

"I don't believe in ghosts," he said matter-of-factly. But he bent and lifted the manuscript, studying it with reluctant interest. "But I pity the poor chap if he couldn't find an ending."

"He was a frustrated playwright. Perhaps you can help him rest in peace when your play is performed. But of course that means someone will have to know . . ."

He shook his head. "I'm using a pseudonym, and I have a trusted man to deal with anything in my place."

"So it will not concern you that no one will know you created this masterpiece?"

"It's not a masterpiece," he said quickly, then he studied her more carefully. "We have opposite goals for the success of our writing. You want your father to know you are capable."

"I also want the world to know that a *woman*

is capable," she said firmly, chin lifted with determination.

He smiled. "You're more than capable of doing anything you set your mind to."

Her eyes brightened as they met his, and he was rewarded by the way she seemed to be breathing too quickly.

He took her hand. "Does anyone know you're with me?" he whispered.

Solemnly, she shook her head. "They think I'm hunting alone."

"Are you supposed to return?"

She leaned against him, and he fumbled to set the old manuscript on the nearby washstand.

"Gwen won't miss me. She's with Mr. Wesley."

He slid his arms around her, then lowered until he cupped her perfectly rounded ass. "So you're hunting alone?"

"I think I found my prey."

She came up on tiptoes, and he groaned as he bent his head to kiss her. Their tongues performed an intricate dance; Abigail had learned so quickly. She entranced him, seduced him, and he wanted to think of nothing but pleasing her.

He lifted his head to stare into her dazed eyes. "Last night, I didn't take the time to—I wasn't fair to you."

She cupped his face in her hands. "And I enjoyed every minute of it. So does that mean that tonight I will faint with ecstasy?"

He grinned, pressing her hips even tighter against him. "Or scream with ecstasy."

She swayed against him, shuddering, and he bent to lift her off the floor. With a gasp, she clutched his shoulders, and he wasted no time passing through the door into his bedroom. He tossed her onto his bed, and she gave a deep laugh, spreading her arms wide.

For a moment he paused, holding on to the bed-post as he looked down at her. Something inside him softened, eased, and it felt good.

"You're wearing too many garments," he growled, leaning over her.

She smiled. "I made it too easy for you last night."

"Then let me show you what an expert I am at removing clothing."

He rolled her onto her stomach, and although she started giggling at the way he tugged at her hooks, eventually she emitted sighs of pleasure as his fingers explored what he revealed. He pulled her up onto her knees, and from behind her, he began to slide her gown and corset and chemise down her body. He caught a glimpse of the two of them in his standing mirror, saw her expression of expectation and pleasure as she, too, watched their reflections. He pulled all the pins out of her hair, watched it fall around her. Her breasts, high and proud on her torso, captured his attention next. When he cupped them, fondling and caressing, she closed her eyes, as if she were too shocked to watch anymore. But she peeked at the mirror again through half-closed eyes as his hands slid down her torso, and he reached between her thighs.

Suddenly their eyes met in the mirror. She blushed and stiffened, but he only gave a wicked smile, and held her captive with his gaze. He stroked her, sliding his fingers deeper into the moistness of her. She was so warm, so ready for him, and it took everything in him not to tear his clothes from his body to have her. But her satisfaction was more important than his need. He continued to caress the soft nub of her pleasure while his other hand circled and plucked her nipple. She moaned, her head falling back on his shoulder but her eyes never breaking with his. Losing himself, he rubbed his hips into hers from behind.

He watched her face, saw her gasp, knew her climax would soon take her, but suddenly she looked panicked.

"You aren't—" she gasped. "Shouldn't I . . . lie down?"

He pressed his mouth against her ear, giving a strained chuckle. "There isn't a rule that you be on your back, my love. Trust me to show you everything."

That word "trust" seemed to ring between them, and her eyes clung to his. But when she nodded, he picked up his pace, and she came almost immediately, shuddering in his arms. He watched the quiver of her breasts, the ecstasy on her face, and felt as if he could spill himself before he was even inside her.

When she collapsed forward, he helped her pull her clothes away from her body, heedless of where they landed on the floor. He stripped off his coat and waistcoat, was struggling with the buttons of his shirt, when suddenly, her fingers were taking over the task for him. He felt her breasts against his chest, looked up into her eyes.

She seemed to be searching him. "Let me," she whispered, then her shy smile blossomed into something wicked.

And inside his chest, his heart turned over. He ignored it, telling himself he only cared about his body's response. He realized he was actually trembling. Watching her delicate fingers move over him made him so hard it was almost painful. He'd never been with a woman who wanted to explore him for her own pleasure. She helped draw his shirt over his head, then her hair brushed him as she licked his nipple.

He groaned. "Abby, what you do to me."

And then those clever hands were unbuttoning his trousers, reaching inside to touch him. He gritted his teeth, let her explore because he knew she was so curious about everything. Sex wouldn't be any different.

At last he kicked his trousers and drawers off and climbed up onto his bed. He stretched out on the pillow, hands behind his head. Although she smiled, she also looked uncertain.

"I told you you wouldn't always be on your back, Abby. Take me."

Her dark eyes went wide. "Pardon me?"

He grinned. "You don't have to be so polite in my bed."

Then he drew her to him, pulling her leg across his body until she straddled his thighs.

His voice went hoarse. "Touch me, Abby. Take me into you."

And then her hand circled him, and he didn't remember how to speak. She lifted herself, awkwardly tried to guide him, then, at the right moment, he pulled her hips down as he buried himself inside her.

"Oh, God, you feel wondrous," he said, thrusting up inside her and retreating.

In a few moments, she realized how to lift herself, and she wholeheartedly joined in the ancient rhythm. "This feels . . . you feel . . . I can't even describe it."

Gritting his teeth, he murmured, "You, a writer, and you can't even come up with words?"

She threw her head back, gasped more than laughed, then cried out when he cupped her breasts again. Then there was no more talking, no more thinking, only her hot, wet body sheathing him. His climax overpowered him, tore through him, leaving him spent and fulfilled. At last he brought her down to rest against his chest, still joined so intimately together.

He held her, stroked her hair, kissed her forehead, her nose, whatever he could reach. She looked up at him in quiet surprise, and he remembered how last night he had simply left her, and she a virgin.

"Forgive me for last night," he whispered into her hair. "My haste, the way I left you . . ."

Her mouth quirked as she looked up at him. "Your actual haste was rather exciting."

He gave a low laugh, amazed at how she eased him, how understanding she was. He tried to draw a counterpane up over her, but she sat up, sliding off his body.

"I should leave. Someone might come."

He drew her back. "I told my valet I did not need him this night."

She braced her hand on his chest, her hair wild about her shoulders and breasts. "Confident, were you?"

"Determined."

She smiled as he sat up, bracing himself with pillows, then pulling her against him where she nestled beneath his arm.

Abigail lay still, heated by his big body, feeling so at peace it was as if the rest of the world didn't exist. But their silence began to confuse her, made her think of things that had no place in his bed. Softly, she said, "I do not know what people are supposed to talk about after . . ."

"Lovemaking?"

She nodded, tucking her hair back behind one ear.

"What do you want to talk about?" he asked.

She glanced up at him, felt amused by her idea, but tried to be serious. "How did you know you wanted to write? From when you were a child, as I did?"

"No, nothing so simple." He leaned his head back and looked up at the canopy, as if he were thinking back. "Even when I was a child, I felt the need for constant activity. Being confined at Eton with boys who thought I did not fit in kept me far too busy truly to immerse myself in my studies."

"How could you, a future duke, not fit in?"

"You might not have noticed, but I have darker skin than most." He grinned, flashing his white teeth. "And the fact that my mother wasn't English made them all think of me as a half-breed. My status as a marquess mattered less than my ability to defend myself. And I relished the chance to prove what I could do."

She watched his face, saw the troubles that passed through his eyes. She had not meant to make him relive whatever scandal he'd been a part of, but she thought it best to let him simply speak.

"I took too many risks," he said with a sigh, "all for the amusement of my friends and my pride in my prowess. I was too quick to respond with my fists."

A spasm of old grief passed so swiftly over his face she wasn't sure she saw it. She knew he was not going to talk about it, and she did not ask it of him.

"I earned a terrible reputation. They said I had 'wild Spanish blood,' as if it were a disease. And then my father died when I was eighteen, and I realized he must have thought I would further ruin the family name with my uncontrollable temper."

She tried to lighten his sadness. "I cannot imagine you with such a temper. You seem impervious to everything."

He arched a brow and smiled. "Only through great practice. I quickly realized I had given Society another reason to disparage my mother. It shamed me. After that, I changed. I was responsible for the entire family and took the heavy weight of it seriously. I educated myself in land management, business, and politics, listening to the experience of my skeptical elders. I could not attend Cambridge because of the ducal responsibilities."

"Did you get to the Continent? I heard young men of your class always take a grand trip."

"My father did," he said with a grin. "It was where he met my mother. But I couldn't, not then, although I have been there a time or two more recently. I closed off every wild emotion, determined to be the perfect duke."

"The perfect duke?" she echoed. "I did not know there could be such a thing."

"Didn't you? Isn't that why you chose me from the beginning?'"

Gently she caressed his chest, snuggled closer. "I guess so."

"I stayed away from Society at night, far too busy for pleasure. I felt that everybody was waiting for my old temperament to surface. And I wasn't yet in the market for a wife. Staying home was easier. But the nights were sometimes too quiet, and the restlessness I tamped down all day threatened to surface."

He hesitated, and she held her breath, wanting his confidence yet knowing she didn't deserve it.

"I was proud of what I'd done, but there was still an . . . emptiness inside me. I found myself drawn to the library, reading the books I'd never had time for at Eton. I discovered plays and regularly attended the theater. And then I realized that late at night, as my mind emptied, I began to hear my own stories."

"Yes, oh yes, I understand," she whispered.

He smiled at her, really saw her, and she realized he must never have shared this part of himself before, not even with his family. She felt closer to him than she'd ever imagined feeling to a man, and for a moment, she had the frightening thought that she could fall in love with him if she let herself. She chased that thought away.

"And then?" she prodded. "You wrote them down?"

"If only to make them go away. But the writing itself began to intrigue me. The characters could do whatever I wanted them to, behave as I wished."

"Perhaps they could have the emotions you kept denying yourself."

He shot a surprised glance at her, suddenly wary.

"I'm sorry for interrupting," she hastily said.

"No, no, I . . . see what you mean. It's an interesting speculation."

"But not one you're ready to agree with."

"Exactly." He kissed the top of her head. "I've already said the rest. I began to have dreams that my play was worth being performed, and, using a pseudonym, I sent it out to various acting companies. I wanted people to enjoy what I'd created, just like I had enjoyed the works of others. I wanted to improve the reputation of theaters that showed more melodrama and farce than Shakespeare."

"And now your dream is about to come true. Why haven't you been able to finish the play?"

He touched a finger to her nose. "Someone seems to be distracting me."

"Me?" she gasped, trying to push away in indignation.

He caught her back in a hard embrace. "I am teasing. My dilemma with the plot began long before I met you. I came here to write in peace, only to discover a house party orchestrated without my knowledge to help me choose a wife."

"What a good transition to my next question. What is going on with Miss Preston, your newest guest? Elizabeth told me she wanted to marry you, and you refused. Seems opposite the traditional way of proposing."

He sighed and didn't meet her eyes. "You have it all," he said.

She heard the distance in his voice, and knew this touched too closely to the other secret he'd kept his whole life. "You still have my help, you know. I can keep you distracted from her."

"Oh, you're keeping me distracted. But don't worry about Madeleine. She's already gone."

He caressed the side of her breast, and she was amazed at how quickly her mind sank back into remembered pleasure. He rolled her onto her back, and she stopped him from kissing her with a hand on his chest.

"Chris, about your play—let your hero live. Let him triumph. I've reviewed too many depressing or unbelievable plays."

"But it's often real for life to be a tragedy, isn't it?" he asked softly. "We can't all have what we want."

She whispered, "I think you've learned that lesson too often."

They looked into each other's eyes, and Abigail knew that their time together would be too fleeting. Even if he offered to keep her as a mistress, she wouldn't do it. She could not shame her family—or herself—like that.

So she reached up and enfolded him in her embrace, living for the moment, enjoying their intimacy and mutual pleasure, because it was all they would have.

After Christopher escorted Abigail back to her room, he found he couldn't sleep. He thought about the ancient manuscript, even read a couple pages carefully. It seemed to be a comedy, which was ironic. The ghost—if there was one—was surely part of a tragedy.

He thought he would feel uneasy now that Abigail knew that he was a secret playwright, but it paled in comparison to the whole world knowing about the indiscretions of his youth. He hated feeling so little in control. He couldn't let Madeleine and the article stop him from enjoying the success he'd achieved in his life.

Or he'd end up like the ghost, so unhappy that he couldn't rest.

Chapter 22

When Abigail awoke in the morning, she was pleasantly achy with sated passion. She bathed and dressed in a fog, remembering Christopher's kindness, his gentleness, the way he focused on making her happy.

And he'd called her "my love."

At the time, she hadn't thought about the endearment, but later it had kept her from falling asleep easily, and now she could not stop thinking of it.

What had he meant? Surely it was only a slip of the tongue, an accident that had no meaning for him. He would never allow himself to love her, not he, the "perfect duke."

Would they both only hurt each other in the end?

Before she reached the breakfast room, she found Elizabeth in the entrance hall, gaping at the morning's newspaper with tears running down her face.

Abigail rushed to her. "Elizabeth? What is wrong?"

Absently, she wiped one tear-stained cheek with the back of her hand. "It is a terrible article about my brother."

Abigail felt cold inside, remembering Mr. Walton and his threats. She came to Elizabeth's side and read over her shoulder. The headline screamed, "The Scandalous Duke of Madingley," and the body of the article was worse. Christopher was called a champion of the underprivileged, the voice of reason in the House of Lords, but also someone with a vicious enough temper to paralyze an innocent man.

When she read that part, Abigail gasped aloud and looked into Elizabeth's weeping face.

The girl nodded. "It's . . . true. Oh, Michael Preston wasn't innocent, but he was terribly injured."

"Michael Preston? Related to Madeleine?"

"Her brother."

It all made sense now, why Madeleine thought she should be entitled to wed Christopher. Abigail continued reading the article, which claimed that as a young man Christopher was known for his uncontrollable brawling at Eton. Several witnesses were interviewed as proof. They were all there the day that Christopher savagely beat Preston. The fact that Preston had never recovered the ability to walk had not been revealed until now, because the previous duke had paid to make certain that Preston retired to Scotland permanently.

"Our family knew what had truly happened to Michael, of course," Elizabeth said forlornly. "But not that my father had . . ." Her voice trailed off, and she swallowed. "Right after the fight, Michael admitted his own culpability and claimed he did not blame Chris. But Chris blamed himself, of course, and never forgave himself for what befell Michael. He has supported Michael in every way possible, and they are now friends. Chris travels to Scotland several times a year to visit. He's *proved* himself!" she finally cried. "He's done everything good and right since then, and now they're punishing him."

Abigail thought that it was rather coincidental that Madeleine arrived just before this article—and just after the journalist. She was even quoted, relating how her brother continued to suffer. Had she tried to blackmail Christopher?

She forced herself to finish the article, which talked about Christopher using a front to hide his true nature, that when Mr. Walton tried to question him, the duke had been unable to control his "vicious temper" and had bodily thrown him out.

Abigail winced. Christopher was a man who'd bettered himself, who'd tried to live a good life after a terrible mistake in his youth, who protected his family, yet was sensitive enough to write plays. In his play, he could control the world, unlike real life. She ached for him as if his pain were her own. She wanted to soothe him, to help him survive it—to help him counter it. And then she realized the truth: somehow she'd fallen in love with him, even though she knew common Abigail Shaw could never marry a duke.

And why would she want to lead this sort of repressive life, where the threat of scandal could ruin a person, where one's life was so rigid? In this Society, she would never be allowed to write anything but letters.

And Christopher already felt that his father's scandalous marriage caused too much notoriety. Marrying a commoner—a journalist—would be even worse.

"Is this the only newspaper?" Abigail asked.

Elizabeth sniffed loudly as she shook her head. "Because of the party, Mother had ten extra delivered every day. I imagine the men in the breakfast room are devouring it as we speak. Oh dear, they'll all be talking about this."

"Do you think your brother has seen it?"

Elizabeth's wet eyes went wide. "There's always one on his desk first thing in the morning. Oh, I don't even know what to say to him!"

"Let me speak with him. I might be able to help."

Elizabeth nodded, her expression full of confusion, then she looked back at the newspaper again as her lips began to quiver.

Abigail found Christopher in his study, sitting at his desk, looking out the window. The *Times* was spread before him. She closed the door and leaned against it, and only then did he slowly turn his head and look at her.

He smiled, but it didn't touch his solemn eyes. "I guess you were right about the interest in me. Front page. I imagine you regret it couldn't be your article."

"No, I don't," she said, walking forward. "And my article would have been much less sensational in nature."

"So you like to think."

She winced but tried not to take offense. He was suffering, and wondering how his life was going to be, and worried about how much this had hurt his family.

"So what are you going to do?" she asked.

"I've been giving that much thought this morning," he said, too calmly. "I've got to go to London, of course. Can't hide out here. I have business investors to calm, politicians and friends to reassure, enemies who need to realize that I won't flee to the Continent."

He spoke without emotion, too distant, as if he were already beyond her reach. The sweet man from last night was gone. But she *needed* to reach him.

"I assume this was why Madeleine was here yesterday?"

He nodded, his smile grim. "She was giving me one last chance to take her to wife. And when I wouldn't, she told me she was the one who put Walton on the scent of the story. I supposedly 'owed' her and her brother, even though Michael and I came to peace long ago."

She sat on the edge of the desk. "Would you tell me what happened?"

"You didn't read every lurid detail in the *Times*?"

"I would like to hear it from you."

He pressed his lips together, and for a moment she didn't think he would answer.

"I was seventeen and so foolish," he said in a low voice, and he turned again to look out the window as if he relived that time. "It was ten years ago, yet it seems like . . . forever. I was used to fighting. In fact I rather enjoyed my reputation, and there were few who could intimidate me. Michael was much like I, only he was a boy who took delight in abusing others, whereas I tended to respond— quite willingly—rather than instigate. We got into more than one brawl. In fact, the students tended to congregate when we were together, just to see what would happen. Witnesses, you know," he said dryly, nodding toward the paper. "I guess I was getting immune to his 'half-breed' gibes because he let loose with a particularly vicious slur against my mother."

She inhaled sharply, knowing how much he loved and respected the duchess.

"So I hit him, several times," he said broodingly.

"And he hit me. I was winning, but I didn't stop. I was furious, convinced that's what all the boys wished to say to me."

"Oh, Chris." She tried not to tear up, knowing he wouldn't want her pity, that he was still so angry with himself after all these years.

"And with one last blow, I knocked him down. He hit his head hard on a rock. He never walked again." He gave her almost a savage glare. "And don't tell me it was an accident. I knew I had already won, that there was nothing left to prove. But my temper was ungovernable, and in my mind, that was my excuse for fighting."

He crossed his arms over his chest, glowering at her, daring her to pity him.

"But no one else knew the extent of his injuries."

At last he sighed. "No. It took several days for the doctors to realize he would never walk again. His father moved him to Scotland, even claimed to be ashamed of his son's conduct and participation in all the fighting. It made sense to me. Why stay where your friends are only going to stare at you in pity?" His lips twisted with bitterness. "At the time, I didn't know about my father's . . . influence."

She inhaled on a gasp. "Oh, Chris . . . when did you find out?"

"Years later. I came across the paperwork and realized what had happened. You have to understand, Abby," he said earnestly. "My father was such a good man! The only scandalous thing he ever did was to marry my mother, a woman he loved. And after my terrible behavior, he found himself forced to violate every principle he held by paying off the Prestons in secrecy."

"He made that decision himself," Abigail said with gentle firmness.

"But I brought him to it. And within the year, he was dead." His black eyes were stark with grief and regret for only a moment, before he blocked all his emotions. "That's all he knew of me. He never saw what I became. And now everyone knows what I did and what he was forced to do."

"Michael didn't speak against you in the article," she said calmly. "Elizabeth tells me you've become friends."

Gradually, his tension eased, and he sighed. "We have. Thank God. I visit as often as I can. He gets around well in a wheelchair. And we've discussed his move to Scotland, how it turned out for the best. He's a successful businessman there. He later told me that his family was about to be ruined before he and I fought. A steward had embezzled all of their funds, and his father was too 'honorable' to let anyone know." He sighed. "Michael always says my father saved his family. I try to believe that. And he doesn't assume I must marry Madeleine. In fact, he sent me a letter, warning that she might cause trouble. I just didn't anticipate what she'd do."

She let him think in silence. Casually, she walked

back to the door, as if she were leaving him. And then she turned the key in the lock.

He watched her intently as she returned to him.

"You're thinking too much," she whispered, putting her hand in his hair, tilting his head back until he looked up at her.

Gently, she kissed his forehead, his nose, his lips, trying not to think that this might be the last time she would touch him. The party was almost over, the ghost mystery solved, and they were all going back to London. She could not continue to see him in private, and she would never move in his circle of Society. This would be their last good memory together—especially when he heard her plan.

He still didn't touch her, but she noticed that his hands were gripping the arms of his chair.

"Abby, are you trying to distract me with seduction?" he asked hoarsely.

She loved when he said her name so intimately. "Is it working?"

He slid his arms around her, pulled her up until she straddled his lap, her skirts puffing all around them. "Yes," he breathed, then kissed her hard.

"Just don't disturb my hair," she murmured against his lips, "or everyone will know what I've been doing."

He gave a laugh that sounded rusty, then began to touch her, loosening her bodice and corset so that he could reach her breasts. She pulled his shirt out of his trousers to touch his bare skin, felt the tension of his muscles as he restrained himself. With kisses and caresses, he readied her for him, and she reveled in his wildness and his desire. He was inside her faster than she'd imagined, groaning his need of her, teasing her breasts with his lips, guiding her pace with his hands on her hips. They came together in a wild rush of pleasure, kissing to stifle their moans of release.

Panting, Abigail leaned against him. "Oh, my, perhaps you should be upset more often."

To her shock, he stood up, still holding her inside him. She gripped his hips with her knees until he brought them both to the sofa, then he sank back against it. With a sigh, she slid off him and sat back into the corner so she could see him. He buttoned his trousers.

"You are quite the expert," she said, trying to ignore the rising tension of what she was about to tell him. "I didn't even remove my drawers."

"Whoever designed them saw many uses for the slit in the fabric."

Christopher could tell he'd shocked her, for her face reddened, and he couldn't help but laugh. She was very good at distracting him, amusing him, trying to make him feel better. He knew that soon enough he would have to confront the mess of his life, but for right now, here in his sunlit study, he only wanted to look at Abigail.

"Let me tighten your bodice in case we have a visitor."

She gave him her back, and when he was finished, she turned to face him again. Her expression softened.

"I didn't want to be a journalist for stories like that," she began quietly, gesturing to the newspaper on his desk, "much as you may think otherwise."

He thought he would tense as the painful subject came up again, but he was too curious about what she would say.

"When I was a little girl, I was in my father's carriage when he had to stop at a factory that was central to a story that one of his journalists was working on. He talked to me like I was an adult, telling me of the children who had to work long hours in that factory, and how it was up to the newspaper to show their plight so that something could be done to help them. I saw what those poor children looked like, no older than I, dirty and bedraggled and exhausted. That article helped change lives. I devoured the paper each night, reading the letters to the editor and the report of the discussion in Parliament. I was so proud of my father because he did more than just donate money to charities. He and the *Morning Journal* were trying to make London a better place."

He could almost see her as a too-curious, intelligent little girl. Where some women would be happy knowing that their lot was not so terrible, she wanted to make things better for others. He didn't know if he'd ever met another woman like her. He put his hand on her thigh, opened his mouth to speak, but she shook her head.

"Let me finish, Chris. I told you this story to show you how important a newspaper is in society, and how hard I worked to be good enough to write for it." She took a deep breath. "And so I'm going to write a story to counter the one about you in the *Times*."

He blinked for a moment, stunned, feeling the rise of his anger—his infamous temper—sweep over him. But he'd spent ten years learning to control himself, and he would not let even this ruin what he'd accomplished. She didn't understand what she was saying.

"No," he said slowly, with deliberate force. "I won't allow that."

"Oh, Chris, by saying nothing in rebuttal, you make everything worse. You can trust me! I can make this work, show the world that you've become a decent man, regardless of what happened in your youth."

"You would just feed the fire. I won't have it."

She drew away from him a bit, pulling up her knees as if she wanted to hug herself. There was hurt in her voice as she said. "I won't write about your play. I'll show you as the man I know."

"Don't do this, Abigail," he said, feeling the coldness in his voice settle into his heart. "You will be betraying me."

"I will not!" She shot to her feet as if she had to

pace out her frustration. "Why can't you let others help? Or is it all about control? After all, perhaps you want to see your play performed because you can manipulate to your heart's content." Her voice softened. "It doesn't always have to be you saving everyone. Let me do this for you!"

He stood as well, knowing that he was trying to intimidate her. But he hadn't been able to do that with Abigail. "I'll never forgive you if you do."

She flinched as if he'd hit her, and though he felt a momentary guilt, his anger and feelings of betrayal overrode all else.

"Well, considering we can never see each other again after this house party," she said, "then I guess I'll have to live with that. But I have to do what I think is best."

"You mean best for your father's newspaper."

Now those wide eyes glistened with tears. "How can you—no, I understand why you'd think that. I never thought you could really trust me, not after everything that's happened. But I'm writing this, Chris, although it's obvious you won't allow me to interview you. I'll make it work, you'll see."

She walked past him, holding her head high.

"I could keep you here," he said tightly.

Without looking back at him, she said, "I don't think you can."

And she was right, damn her to hell.

Chapter 23

Abigail didn't know how she kept her tears inside until she reached her room, but somehow she did. And then she cried as she hadn't since she was a little girl. She'd known her affair with the duke could never last, but hadn't imagined how tragic and sad the ending would be.

At last she dried her tears, washed her face, and concentrated on her resolve. She could never have him, never let him know she'd fallen in love with him, but she could write this article and counter the blows to his reputation.

His mistrust hurt, she could not deny it. But as she became more rational, she understood and even accepted it. He was a private man whom she was once going to betray. Because of her promises, he'd thought she wouldn't, had thought their intimacy was more important than a story, and now she was proving him wrong.

When he read it, he would understand. It was the last gift she could give him.

There was a soft knock on her door, and for only a moment, she thought it might be he. But she knew better.

Gwen peeked in. "Are you alone?"

Abigail smiled grimly. "Shouldn't I be?"

Gwen shrugged as she shut the door. "I thought perhaps you were having better luck with the duke than I was having with the vicar."

"Still no proposal?"

She shook her head, but her confident smile had returned at last. "But I think he finally understands how I feel about him. At least my kiss should have shown him. Perhaps he means to ask my father's permission to marry me first." She lifted her chin.

Abigail grinned. "I am so happy for you." Then she sobered. "But you need to know that I must leave today."

Gwen sat down beside her with a tired sigh. "So you saw the newspaper article."

"Hasn't everyone?"

She nodded glumly. "And the duke didn't believe that you wouldn't write one, too?"

"I told him I was going to."

Gwen's head came up in shock. "But—oh, I see, you're going to write a better one, one that will show what kind of man he is."

Sighing, Abigail nodded. "At least you see what I mean to do. You trust me; Chris doesn't."

"And yet you're still going to write it."

"I have to. It's something I can do for him."

"Because you can't be with him again?" Gwen said softly.

Abigail's eyes stung, and she gave her friend a mock glare. "Now do not start with me. I am not a fool. There is no future for a journalist and a duke."

"But you love him."

Abigail shrugged, feeling rueful. "It doesn't matter."

"Of course it does! Doesn't he understand that?"

"He doesn't know. How could I tell him something that would hurt him?"

"But he had no problem hurting you, if your swollen eyes are any evidence."

"Do not blame him, Gwen. He is hurting. But I can make it better. He'll see that. You'll . . . tell me how he is occasionally, won't you?"

Gwen gripped her hand and nodded.

"Could I borrow your carriage? I will send it right back."

"Of course! As I said, I'm not going anywhere. And I have to see who won the ghost contest."

"I think the four of us did."

"Really? And when will two of us hear what two of you discovered?"

"Probably this afternoon, when Lady Elizabeth calls for the results. Do tell Miss Bury that I hope she finds love at last with Mr. Fitzwilliam. And that I thank her for her belief in me."

"Of course!"

"But now I must pack. Write to me as soon as you can and tell me everything."

They hugged fiercely.

By the afternoon, Abigail was all packed and ready to leave. She'd had luncheon served on a tray in her room, and Gwen stopped by again to say that almost everyone was trying to act as if nothing had happened. Why wouldn't they want to stay and see what would unfold next?

A footman took her baggage to the carriage, but she didn't feel right about just sneaking away. So she stood in the corridor outside the drawing room and listened as Christopher displayed the manuscript he said he found alone, using clues provided by Abigail, Gwen, and Mr. Wesley.

"Why, Madingley, you win!" said Elizabeth with forced enthusiasm.

"I did not discover the clues, so I cannot claim the credit," he said, gesturing toward the blushing Gwen.

"So you think the ghost was a playwright?" Lady Swarthbeck said with obvious disapproval. "How shocking."

Abigail wanted quite childishly to pull the old woman's hair.

The duke only laughed, as if nothing in the world could bother him.

Abigail's tears were threatening again.

"Miss Shaw?" said a voice behind her.

She turned to find the duchess standing in the corridor watching her.

"You look dressed for travel," she continued. "Did you plan to leave without saying good-bye?"

"Oh, no, Your Grace! I was waiting for Lady Elizabeth to be finished, and then I had hoped to speak with both of you."

"Then please proceed to my morning room, and I'll bring my daughter."

"Would you mind . . . not telling the duke? It would only upset him. I promise to explain why."

Dark Spanish eyes regarded her solemnly, curiously, but at last she nodded. Abigail went to the morning room, where the wait seemed endless. She kept fearing that Christopher would barge in and make everything worse.

But at last the duchess was preceded by her daughter, and the three of them sat down to face each other.

Abigail took a deep breath. "Your son already knows everything I'm about to tell you, so please do not think I am going behind his back. I am not a gentleman's daughter; my father owns the *Morning Journal* in London."

Elizabeth's eyes grew wider and wider, but the duchess's expression only showed reserved interest.

"I came here in disguise because I thought I could discover the secret in Madingley's past and write an article to save my father's newspaper."

Elizabeth gasped.

"I didn't write it, obviously, because once I grew to know and understand the duke, I could not betray him—or his family. I was foolish ever to think I could go through with it, but you must understand how desperate I'd felt. And then Miss Preston made sure a far worse article was published, all to punish the duke."

"I knew she'd done it!" Elizabeth said with heat.

"But it could have been you, Miss Shaw," said the duchess in an impassive voice.

Abigail could not hide her guilty blush. "Yes, it could have been, until I came to my senses. But now I think the best way to counter it is to write a better story, one telling the full truth."

"And you've told this to my son?" the duchess asked.

Abigail nodded. "And he wants nothing to do with it. Understandably, he doesn't trust me. But I'm a good writer, Your Grace. I can interview Madingley's allies to show that he's changed and matured, that he's done good for so many people. And more importantly, I can interview Mr. Preston for his side of the story. I am sure you are aware that he did not participate in his sister's scheme. But I would need a letter of introduction."

Elizabeth's expression seemed to vary over the next minute of silence, from confusion to curiosity to understanding. Abigail wished her feelings for

Christopher were not so open to these two proper ladies, but it could not be helped.

Though Elizabeth, with her romantic streak, might favor Abigail, the duchess was a mother of a son who'd been hurt once too often.

"Let me make this right, Your Grace," Abigail pleaded.

"Very well," the duchess said at last. "I will pen it myself. Give me a moment."

Abigail met Elizabeth's happy eyes and sighed with relief. Elizabeth came to her and bent to touch cheeks.

"Regardless of why you came here," the young woman said, "I am glad I had the chance to know you. Thank you for wanting to help my brother."

"It is the least I can do."

After Elizabeth had gone and the duchess had finished her letter, she placed it in an envelope, wrote Mr. Preston's name on the front, and sealed it with her insignia pressed into hot wax.

When she handed the letter over, Abigail smiled. "Thank you so much, Your Grace. I regret that we must part so abruptly and under such strained circumstances. It has been a pleasure meeting you."

"Take care, Miss Shaw, and go with God. I hope everything you wish to happen comes true."

Before dinner, Christopher was sitting alone in his study, contemplating nothing but the emptiness that was seeping into his life again. Though close friends would understand the scandal of his youth, others would look at him differently now.

And Abigail had gone. She had not come to him again, and he couldn't blame her, not after he'd threatened to hold her captive like a barbarian.

God, he hated how desperate he'd sounded.

Someone knocked on the door, and he was tempted to pretend he wasn't there. "Come in."

His mother entered.

"Not even a greeting, Christopher?" she said mildly.

"Mother, I didn't know it was you."

She sat down before the desk. "I've come to speak with you about Miss Shaw."

He wanted to wince.

"She came to talk to me before she left."

"And what did she tell you?" he asked warily.

"About why she'd come—and why she was leaving."

"Then you must be happy she left."

"Of course. She is doing something that she thinks will help you."

He stiffened. "You cannot believe that. More publicity will only—"

"I think a woman who loves you will write something to honor you."

He blinked at her, then his brain started to work again. "*Madre,* what are you talking about? She didn't tell you that she loves me."

"No, she didn't. But a woman does not risk your wrath lightly."

"She risked it—and experienced it. I really don't wish to say any more. And she doesn't love me."

She only arched a brow at him.

"Her betrayal is far worse than what Madeleine did in the *Times*."

"Really?" the duchess said with interest. "And that would be because you love her?"

He couldn't love her. There was no use loving her, no future in it. His mother had suffered being an outsider in Society. Abigail certainly wouldn't accept that lightly.

And she didn't love him. If she did, she would have accepted his position and not gone to London.

But she wasn't the kind of woman he was used to—the kind he'd thought he'd wanted. She would never obey him mindlessly; she would always have her opinions, and she wouldn't care what others thought.

He cared too much. When he was young, he hadn't been that way. Where had that young man gone?

He'd been buried beneath guilt and duty and responsibility, and he'd let that guilt make him into a man too afraid to step over the line of respectability.

He felt confused—he felt like a fool.

"*Madre,* I can't love her," he said softly. "It would hurt her too much."

*   *   *

Abigail returned home in time to prepare for dinner with her parents. It was strange to be herself again, she thought as she changed out of her traveling clothes. She felt humbled by what she'd originally meant to do to Christopher and his family, grateful that she'd stopped in time.

And still partly angry that he didn't trust her to make things right.

And so sad, because her life seemed dark and drab without him. There would come a day when her carriage would pass his. Would he smile at her? Or even nod? Or they could encounter each other on Bond Street. Perhaps he would even pretend they were acquaintances, and that might be worse.

Someday she'd read his engagement announcement in the paper.

Before the tears could start, she descended to the dining room and gladly kissed both her parents.

Her father cleared his throat. "I wish you had let us know in advance of your return, my dear. I could have asked Mr. Wadsworth to attend this homecoming dinner."

Abigail shot a glance at her mother, who gave her a painful smile. If Abigail could stand up to a duke, she could stand up to her father.

"Papa, you know how much I love you, but I am uninterested in marrying Mr. Wadsworth just because he is a gentleman. I would rather be a spinster."

He inhaled as his face mottled. "It might come to that if you keep up this foolishness."

Softly, kindly, she said, "When you first started parading all these men before me, insisting I was going to marry, I thought you were trying to force your will on me for no better reason than that you could."

Shocked, he opened his mouth.

She wouldn't let him protest. "I don't think that anymore. I know you just wanted my security—and Mama's security, too, with my good marriage. I know all about the problems at the newspaper."

Her parents exchanged a glance of recognition, and Abigail was relieved that her mother already knew the truth.

"There are no problems," he said stiffly. "We had a slow quarter, but—"

"I know about the problems, because I've been writing for the *Journal* for the last year."

Her father gaped at her, and for once, he seemed to have nothing to say.

"I started as the literary critic, then moved on to plays. I wanted to prove myself as a writer, and your managing editor allowed it since I could write anonymously. Do not blame him, for I worked my will upon him."

"I'm sure you did, dear," said her mother.

Abigail couldn't miss the woman's pride, and she gave her a brief smile. "But then he had to tell me I could no longer be paid. He confessed the problems. I wanted to help. I knew scandal sold newspapers—"

"The *Journal* has never been a newspaper to cater to that sort of thing," he said indignantly.

"I know, Papa. But perhaps that was why your circulation was shrinking. I heard rumors about the one nobleman supposedly without scandal— the Duke of Madingley." Even saying his name made her want to weep, the pain was so real to her. She controlled herself. "So Gwen took me to a house party at Madingley Court."

Her mother gasped in obvious pleasure, and even her father slowly smiled.

"Abigail, what a wonderful opportunity!" he said. "I am certain you met so many eligible men."

"I did *not* come home with a marriage proposal."

He seemed genuinely shocked, as if he thought every nobleman would want her for a wife. She could have cried, she loved him so for believing in her.

Abigail held up a hand. "I went pretending to be the daughter of a Durham gentleman. I'm sorry that the lie was necessary, but I needed to help you, Papa."

"You've been there for a week, pretending?" her mother asked in shock.

She nodded. "I was investigating the duke so that I could write my own article. To save the paper, Papa," she said earnestly.

He rubbed his eyes. "Oh my dear, you put yourself at such risk. It was not necessary."

"I thought it was. But if you saw the *Times* this morning, you know that someone else wrote a terrible article about the duke."

"So you were beaten to the story," he said heavily. "It was for the best. Such a terribly tragedy, and you would have suffered with Madingley's wrath." He tried to smile. "But your instincts were good, because obviously there *was* a story."

"There still is, and I'm going to write it. I lived there for a week, and I know more about him than that—bounder, Walton, does. I'll show the kind of man the duke is, the one who's changed his life for the better. And I have the duchess's letter of introduction so that I can interview Mr. Preston, the man who was paralyzed in the fight."

Before her father could speak, her mother said sharply, "You have the approval of the duchess?"

Abigail tried not to blush. "To write this article, I do. But I don't have the duke's approval. He is against any more invasion of his privacy. But he's wrong."

Slowly, her father said, "You do not think a duke knows better what would satisfy him?"

How could she explain what she'd learned about Christopher, why she knew him better—maybe better than he knew himself?

"He'll understand when he reads it. And he'll be satisfied." She met her father's confused gaze.

"Do I have your support, Papa? Will you publish this article? After the frenzy of today's news, surely the public will want my story, and thereby increase your circulation." She could help everybody.

"I—" He broke off and met his wife's gaze once again. After awkwardly clearing his throat, he said, "As long as I approve it."

"As any publisher should," she said with satisfaction. "Have no fear, Papa. It will be good enough."

And then she started to eat, for she hadn't eaten all day in nervous expectation. She knew her parents watched her, but they hadn't stopped her from her plan. And she was grateful.

Now she just had to write the best article the newspaper had ever published. She gulped.

Chapter 24

Over the next week, Abigail conducted many interviews, the first—and the most important—of which was with Michael Preston. Though she'd been prepared to take the train as far north as she had to, Mr. Preston had already arrived in London, fearing his sister's plans. The duchess's letter of introduction made him treat Abigail as a valued friend, and she was so taken aback and flattered that she wished she knew what the duchess had written about her. Mr. Preston humbly admitted that he'd been a bully, and that Christopher was justified in fighting him. After his initial shock and acceptance of his condition, he had not blamed Christopher for what he considered an accident, and it had taken a long time for Christopher to forgive himself, so that they could become friends.

But what was most revealing—and what had made Madeleine truly desperate to take her last chance to marry the duke—was that after many years of effort, Mr. Preston's condition was improving. He could wiggle his toes and had begun to put pressure on his legs. His doctors felt that in time, he might be able to walk again.

"Certainly not run about, Miss Shaw," he said affably. "But I know Madingley will share my joy. I haven't had the chance to tell him about the improvement in my condition yet. I will be satisfied knowing the first place he'll read it is in your newspaper."

Abigail could only nod her acceptance because she was too busy fighting back tears. This news would ease Christopher's mind in a way that nothing else could.

After that, every interview was a joy to her. She spoke to men Christopher had gone to school with, as well as his political allies in the House of Lords. Several charities he sponsored contacted the newspaper in hopes someone would help them publicize the duke's good deeds, and Abigail gladly interviewed them as well. No one blamed him for his father's actions to protect him.

With her concentration on Christopher's life, he was never far from her thoughts. She heard nothing from him, nor did she know if he'd come to London as he'd planned. She didn't want to ask the people she was interviewing, for fear her reaction would betray her emotions. She would have to get used to knowing that they resided in the same city together, yet could never meet.

But . . . how had he ended his play? She had

finally realized why the plot had seemed familiar to her. The hero represented his mother, a woman who braved a new country for love's sake. And she triumphed over Society with her happy—if scandalous—marriage. Could he not see that the duchess felt that her family was worth every sacrifice? The hero of his play should live, thrive—but only Christopher could realize that.

At last she had assembled all of her research, and she began to write. She wrote about Christopher's mistakes as a boy, but she mostly wrote about the man he'd become, his crusades against child labor in Parliament, his friendship and support of the man he'd injured, and Mr. Preston's slow, but miraculous, recovery. When the article was published, the printing presses could barely keep up with the demand.

Abigail felt as if a tremendous weight had been lifted from her. She'd done her part and could only pray that the newspaper's circulation stayed high when readers saw all that the *Morning Journal* offered.

And certainly she must have helped Christopher. She prayed he thought so, that he would look back on their time together with fondness . . . someday.

"Mr. Shaw, come quick!"

Lawrence Shaw looked up from the account book on his desk as the editor's assistant gaped at him in the doorway. It was late in the afternoon,

and the newspaper office was just beginning to
hum with the energy of the coming evening's work
to put the paper to bed.

"What is it?" Shaw demanded absently. He was
busy estimating the effects of Abigail's article on his
circulation numbers after only three days, and the
increase in advertisements. It was looking promis-
ing thus far, and his cautious relief overwhelmed
him. He was so proud of her.

"There's a carriage near the front door, with a
huge coat of arms on the side. There are at least
four footmen!"

Frowning, Shaw left his office and emerged into
the editorial room, where newspapers were stacked
on desks and even on the floor, as the assistants
searched through them for story ideas. But everyone in the office was crowded at the windows. They
made room for Shaw as he approached, and he
watched the porter below speaking to a footman.

Shaw recognized the coat of arms and took a
deep breath. Before he could think how best to
handle the confrontation, someone cried, "It's the
duke of Madingley!"

Several young men gasped with astonishment,
but Shaw could only wonder if an enraged duke
would create havoc in their offices. But no, if a duke
wished it, the damage to his newspaper would be
much slower—and more complete—than that. Yet
he'd never heard the duke called unfair, and Abigail obviously admired him. Too much. He hoped

she would not be disappointed by whatever happened today. Bracing himself to manage the duke's displeasure, he waited with everyone else while the man himself ascended to the third floor.

When the duke entered the room, followed by a footman, he swept off his hat, revealing the dark Spanish heritage he was known for.

But he did not look angry, only raised an eyebrow as he saw everyone staring at him. "I am looking for Mr. Shaw."

Without a word, a path cleared between the two men. Madingley passed through, and when his mouth quirked with amusement, Shaw found himself beginning to relax.

"Your Grace, I am Mr. Shaw," he said, bowing slightly.

Madingley gave a formal nod. "Mr. Shaw, might we speak in private?"

Shaw gestured to his office, allowing the man to precede him. Shaw had already cleared a chair for him, and the duke sat down once Shaw was behind his desk.

"Would you be here to discuss the article, Your Grace?"

"Only indirectly, sir. I am here to talk about your daughter."

Stiffening, Shaw said, "I did not know that she was planning to stay at your home under false circumstances. I do not approve." He hesitated, then admitted, "I didn't even know she was writing for my paper. It would seem that I did not know how to keep control of her actions."

The duke smiled faintly. "I do not believe that is possible."

Shaw blinked. "Oh. Then—"

"But I have a suggestion for how it might be managed in the future."

Abigail sat in the drawing room, writing by the light of a lamp, while her mother sewed nearby. It had been five days since her article was published to great acclaim. Yesterday, for the first time, the managing editor had given her a story to cover about a charity event hosted by the Institute of Popular Science and Literature. It was not a front-page story, but it was a start—especially for a female journalist who would have to continue convincing the public of her abilities.

She told herself that she should be happy. Hadn't this always been her dream? Her father was proud of her, wanted her to work for him. She'd helped save his newspaper. And he hadn't brought a different man to every meal this week.

Perhaps happiness would come as she learned to forget what had happened to her. But she'd been changed. Loving Christopher had made her feel like a different person. It had helped her understand her parents, had helped bring her personal dreams to life.

But at last she'd realized that without Christopher to share in her success, it was somehow less satisfying. She forced herself to return to her work, before her useless tears started again.

The front door closed, followed by the sound of footsteps up the stairs.

"Abigail?"

She turned about in her chair in time to see her father enter the drawing room. He was carrying a newspaper, and although he smiled a greeting at his wife, he moved with purpose toward his daughter and set the paper on the table before her.

"This is tomorrow's paper, the first off the presses. I would like you to approve the front page."

As the main headline was about a railway merger, she gave him a confused glance.

"Keep reading."

Near the bottom was a small notice that made her heart pound with sudden dread. It promised another article about the duke. After the first line, she couldn't read any more.

"Papa! How can you promise such a thing?"

He only grinned.

"And you cannot expect me to write it!"

Before he could answer, a young maid rushed in, curtsied with such excitement she almost toppled over, and said, "Mr. Shaw, there's a fancy carriage comin' to stop before the house. Look out the window!"

Both her parents reached the window first, but

Abigail was moving with slow deliberation, telling herself it meant nothing. It was probably just some fool lost in the wrong section of London. She could see several people gaping from the pavement across the street, as well as heads leaning out windows.

She took a deep breath and looked down at the carriage. It was pulled by four of the most beautifully matched horses she'd ever seen. The coat of arms struck her with a dreadful pang, and she tried to tell herself that Elizabeth must be coming to visit.

Then she saw the tall, lean form of the duke of Madingley, and she had to put her hand on the windowsill to steady herself.

"My," her mother breathed. "Abigail, you never told me how handsome your duke is."

She wanted to protest, *He's not my duke!* But her mouth was too dry to speak. Surely he was not coming to berate her before her parents.

But she realized to her dismay that she would even tolerate that for the chance to be in his presence again, to look into his dark eyes and remember their stolen moments together.

A minute later, the butler solemnly announced, "His Grace, the Duke of Madingley," as if a peer visited them all the time.

Abigail scurried away from the window, not knowing if she should be writing at her table, or—

But when he entered the room, she stopped in

the center of the floor, clutching her skirt in trembling fists. Her mother curtsied, and Abigail remembered to do the same.

"Miss Shaw," he said impassively, then turned to greet her parents in the same polite tone.

"Please sit down, Your Grace," her mother said smoothly, as if her upbringing as a tailor's daughter had never happened. "May I send for tea?"

"That will not be necessary. And I don't believe I can sit at the moment."

Abigail wanted to gape at him. What was going on? His manner was polite, but she couldn't tell what he was thinking. And he couldn't sit? Was he just going to yell at her and leave?

Christopher glanced at her father. "Has she read the article yet?"

Christopher knew about that? Now she was truly confused, especially when her father smiled.

Abigail grabbed the paper off the table and kept reading. It promised news about the duke's latest scandal, and she winced, praying that her father had not somehow discovered Christopher's playwriting. As she continued reading, her whole body started to shake.

"What does it say?" her mother demanded.

"Somehow," Christopher said casually, "the *Morning Journal* discovered that I planned to scandalize all of Society by marrying a lady journalist."

Her mother gasped, but Abigail didn't look at

her. She slowly raised her gaze to Christopher's and saw his gentle smile, and the way his eyes softened as they looked at her—softened with love? Warmth and amazement spread through her until she began to feel giddy with it.

Her father cleared his throat. "Henrietta, I believe our daughter and her fiancé require some privacy."

Though she could hear her mother blowing her nose already, Abigail didn't look away.

And then with two long steps, Christopher enfolded her in his warm, strong arms, and she was surrounded by the scent of him, the memory of which had kept her awake at night.

He kissed the top of her head, her cheeks, then her lips, and she laughed against his mouth and linked her hands behind his neck.

"The article was wonderful," he said, when at last he stopped kissing her. "Michael is recovering! I should have trusted you. I was such a fool."

"No, no, after everything you'd been through, you couldn't know."

"But I knew *you*. Even when you were lying, you couldn't hide yourself from me. I knew you were different from any woman I'd ever known, and since I stupidly thought 'different' might not be proper, I ignored what was right before my eyes."

"So I'm not too bad?" she asked, chuckling.

"Bad?" He gave a sigh and touched his forehead

to hers. "These last days and nights without you have been unbearable. How could I not have realized that the right scandal was worth living for, worth loving for? And to think I had the perfect example of that in my parents' marriage! But instead I focused on the few negatives, not understanding that such things didn't matter to them. The only ghosts I have left are ones of regret for hurting you, for not understanding sooner how important you are to me, for not realizing how much I love you. And Abby, I love you so."

The tears she'd been shedding every night made their appearance again, but they were finally tears of joy. "Oh, Chris, I love you, too. Perhaps I should have told you when I realized it."

"No, I was still too blind then, too intent on what I thought was important." He caressed her face, settled his warm hand on the curve of her neck. "But then I saw that nothing seemed to matter anymore if I couldn't share it with you. I kept finding myself wanting to tell you my ideas for the end of the play, for God's sake! You're all I've been thinking about." He hesitated, and his eyes searched hers. "But, Abby, this is important. Will you mind dealing with the foolishness and pomp of being a duchess?"

She thought she'd be staggered by such a foreign concept, but she was worried about something more personal. "Chris, I need you to understand something. I'll never be perfect. I can't become the kind of woman you think would make a perfect duchess."

"Perfect is boring," he said, kissing her swiftly. "I was a fool when I thought I could make a list, and some woman would fit right into it. I fell in love with you because you had your own beliefs, and you never backed down from them. You were far braver than I've ever been, and your convictions mattered to you. And you make me laugh, Abby, and help me realize that I don't need to take everything so seriously."

"Chris, don't disparage the man I love!" she said with a laugh. Softly, she added, "The man I love cares about his family so powerfully that it brings tears to my eyes. The man I love is honorable and sensitive and a gifted writer, even if no one but me knows it."

He grinned and pulled her even closer. "I vow that I'll never try to make you do anything you don't want to."

"I've realized that someone wanting the best for me isn't always a form of control," she said. "But as for making me do what you want, aren't you doing that right now? You haven't asked me to marry you. You only assumed."

To her surprise, he dropped to one knee.

"Will you marry me, Abby? Will you become the duchess of Madingley and bear my children and read my manuscripts?"

Laughing—and crying once again—she sat on

his knee and put her arms around him. "Oh, yes, I will gladly marry you."

"Good, because if you let me, I'll read your articles, too. I want you to keep writing, to live your dream, just as you've brought my dream to me."

"A duchess who's a journalist?" she said in wonder as she kissed his cheek. "I don't know if London is ready for that."

"You'll blaze the trail, my love. And I'll be proudly at your side."

Epilogue

Six months later . . .

Abigail sat in a private box at the Olympic Theater, anxiously awaiting the start of Christopher's play. It was the opening night, and although many were in attendance, no one knew that the duke's restlessness was due to a budding playwright's nerves.

She smiled and took his hand, and he returned the grip a bit forcefully. She said, "Well, I think the Madingley ghost must be at peace now, since his descendant has succeeded so brilliantly. Look at this crowd!"

"I hope this will begin a new trend," Christopher said. "A serious play that is not a melodrama or farce. It is time for the occasional happy ending."

"Like ours," she said, bringing his hand to her lips. "And there'll be even more. You know about Gwen and Mr. Wesley's engagement, of course, but did you know that Miss Bury and Mr. Fitzwilliam eloped? I wonder if he stayed awake during the wedding!"

"It seems many people found the love of their lives at the Madingley house party," he said with a smile.

"Except your sister. But her turn will come."

"It can wait a while," said Elizabeth's protective brother.

They smiled, then turned together to look at the stage with anticipation.

"I'll write a wonderful review for the *Journal*," Abigail said with a happy sigh.

"You haven't even seen how the play has been presented."

"It will be good. And it would be even better if I could reveal the true identity of the playwright to the public, besides to just your mother and sister."

He rolled his eyes. "Not again. My mother's excitement was more than enough for me."

"Maybe when your next play is ready, you'll consider it."

"I'll think about it."

"Until then," she said, "I'll let you decide how our next production is doing."

She took his hand and placed it on her stomach. He frowned at her, and she knew she felt no different to him—yet.

Then those wonderful dark eyes lit with understanding, and they shared a glad smile and an even better kiss.

At Avon Books, we know your passion for romance—once you finish one of our novels, you find yourself wanting more.

May we tempt you with . . .

- **Excerpts** from our upcoming releases.

- Entertaining **extras**, including authors' personal photo albums and book lists.

- Behind-the-scenes **scoop** on your favorite characters and series.

- **Sweepstakes** for the chance to win free books, romantic getaways, and other fun prizes.

- Writing **tips** from our authors and editors.

- **Blog** with our authors and find out why they love to write romance.

- **Exclusive content** that's not contained within the pages of our novels.

Join us at
www.avonbooks.com

AVON *An Imprint of* HarperCollins*Publishers*
www.avonromance.com

FTH 0708